BETRAYAL

A Roseanna Series Book

Book VIII

VITI LEE TACKETT

Thanks for your Support
Viti Lee Tackett

Copyright---2006 by Viti Lee Tackett
Library of Congress
All Rights Reserved

ISBN 0-9769963-2-4

Royal Family Publishing
High Point, NC

Printed in the United States of America
Faith Printing Company
Taylors, SC

Song: "Where Is My Mountain" written and recorded by Kathy Davis. Used by permission.

Songs: "He'll Calm Your Storm"
"Just Beneath the Cross"
Written by Tommy Curry.
Recorded by Kathy Davis. Used by permission.

Dedication

I gratefully dedicate this book to my faithful readers. Without you the Roseanna Series Books could not have been written. I hope they have been as much a blessing to you as you read them as they have been to me as I wrote them. I also want to thank each of you for your support in not only buying the books, but also for the prayers you have prayed for me over the years. God bless you.

I also dedicate this book to Parker Hines the newest member of our family. Parker even though you're just a baby you have found your own special place in our hearts, and our lives are brighter because of the sunshine you have brought to all of us.

Special Thanks

First and foremost to God, who inspired me to write the books and whose direction guided me through situations to which I didn't know the answer. And for always being there when I needed help and inspiration.

To my grandchildren, Laura Tackett, Josh Hines and Collin Hines for being the models for the front cover of this book.

To Diane Collins, my hairdresser and dear friend whose idea sparked the writing of the second book, 'Belle's Restless Heart' and thus the Roseanna Series was born.

To Kathy Davis and Tommy Curry for allowing me to use their songs in the book.

To all of you whose prayers and words of encouragement lifted me up and kept me going especially through the hard times.

Chapter 1

As Isabelle sped along Interstate 20, she sang along with the CD playing one of her mother's songs. Her heart was singing too. She graduated last night and now she was on her way to Nashville: to Bo. Happy thoughts filled her mind. In a few weeks she would be eighteen; she would marry Bo, and they would live happily ever after. She picked up her cell phone and dialed his number.

"Hi Bo," she said when he answered.

"Isabelle!" he exclaimed, thrilled to hear her voice. "Where are you, honey?"

"I'm on my way to Nashville. I should be there late this afternoon."

"That's great," he said. "What time does your plane land? I'll meet you..."

"I'm not flying," she said, smiling. "I'm driving through---in my new car."

"New car?"

"Yeah, Mama and Daddy gave it to me last night as a graduation present. It's beautiful. I can't wait for you to see it."

"Well, I do want to see the car, but not near as much as I want to see you," he said. "I'll be waiting at the ranch for you."

"Bo, let's meet somewhere private, just the two of us," she said. "You're the first person I want to see when I get there, and I want us to have some time together alone. There's so much we need to talk about."

"Okay, where?"

"Since we're gonna be living in Mama's other house once we're married, why don't we meet there."

"That sounds great. I'll be waiting for you." They talked on for a while, then, hung up. Bo turned to those standing round him. "That was Isabelle," he said. "She's on her way here."

Jeff, one of Bo's new friends, who had also graduated last night, nudged him on the arm. "What's Isabelle gonna say when she finds out that you celebrated graduation by staying here at my house all night, boozing it up?"

Kari, Jeff's girlfriend, was there with them. "Yeah, she may decide not to marry you at all," she teased.

"I'm not worried about that," Bo said. "That girl loves me so much that she would marry me anytime, even tonight, if I asked her to."

"You sound sure of yourself," Jeff said doubtfully. "If you can pull that off, I'll give you a thousand dollars."

Bo looked at him, surprised by the offer. "It's not possible," he said. "I don't have time to get the license, but if…"

"It doesn't have to be a real wedding," Jeff broke in. "It can be a fake one. The only thing is, Isabelle has to believe it's real; and the money is yours."

Jeff, tall and lanky, with light brown hair and a goatee to match, came from a rich family, who gave him a very generous allowance, so Bo knew he wasn't kidding. He would give him the thousand dollars if he could talk Isabelle into marrying him tonight. "How can we pull if off?" he asked, looking over at Jeff.

"I can go online and get a marriage license that looks real," Jeff answered. "I have a friend who owes me a favor, so he will pretend to be a minister and perform the ceremony. Kari and I will stand up for you, and that way, I'll be close by; and I can tell if Isabelle really believes the wedding is for real."

"I don't know about this," Kari said, her short blonde curls bobbing as she shook her head. A hint of disapproval flashed in her big green eyes. "It's a mean trick to play on Isabelle and I'm not sure I want to be a part of it."

"There's nothing wrong with the plan," Jeff argued. "Bo will explain to her after the ceremony that is was all just a joke and everything will be alright; and he will be a thousand dollars richer."

"And, I sure can use that money," Bo said. "I'm sure Isabelle will understand when I explain things to her."

"Well, okay, I'll go along with it, even if it is against my better judgment," Kari said reluctantly.

"Come on, let's get started on that marriage license," Jeff said.

Late that afternoon, Bo was waiting at Roseanna's house when Isabelle arrived driving a shiny red Jaguar. She jumped out of the car and ran into his arms.

He kissed her passionately. "It's so good to hold you in my arms again."

"It's good to be in your arms again," she replied. "Oh, Bo, I've missed you so much. I thought this day would never come."

"I know. I've been counting the minutes 'til you got here, and every minute seemed like an hour."

"I wish we could stay like this forever, and, never be separated again," she said, snuggling close to him.

"Well, there is a way," he said, happy that she had paved the way for him to bring up the subject of getting married tonight.

"How?"

"We can elope..."

"Get married now?"

"Yeah, tonight," he answered, crossing his fingers, waiting for her reply.

"Our mothers would kill us," she told him. "They have been working for months getting ready for our wedding."

Well, at least she didn't say no. Now he had to come up with a plan that would keep their mothers happy, and maybe then she would say yes. He thought a moment before offering a solution. "Honey, we will go ahead with the big wedding on your birthday. We'll keep this marriage a secret and everyone will be happy."

"That could work," she said, still a little skeptical. "We'll need a marriage license. Is there time to get one?"

"I already have our marriage license. I got it early so there wouldn't be a hassle at the last minute. I can wear the suit I wore to graduation," he stated. "We can't ask my pastor to marry us since it is a secret; but I'm sure I can find a minister who will do the ceremony, so the only thing left is for you to say yes."

"Well, it does sound romantic," she said. "I have a dress that will be perfect to get married in, and I have our wedding bands with me. Since you already have the license I don't see any thing standing in our way. Oh Bo I'm so excited. Grab the suitcases and let's go inside and make the arrangements." She picked up a picnic basket from out of the back seat. "My family fixed a basket of food; so let's eat before we get dressed for our wedding tonight."

"That sounds great. I'm starving, and by the way, that's a very nice car," Bo said putting his arm around her and walking inside.

"Mama's Cajun Fried Chicken, Grandma Blanches' homemade rolls and potato salad, and Grandma sent one of her chocolate pies," she said opening the picnic basket and setting the food on the table.

"Only one? I can eat a whole pie by myself," Bo teased. "I remember those pies from when I was a kid and we would spend a holiday with your family."

"They were my favorite pies too, and they still are, so I guess we will have to fight over who gets it."

"May the best man win," Bo said grabbing for the pie just as Isabelle snatched it away.

"The best *man* has won, but I will share it with you."

They chatted happily about things that had happened since they last saw each other, as they hungrily devoured the feast set before them. "Give my compliments to your family. They sure know how to cook," Bo said, wiping his hands and mouth on the napkins Roseanna had stuck in the basket.

"I'll tell them they made you very happy," she said, leaning over and kissing him. "Now, I'm going to clear the table, then, take a shower and get dressed for our wedding tonight."

"You go on and shower," Bo said. "I'll take care of this mess."

As soon as she left the room he cleared the table, then, called Jeff. "It's all set," Bo told him. "Is eight o'clock all right?"

"Eight o'clock is fine," Jeff answered. "I'll call my friend and tell him to be ready. Kari and I will be there waiting. Grab a pen and write down the address."

A pang of guilt hit Bo when he hung up the phone. He was lying to Isabelle. How would she react to his lies? He knew she would be upset with him, but he really needed that money, and after all, it was just a joke. "She'll understand," he muttered, hoping that was the case.

He hurried outside and got a bottle of whiskey and a big mug from his car. He poured cola into the mug, then whiskey. "I need this to get through tonight," he mumbled aloud walking back into the house.

In a few minutes Isabelle walked into the den, wearing her robe and a big towel wrapped around her head. "I've got to get my dress out of the car," she remarked.

"I'll get it," he offered.

"No, you go ahead and take your shower," she told him. "No one lives for miles around, so it's okay if I go outside looking like this. Besides, I know exactly where everything is." She hurried out to the car and got the things she needed, then went into one of the bedrooms and dressed. She looked at herself in the mirror. "This will do nicely," she said aloud, looking approvingly at the outfit. An off-white suit with a cape that buttoned around her shoulders and a slim fitting mid-calf length skirt was just the thing for her wedding. She pulled on off-white stockings and stepped into shoes the same color as the dress. "I think Bo will approve of the way I look," she mused happily, hurrying into the den where he was waiting.

"Wow!" he exclaimed, taking her into his arms. "You look amazing."

"If you think this looks good, just wait 'til you see me in Mama's wedding gown," she told him. "It makes this outfit look like burlap."

"You'd make anything look great, even burlap," he said, kissing her.

"Let's go in my car," Isabelle remarked a little while later when they left for the ministers' house. "Would you like to drive?" she asked offering him the keys.

He would have liked nothing better than to drive that beauty, but he knew he was in no condition to get behind the wheel, so he declined. "You drive honey," he said. "I don't want to concentrate on anything but my beautiful bride to be."

They were soon on their way and arrived at the minister's house a few minutes before eight. Jeff and Kari were waiting outside. Bo took Isabelle's hand and walked over to them.

"Hey, guys, I want you to meet Isabelle," he said. "Honey, this is my good friends, Jeff and Kari. They'll be standing up for us."

Jeff gave Isabelle a big hug. "It's so good to finally meet you," he said. "Bo talks about you all the time, but his description of you doesn't compare with your true beauty."

"Well, it's hard to describe perfection," Bo said, "but I did say she is the most beautiful girl in the world, and as you can see, I wasn't exaggerating." He blushed as he looked over at Kari. "I'm speaking from my point of view, of course," he muttered realizing how his description of Isabelle might insult her.

Kari laughed. "I know what you meant, Bo, and I'll have to agree with you. She is the most beautiful girl I've ever seen."

"Thank you, both, for the compliment," Isabelle commented blushing slightly and glancing at her watch. "It's eight o'clock and we don't want to keep the minister waiting."

They rang the doorbell and in a moment the door opened. The man standing there was tall and pleasant looking with a smile that put one's mind at ease. "Come in," he said pleasantly. "Which of you is the happy couple?"

"We are," Bo replied, taking Isabelle's hand and stepping forward.

"Well, I guess you're anxious to get this over with," the man commented.

They nodded.

"First, I need to ask you a question or two," he said. "Have you talked with a minister or a counselor concerning your decision to get married?"

"My father is a minister and my uncle is a counselor, and I've talked to both of them," Isabelle answered.

"My dad is a policeman," Bo added, "and he's all for this marriage. So, you see we're covered from all angles."

"Good," he said. "Now for one last question; are you kids sure you love each other and want to spend the rest of your life together?"

"We're very sure," Bo said.

"I love Bo with all my heart and I can't imagine going through life without him," Isabelle stated as Jeff and Kari exchanged worried glances.

"Okay, join right hands and repeat after me..."

"Sir, may I say something first?" Isabelle asked. "I've written my personal vows to Bo and I'd like to say them now."

"By all means," the 'minister' answered.

She took hold of Bo's hands, looked deep into his eyes and said: "Bo, I love you. I can't remember not loving you. At first it was a childish crush, but it grew into a much deeper feeling, when in our teenage years we became best friends. I'm not sure the exact moment when it went beyond friendship, and I fell in love with you; but I do know my love for you is good and strong, and it will last a lifetime and beyond. Bo, you are my happiness, the sunshine in my life, and I will spend all the days of my life on earth loving you and making you happy."

Bo felt like a hypocrite, but knowing he had to play along if he wanted that thousand dollars, he searched his mind for words to say. "I'm not too good at this," he said. "I haven't written down anything, so I'll just talk from my heart. Issy, I love you, and I want to prove my love for you every day for the rest of our lives. You're the best part of me and without you by my side I wouldn't want to walk through this life at all. I cherish you and our love, and I will try to be worthy of that love all the days of my life." The words were all true, but he still felt hypocritical saying them under these conditions.

"Okay, repeat after me," the minister said and administered the wedding covenant to them. They repeated the vows and exchanged rings. "I now pronounce you husband and wife. Bo, you may kiss your bride."

The liquor was taking effect as Bo took her in his arms and kissed her. It felt good, holding her like this, and knowing that she belonged to him now made it even better. All other thoughts crept from his mind as he kissed her again.

"Thank you," he told the minister, placing a bill in his hand.

"This one's on me," the man answered, handing the money back to Bo.

Amid congratulations and hugs, Jeff slipped a wad of bills into Bo's hand. "Way to go, buddy," he said, winking at him.

After goodbyes and well wishes, Isabelle and Bo walked to the car, hand in hand. She offered him the keys. He shook his head. "No, you drive," he said.

"What's the matter, don't you like my car?" she asked, puzzled by his reluctance to drive it.

"Oh, I love the car," he answered trying to cover up the fact that he was too drunk to drive. "And, I don't want to chance messing it up. You know how I drive." He took a big swig from the mug.

"Okay," she said, sliding in under the wheel. "It drives like a dream," she added. "You don't know what you're missing."

"Yeah, your car makes my old heap look like a pile of junk."

"Bo, I hope you know that this is our car, not just my car. What's mine is yours, now that we're married."

"And all my meager belongings are yours," he answered teasingly. He lifted the mug to his lips and took a big swallow. There was something in his head that nagged at him, but his mind was boggled from the booze and he couldn't remember what it was. Was it something important? He tried to force his brain to remember but he drew a blank.

She pulled into the yard of Roseanna's house. "Do you want to stay here tonight or go to a hotel?"

"Whatever you want is okay with me," he answered, still trying to clear his head of the cobwebs that covered his brain.

"What better place to spend our wedding night than in our own home," she answered. "At least it will be ours after we're officially married on my birthday."

"Sounds good to me," he said getting out and opening the door for her. He took her in his arms and kissed her when she stepped out of the car.

"You know you have to carry me over the threshold," she said as they walked up to the door, arm in arm.

He nodded, and reached to pick her up.

"Maybe you'd better open the door first."

"Oh, yeah," he said, taking the key and unlocking the door. He picked her up and stepped inside. "Welcome home, Mrs. Abbott," he said, kissing her and pushing the door shut with his foot.

Chapter 2

The sun was shining through the window the next morning when Isabelle awoke. "Bo," she whispered, turning over to face him, only to find that he was gone. "Bo," she said aloud, getting out of bed and pulling her robe around her. "Bo," she called a little louder. When he didn't answer, she went looking for him. The house was quiet and Bo was nowhere to be found. She glanced out the window and saw that his car was gone. "Where are you, Bo?" she sighed, walking back to the bedroom and looking at her watch. "Nine o'clock," she muttered. "I overslept. He's probably already at work."

She dialed his cell number only to hear it ringing. He had left his phone on the bedside table. "Oh well, I'll call him later," she mumbled, dropping his phone into her purse. She showered and dressed, then after tidying up the house she got into her car and drove toward the ranch.

"I've got to call Mimi," she exclaimed aloud, realizing she had not called to let her know she wasn't coming out to the ranch last night. She dialed her phone.

"Where are you?" Mimi asked when she heard Isabelle's voice.

"I'm on my way to the ranch and I'll explain everything when I get there."

"It had better be good," Mimi said sternly and hung up the phone.

A little while later Isabelle drove into the yard at the ranch dreading to face Mimi and the questions she was sure to ask. "I may as well get it over with," she mused aloud. "I'm here, Mimi," she called, opening the door and stepping inside.

"Where did you spend the night?" Mimi asked sharply. There was no hello or hugs, just the demand to know.

"I stayed at Mama's house."

"Alone?"

Isabelle knew it was coming but she hesitated before answering. She couldn't lie to Mimi and the abrupt question left no room for beating around the bush. It could only be answered with a simple yes or no.

"No, I spent the night with Bo."

"Did you sit up all night talking?"

Isabelle shook her head. "No, we slept together, but..."

"There are no buts, young lady, you know I won't tolerate that kind of behavior and..."

"Mimi, it's all right. See," she held out her hand so Mimi could see the ring. "We're married. We eloped last night."

"What have you done?" Mimi gasped and sank down on the couch, holding her hand over her heart. "Your mothers are going to kill both of you; running off and getting married, after all the work they've done to plan that big special wedding on your birthday. And Brad and Roseanna will hold me responsible for this."

"No, they won't if you promise not to say anything," Isabelle said, putting her arm around her. "We're keeping our marriage a secret. We'll go ahead with the wedding on my birthday just the way we planned, and everyone will be happy. So it's important that no one finds out that we're already married. You will keep our secret, won't you?"

"I'll keep your secret, but only because it would hurt your families too much if they learned the truth."

"Thanks, Mimi," Isabelle said, leaning over and planting a kiss on her cheek.

"You're not off the hook yet, young lady," Mimi said sternly. "And, by the way, where is Bo? He's in on this too."

"I suppose he's at work. He was gone when I woke up this morning and he left his cell phone behind so I haven't been able to get in touch with him. I'll call him later."

"Okay, then you explain why you did this when your regular wedding is just a couple of weeks away?"

"It felt so good being together again after all those months and we didn't want to be apart any longer so Bo suggested we get married last night."

"So this was his idea?"

"Yeah, but I liked the idea too. The decision to elope was a joint one and I'm not sorry. I'm so happy."

"I can see that," Mimi said. "But why didn't you call and let me know you weren't coming home last night. I was worried sick wondering where you were, and, if something had happened to you. I tried calling you on your cell phone."

"I turned my phone off when we left for the minister's house and I forgot to turn it back on. I'm sorry, Mimi, I should have called you."

"Well, maybe things will turn out all right," Mimi conceded. "Remember how we all fretted when Rex and Ellie ran off and got married; and that has certainly turned out well. One look at the two of them and you know they are so much in love and blissfully happy. And there's a special glow about them since little Melissa came---you'd think they were the only couple to ever become parents."

"I can't wait to see her," Isabelle said. "Do they call her Missy?"

"They usually call her Lissie. I don't know if that name will stick but anyway she's the most beautiful baby in the whole world," Mimi said braggingly. "Of course I'm speaking from a grandmother's point of view."

"Well, I'm sure I will agree since she's my cousin," Isabelle said, as the cell phone in her purse rang. "That's not my ring so it has to be Bo's phone. He's probably calling, trying to locate it."

"I'll go finish up in the kitchen," Mimi whispered, leaving the room.

"Hello," Isabelle said, answering the phone.

"I must have the wrong number," a lady's voice answered. "I was trying to reach Bo Abbott."

"You've reached his phone. This is Isabelle."

"Hey Isabelle. This is Kari," she said excitedly. "How did last night go?"

Isabelle stood there momentarily stunned. She barely knew Kari and she was asking about her wedding night. She would never talk to an almost stranger about something as personal as that. She didn't want to appear rude and knew she had to reply, so she asked a question in return. "What do you mean?"

"You must have been really upset when Bo told you about the trick they played on you."

"Trick?"

"You know...about the fake ceremony. Jeff's friend, Bryan did such a great job playing the part of the minister that he almost had me convinced; and the marriage license sure looked like the real thing. I can see how you were fooled into believing that it was a real wedding ceremony. Did Bo explain about the thousand dollars Jeff gave him for pulling it off? That's the reason Bo agreed to do it; he needed the money so badly and he felt sure you would understand." She hesitated a moment, then when Isabelle didn't answer, she continued. "Isabelle, don't be too mad at Bo. He and Jeff had been drinking heavily and he wasn't thinking straight, or else he never would have agreed to con you into that fake wedding. Just think of it as a rehearsal for the real one in a couple of weeks and..."

Isabelle stood there unable to move. The phone slipped from her hand and landed on the floor. She couldn't believe what she had just heard. The wedding last night was a hoax. Bo had tricked her. They weren't married. It was all a joke, a thousand dollar one. "No," she cried, falling to the floor. "No! No!"

Mimi heard her cries and came running into the room. She knelt beside her and pulled her into her arms. "What's wrong? Has something happened to Bo?"

Isabelle clung to her and wept hysterically. She shook her head. "It—it--was all a joke—Mimi—last night—was fake—the ceremony—Bo tricked me---we're not really married."

Mimi couldn't believe the words she'd heard. Anger, like she'd never felt, boiled up inside her. "And to think I helped raise that boy," she fumed. "I'd like to get my hands on him right now. I'd..."

"Mimi, I slept with him and he's not my husband," Isabelle cried out painfully as the realization hit her. "Oh, God, I'm sorry. I didn't know. I thought we were married. Please forgive me. I didn't know."

Mimi clasped Isabelle's face in her hands and looked her straight in the eye. "Listen to me. You did nothing wrong. You slept with Bo thinking he was your husband. You trusted him. There was no reason to think that he would betray you. Don't you go feeling bad about this. You're not to blame, Bo is. He's the one who should be praying for forgiveness, not you."

"Then why do I feel so dirty?"

"Honey, Bo did a terrible thing to you and I understand how you feel, but there's no shame in what you did. All the shame lies on Bo's shoulders."

"Mimi, I loved him so much, why couldn't he love me back?"

"Honey, the way he acted it seemed as if he loved you with all his heart. I've seen girls flirt with him, but he made it clear that he wasn't interested. He hasn't looked at another girl since the day you two got engaged."

"Well, he changed his mind somewhere along the way or else he wouldn't have plotted to betray me, not even for a thousand dollars." Isabelle wiped tears that rolled down her face. "How can I face people after last night? My life is over. I might as well be dead."

"Don't you go talking like that, Isabelle," Mimi said tenderly. "You'll get through this and someday it will be just a bad memory."

"No, I'll never get over last night," she sobbed. "How could he do that to me knowing how I felt?"

"I don't know, honey, but he will have a lot of explaining to do when I see him," Mimi replied. "And I hate to think of what will happen when your daddy gets his hands on him."

"No! Daddy must never find out," she cried hysterically. "No one can find out. Please, Mimi, don't tell."

Mimi grabbed her and pulled her close. "Of course I won't tell. But don't you think your family has a right to know," she asked. "Honey, Bo committed a crime against you last night. Since you're underage it's called statutory rape and he should have to pay for it."

"No, Mimi, I'll die if anyone finds out about last night."

"Okay, it's your choice, but you are going to have to call Mavis and Roseanna and tell them the wedding's off so they won't go ahead with the plans."

"No, I can't talk to them."

"You want me to call?"

She nodded. "Thank you, Mimi." She leaned over and gave her a kiss.

"Brad and Roseanna will insist on coming here and Mavis will hurry right over…"

"No, I don't want to see anyone. Tell them not to come." There was panic in her voice.

"Okay, I'll come up with something."

"Thanks, Mimi," she said, walking down the hall to her room.

Mimi sighed heavily, dreading the task she had to do. It would be easier talking to Mavis, so she dialed her number first. When she answered, Mimi took a deep breath before passing on the bad news.

"Mimi, has something happened?"

"Well, yeah, I've got some bad news. The wedding is off. Bo and Isabelle are not getting married."

"Are you sure?" Mavis gasped, too stunned to grasp what she had just heard.

"Yes, I'm sure. Isabelle just told me."

"What happened?"

"I don't have all the details," Mimi answered cautiously. She couldn't betray Isabelle's confidence but she couldn't tell a lie either, so she had to weigh her words carefully. "Isabelle said Bo had been drinking and I suppose that led up to it."

"I'm coming right over."

"No, Mavis," she said quickly. "Isabelle is in bad shape and she doesn't want to see anyone. Maybe later when she has calmed down a bit she'll be able to see you. I'll have her call you."

After saying goodbye to Mavis she whispered a prayer as she dialed the phone. Roseanna and Brad wouldn't be put off so easily. They would insist on coming to Nashville as soon as possible.

"Hello." Brad's voice unnerved her even more. She was hoping Roseanna would answer.

"Brad, is Roseanna there? I need to talk to her about the wedding," Mimi said, getting right to the point.

"I'm sorry, Mimi, but she's on her way to New Orleans. She's taking care of some things for the wedding. I think she mentioned the caterers and…"

"Can you get in touch with her right away?"

"Yes, she has her cell phone," he said, a little worriedly. "Is something wrong, Mimi? Has something happened to Isabelle?" There was fear in his voice.

"No, she's okay physically but the wedding is off and…"

"I want to talk to Isabelle."

"Brad, she's in a bad way and doesn't want to talk to anyone."

"I'll call Roseanna and tell her to meet me at the airport in New Orleans and we'll be there in a few hours," he said. "Tell Isabelle we're on our way."

"No, Brad, she doesn't want you here." Mimi's voice was strained. "She told me to tell you not to come. She wants to be alone."

"But she needs us," he argued.

"You know that and I know that, but unfortunately Isabelle doesn't know that. I'm sorry Brad, but I think we have to respect her wishes. Maybe in a few days she will feel differently and will want you here with her."

"Well, I'll call Roseanna and tell her the wedding is off before she makes any more plans. Thanks for calling Mimi and tell Isabelle I love her and I'm here if she needs me. We both are."

Brad dialed Roseanna's number as soon as he hung up the phone.

"Hey, honey, what's up?" she asked as his number came up on her phone.

"Brace yourself sweetheart," he answered. "You're not going to believe what I'm about to tell you."

"What's wrong, Brad?"

"Mimi called. The wedding is off."

"Isabelle and Bo's wedding?"

"Yes, sweetheart and I..."

"I'm coming right home," she blurted out, making a complete turn around on the highway. "My poor baby, we've got to get to her as soon as possible."

"No, honey, she doesn't want us to come. She wants to be alone and Mimi thinks we should abide by her wishes."

"But, she needs us."

"I know," he said, "but until she realizes that, we have to stay put."

"Well, if you think that's best," she said with a sigh. "Do you know what happened?"

"No, but Bo must have done something awful for her to call off the wedding."

"You're sure it's his fault?"

"It certainly could not be Isabelle's. She was too happy about getting married to call off the wedding without a good reason."

"You're right about that," Roseanna conceded.

"Well, maybe we can go out for her birthday and..."

"Oh, Brad---her birthday," Roseanna cried. "It was supposed to be her wedding day. It's gonna be rough on her. We've got to be with her. I don't think she will come home since she was going to be married in the church here, and it would be a painful reminder, so we'll plan to go to Nashville and take some of the family with us. We'll try to make it as festive as possible."

"We'll throw her a party with lots of presents," he added.

"I'll be home in a little while and we'll start planning it."

"Wait 'til I get my hands on that Bo Abbott," Brad said. "He's got a lot of explaining to do, and it had better be good, or else he will answer to me for hurting my little girl like this."

"He'll answer to both of us."

Chapter 3

Isabelle's birthday dawned bright and clear. She awoke with a frown dreading to face the day. This was her eighteenth birthday and was supposed to be her wedding day. A tear rolled down her face. How did things get so mixed up? What should be the happiest day of her life was now a nightmare as her dreams lay shattered around her.

"Oh Bo, where are you," she whispered aloud. Her anger at him was now mixed with dread. No one had seen or heard from him since the day he left. Had something happened to him? Mavis thought so. She was worried sick that drug dealers had caught him and killed him in order to send a message to others, so they would not betray them as Bo had done. Kent tried to dispel her fears by pointing out that the body would have already surfaced if the drug dealers wanted to send a message, but Mavis wasn't convinced.

"I'm with you, Uncle Kent," she muttered as if Kent were there in the room with her. "I don't believe Bo is dead. I think he ran away because he didn't love me. He wanted the thousand dollars so he planned the fake wedding and when he got the money he took off." She had to believe Bo was okay; even though he had betrayed her, she didn't want him to be hurt or dead.

She crawled out of bed, sighing deeply. She showered and dressed. There was somewhere she had to go today. Even though the thoughts of it tore her heart out; she had to go there and be alone with her thoughts; her memories.

"Good morning, Mimi," she said walking into the kitchen a few minutes later and pouring a cup a coffee.

"Good morning," Mimi replied, even though she knew it wasn't a good morning for Isabelle. "I'll fix breakfast," she added, hoping to entice her to eat.

"Thanks, Mimi, but I'll just have coffee."

Mimi frowned. "Here, at least drink some orange juice," she pleaded setting a glass of juice in front of her.

"I'm going out for awhile," Isabelle said, after finishing the juice and coffee.

"You will be back by noon, won't you?"

"Why? Is it important for me to be back by noon?"

"This was supposed to be a secret but I guess I'd better tell you," Mimi said reluctantly. "I know you don't want a big fuss made, but I couldn't let your eighteenth birthday go by with out some kind of celebration, so I'm having a few friends over for a cookout. Ellie is making a cake and she will be devastated if the guest of honor is not here to blow out the candles."

"Thanks, Mimi. I wouldn't miss this party for anything so I'll see you at twelve o'clock sharp." She kissed her on the cheek and walked out the door.

Soon she was out on the highway that led to the mountains outside of Nashville. The music coming from a CD player couldn't drown out the thoughts that were going through her head; thoughts of today; of Bo. She felt alone, like part of her was missing. Her thoughts turned to home and Mama and Daddy. She missed them so much. She needed them today of all days. But she had asked them not to come. Now she regretted it.

She reached her destination and pulled the car over and parked at the foot of a mountain. She got out and walked to the top. The wild flowers growing there gave the same beauty and pleasant aroma as they did last year, but she didn't notice. She walked over to the wrought iron bench and rubbed her hands over it as tears streamed down her face. She was drawn here today, back to the place where Bo had proposed. "Oh, Bo, why?" she cried as memories from that day, almost a year ago, flooded her mind. It was if she could hear his voice once again.

"This bench has a legend behind it," he said. "Legend has it that if a young man proposes to the girl of his dreams sitting on this bench, she always says yes."

"I don't think the legend works unless you actually propose," she teased. Then he proposed and she accepted, and they sealed it with a kiss. More tears streamed down her face as memories of those kisses consumed her. "Oh, Bo, I loved you so much and I thought you loved me too," she cried aloud. "Was it all just a game to you? Did you ever love me? Did you mean any of the words you said to me that day?" She sat down on the bench and let go of the feelings inside her. She wept 'til there were no more tears left, just a feeling of emptiness and fatigue.

"I've got to stop this," she resolved aloud. "Bo doesn't love me, he probably never did, so I've got to put my feelings aside. I have to forget him and the plans we made. I've got to get on with my life." She stood and walked back down the hillside, got in her car and headed for the ranch. There were people there who loved her, who wanted to celebrate her birthday, and help her get through today.

A little while later she drove into the yard at the ranch. She saw four cars parked there. There was one she didn't recognize. The others belonged to Kent and Mavis, Big Jake and Sam, and Rex and Ellie. She was glad they were here even though she had insisted that they not make a fuss over her birthday. Now she breathed a sigh of relief knowing she wouldn't have to face this day alone.

"I'm home," she yelled, walking into the den. It was empty. There was a note lying on the coffee table. She picked it up and read aloud: "We're in the back yard. Come on out."

She stepped out into the yard and stopped dead in her tracks. There were people everywhere.

"Happy Birthday!" they shouted in one voice.

Too stunned to speak, she stood looking around at her family and friends gathered there. Brad and Roseanna rushed over to her.

"Sweetheart," Brad exclaimed, throwing his arms around her. "It's so good to see you."

"Daddy. Mama," she said, pulling them close. "It's good to see you too."

"Happy birthday baby," Roseanna said, kissing her on the cheek. "I hope you don't mind that we're here, but we just had to do something for your eighteenth birthday; and all the family and some friends wanted to come to your party."

"Of course I don't mind. I'm glad you're here," Isabelle assured her. "But how did you manage to get all of them on one plane?"

"Lance and Andy brought their company planes too so there was plenty of room for everyone *and* presents," Brad laughingly told her.

"Thanks for coming everyone," Isabelle said, then went to each one hugging them as tears of joy streamed down her face. She made it around to all the family and friends from back home. Then she spoke to Kent and Mavis, Big Jake and Sam. "I'm so glad you're here," she said to each couple. She hugged Ellie. "I hear you made a birthday cake for me."

"It's my first try at baking a special cake like that," Ellie said. "I hope it tastes good."

"I'm sure it will be a big hit Aunt Ellie."

Isabelle spotted a man she didn't recognize standing off by himself. She walked over to him. "Forgive me, but I don't remember your name."

He smiled. His smile was warm and friendly. "There's nothing to forgive," he said, extending his hand. "We've never met. I'm Brock Mitchell. I'm the new youth minister at church and Mimi invited me to come to your party."

"Welcome," she said, shaking his hand. "I'm glad you came."

Andy rang a bell to get everyone's attention. "Come and get it," he yelled.

"Are you here with someone, Brother Mitchell?" Isabelle asked.

"No, I came alone, and, please call me Brock."

"Okay, Brock, would you like to sit at the table with my friends and me?"

"I'd love to," he answered taking her arm as they walked over to a table where Cassie and Duke and Brianna and Lee were sitting.

"Hey, gang, I'd like you to meet Brock Mitchell," Isabelle said. "He's the new youth minister at church." She pointed to each of them as she introduced them to him. "This is Brianna and Lee and this is…"

"I know Cassie and Duke already," he said. "I hear you two will be leaving us soon."

"Yes, we're moving to south Louisiana," Duke explained. "I'm going to teach school there and Cassie is going to intern with Lee's sister in her clinic."

"That sounds very exciting, but we're going to miss you," he said.

"Yeah, they're leaving just when I'm moving here," Isabelle said pouting playfully just as Andy walked up.

"I seem to remember our birthday girl likes chocolate milkshakes with her hamburgers," he said, setting one down in front of her.

"Thanks, Uncle Andy," she said, giving him a kiss. "This looks great."

"He makes the best milkshakes in the world," Cassie said, remembering the time he rescued her from the clutches of the man from the porn ring, and the milkshakes he'd made that night. "Do we get one too?"

"I believe that can be arranged," Andy said just as Jesse walked up with a platter that held all the fixins' for hamburgers.

"This table gets special treatment," Jesse said, setting the platter down in front of them. "Everyone else will have to stand in line to get served, but we're bringing your food to you since the guest of honor is sitting at this table."

"Thanks," they uttered in one breath.

Isabelle stood and hugged him. Of all her uncles, he was her favorite. "Thanks, Uncle Jesse," she said. "I'm so glad you came. It makes me feel better having you here."

"I wouldn't have missed it," he said, giving her a kiss on the forehead. "You're special to me and so is your birthday."

Brad said grace and as the others lined up and filled their plates, Isabelle and the ones at her table started eating and chatting, catching up on all the news since they had last seen each other.

Isabelle stopped talking suddenly and looked over at the newcomer. "I'm sorry, Brock," she said. "I'm being a terrible hostess. We're ignoring you completely with all this reminiscing. Please tell us about yourself."

"There's not much to tell," he said. "I grew up in a small town a couple of hundred miles from here and I'm afraid I just lived an ordinary life."

"How do you like Nashville?" Lee asked. "I guess it takes some getting used to after living in a small town."

"I was a bit overwhelmed at first but I'm getting adjusted now, and I like living here," Brock said. "It's nice to be able to get the things I need without driving several miles or ordering them online."

"I know what you mean," Lee said. "This town still overwhelms me and I've spent a few summers here. I'm from a small community in south Louisiana known as Bayou Country, and we have to drive several miles just to get to a small town."

"Yeah," Brianna said, "Nashville is like a whole new country to us, being the country hicks that we are."

They all laughed then settled down to enjoy their meal and each other's company.

About thirty minutes later Mimi stood up and banged on a table with a big spoon. "I believe everyone has finished eating so let's go inside. There's a big birthday cake waiting to be eaten and presents to open."

Isabelle blew out the candles while they sang "Happy Birthday" to her. The cake was cut with her getting the first piece. "This is delicious, Aunt Ellie," she remarked. "Thanks."

"It was my pleasure," Ellie replied. "It's not every day that one of my favorite people turns eighteen."

After the cake was eaten and all the presents opened, it was time for the family and friends to leave for the airport and the flight home. Only Brad and Roseanna, Will and Alex would be staying over. Goodbyes were said; hugs and kisses were given as several taxi cabs pulled up to the ranch to escort the guests to the airport.

"It's time for me to be going too," the young minister remarked as the last of the taxis' pulled out of the driveway.

"I'll walk you to the door," Isabelle offered, placing her arm through his. "Thank you so much for coming," she added when they reached the foyer.

"I have a gift for you," he remarked, taking an envelope from his pocket. "I waited 'til we're alone to give it to you so you can say no if you wish, without an audience watching."

Isabelle eagerly opened the envelope and read the note aloud. "Isabelle, I'd like to take you to dinner tonight as my birthday gift to you. Brock Mitchell."

"You don't have to accept unless you really want to," he stammered. "It was presumptuous of me to ask you out when we've only just met, and I realize it's not much of a birthday gift, so..."

"It's a lovely gift and I'd love to have dinner with you."

"You would?" He was obviously relieved and delighted. "Where would you like to eat?"

"You choose the place but I do have one request. Please find a restaurant where there will be no reporters. They're bound to have questions and I'm not ready for my picture or my canceled wedding to make the gossip column."

"I know just the place," he replied after thinking a moment. "It will be perfect. It's off-limits to the media so you can relax and enjoy your meal. But you will need to wear a fancy dress," he added as an afterthought.

"And, I guess that's all you're going to tell me."

He nodded. "It's a birthday surprise. I'll pick you up at seven if that's okay."

"Seven is fine," she told him then waved as he walked to his car and drove away.

She leaned against the door. For the first time in weeks she felt like smiling. Brock Mitchell would be good for her, she was sure of it.

Chapter 4

Isabelle looked at Brock as they drove away from the ranch. He looked handsome in the dark grey suit he was wearing. "Do I look okay?" she asked. "Is this dress all right for dinner?" She had chosen an ankle length silk dress. It was slim fitting with slightly off the shoulder sleeves. The sky-blue color brought out the sparkle in her big blue eyes. Now she questioned if she had made the right choice.

"You look great and the dress is perfect." A frown knitted his brow. He was having second thoughts about his plans for tonight. Would Isabelle be disappointed? Should he have planned something else?

Isabelle was having troubling thoughts of her own. Why was she so nervous over this date? Was it even a date? He had asked her out to dinner as a gift for her birthday; did he consider it a date? She wasn't sure, but she was sure of one thing; she wanted to spend more time with him and she hoped he felt the same. Her thoughts were interrupted when he pulled into the driveway of a red brick house and stopped the car.

"I don't remember this restaurant. Is it new?" Isabelle asked, looking around for a sign with a name on it.

"No, this is where I live," he explained, getting out of the car and opening the door for her. "Come on in."

She walked beside him toward the house and stepped inside when he opened the door. "So this is what a bachelor's pad looks like," she commented looking around the room. "I like..." She stopped suddenly as two men dressed in waiter's uniforms stepped into the room.

One of the men walked over to her, took her hand and kissed it. "Welcome ma-dam," he said, bowing low before her.

Before she could compose herself another man stepped into the room and started softly playing strands of Happy Birthday on a violin. The men joined in singing the stanzas of the song.

When the song ended the first waiter took her arm and led her into the dining room where a table was set with fine china, crystal and silverware. Flowers and candles finished out the decor. The waiter pulled out a chair and motioned for her to sit down while the man played softly on the violin.

Brock pulled out a chair across from her and sat down. "I hope you're not disappointed that we're eating here instead of going out to a restaurant," he said, still pondering the wisdom of his decision.

"Disappointed? No way. This is much better than a restaurant."

"I hope you like pasta, because that's what I ordered for tonight."

"I love pasta. It's one of my favorites."

"I hear this catering company does great things with pasta," he commented. "I guess we're about to find out," he added as the waiter walked in with a big tray laden down with food.

He set a salad down in front of each of them. Then he set platters of several kinds of pasta on the table along with a basket filled with different kinds of garlic bread. "Which pasta do you prefer," he asked looking at Isabelle.

"It all looks good so I'm going to try all of it."

"May I help your plate?" The waiter asked, ready to serve her.

"No, thank you," she answered smiling up at him.

"Very well, ma-dam," he replied. "Enjoy your dinner and ring if you need anything."

"We will, and thanks," Brock said as the man left the room.

"I hope I didn't offend him by refusing to let him help my plate," Isabelle said with a worried look. "I'm not used to being pampered like this."

"That surprises me. With your family being rich, I'd think you were used to being pampered."

"Well, our family has had money all my life but we have lived a pretty normal life. Money never meant that much to Mama and Daddy, and they didn't spoil us kids by giving us everything we wanted. The one time that Mama did go all out was on our birthdays. We had very elaborate parties---there was this one time she and daddy flew me and several of my friends to Florida for a week-end at Disney World."

Wow, that must have been some party," Brock said. "Of course the one today was no slouch. I've never seen so many presents at a birthday party."

"It was great, wasn't it?" Isabelle answered. "The presents were nice but the best part was having my family and friends there to celebrate my birthday with me." A faraway look clouded her eyes. "This was supposed to be my wedding day."

"I know, and I'm sorry things turned out the way they did, but I'm glad your family and friends could be there for you."

She nodded. "Now, let's change the subject. I'm feeling too good to let thoughts of Bo spoil this day for me."

"How's the food?" he asked, changing the subject abruptly. "I do hope you're enjoying it as much as I am."

She nodded. "I'm eating way too much but I can't help myself; it's so good. I haven't enjoyed food this much in a long time. I'll have to starve myself for a week but it will be worth it."

"It's a relief to hear you say that cause I was worried that you might not like the evening I planned for the two of us."

"Is there more?"

"That depends," he answered. "I have a couple of videos that are guaranteed to make you laugh 'til you cry. I hope you'll stay and watch them with me."

"Of course I'll stay," she said. "I've moped around much too long. It's time I get on with my life, and a night of good old fashioned laughter sounds just like what the doctor ordered."

"Which video would you like to watch first," he asked, after they finished eating.

"Can we just sit and talk awhile?"

"Of course we can," he replied, sitting down on the couch beside her. "You know, Isabelle, sitting here beside you like this, it's hard for me to believe that you are the same little girl who was stranded on the island with your father for all those months."

"You knew about that?"

"Yeah, it was my senior year in high school and I…"

"You were a senior in high school," she exclaimed. "I was only six years old then."

"I know," he said. "My family kept up with all the news on the accident and the search for you and your dad; and we prayed for you everyday until there was seemingly no hope for you to be rescued. We continued to pray for Roseanna. I think all of America suffered right along with her. We were so thankful when you and your dad showed up alive and well."

"And you were a senior in high school? That would make you around thirty."

"Yeah, I'm thirty. Does that bother you?"

"No, it doesn't bother me," she assured him. "I just can't picture you being eighteen when I was six."

"Can we please drop the subject of my age and talk about something else?"

"Of course we can," she said with a little grin. "How about the women in your life…have you ever been in love or is that subject off limits too?"

"No," he said and a smile covered his face. "There was this girl a long time ago. Her name was Susan and we were in love."

"That sounds very interesting. Tell me more."

He sighed. "I haven't thought about her for a long time. Her family moved next door to my family when the two of us were in kindergarten. We grew up being best friends. When we were little we played together. As teenagers we went everywhere together---school functions, church outings---where you saw one of us you saw the other. We never dated anyone else until we were in our junior year in high school."

"What happened?"

"Susan decided we should go out with other people to test our feelings for each other. I didn't know it, but the captain of the football team had asked her out. He was tall and very good looking and the heart-throb of every girl in school, so naturally Susan wanted to go out with him. When I found out about her date, I made a date of my own with Sylvia, clinging vine, Johnson."

"Clinging vine?" Isabelle laughed at the image that conjured up in her mind.

"Yeah, I'd heard other guys refer to her as the clinging vine but I didn't know what they meant until I got involved with her."

"What happened?"

"After our first date she stuck to me like glue. Everywhere I went she was there. At first all the attention she gave me was flattering. She was a very pretty girl and I did relish rubbing it in on Susan who had found her football prince to be anything but charming. After their first date she refused to go out with him again and wanted to make up with me, but I wanted to teach her a lesson so I made another date with Sylvia. That was a mistake. Since I had asked her for a second date she decided that we were an item and planned our future together."

"You're kidding, right?"

"No, she thought of everything," he said shaking his head. "We would get married over the summer vacation and finish our last year of school together. Since she came from a large family and I was an only child, we would live with my parents, and we'd both work part time in my father's drugstore during the school year, and would work there full time after we graduated."

Isabelle laughed. "How many kids were you going to have?"

"She never got that far in her plans."

"How did you get away from her?"

"It wasn't easy," he answered. "I didn't want to tell her that I was just using her to get back at Susan so I tried telling her we were moving too fast; that we were just kids and didn't really know what we wanted."

"She didn't buy that?"

He shook his head. "She was convinced that we were meant for each other and nothing could change her mind. She even went as far as to put our pre-engagement announcement in the local paper."

"How did you handle that?"

"I panicked. I couldn't see a way out so I went to Susan and begged her on bended knee to help me get out of that mess."

"And did she?"

"Not right away. She made me grovel," he said. "Usually, I would not have humbled myself like that, but I was desperate. I could see myself going through life with clinging vine Sylvia by my side, so I groveled."

Isabelle laughed again. "How did you finally get rid of her?"

"Susan went to Sylvia and told her to buzz off; that I was her boyfriend and we were promised to each other; and then she told Sylvia what she would do to her if she didn't stay away from me."

"And it worked?"

"Like a charm. Sylvia was afraid to tangle with Susan so she backed off from me and went after another unsuspecting guy."

"And you and Susan patched things up?"

"Yeah," he said. "We had both learned a good lesson and we never dated anyone else after that. It was a well known, though unspoken fact, that we would get married one day."

"But you didn't."

He shook his head. "Susan had her heart set on becoming a teacher and had gotten a full scholarship from a college on the east coast so she moved there right after graduation in order to get an early start on her education. She wanted me to move there and get a job, but I felt like I was needed at home. My father had suffered a heart attack so I stayed and took care of the store. Susan and I kept in touch for awhile and the promises we'd made to marry stayed fresh in our hearts, but those promises were not to be. My dad died a few weeks later and we sold the store, but by that time I had the call into the ministry, and my mother insisted that I take my share of the money from the sale of the store and pursue my ministry. Susan and I had almost stopped communicating by that time and eventually we stopped altogether. I don't even remember which one of us wrote the last letter." He got a far-a-way look in his eyes. "I feel certain she is married by now and probably has two or three kids."

"Would you like to see her again?"

"Yeah," he said. "We were best friends and we didn't part out of anger. We simply drifted apart, and, it would be good to see her again."

"Is there some way you can find her; maybe through her family?"

"No," he said. "She had two older sisters, but they moved away years ago when their father died. They took their mother with them and I don't know where they are. I don't even know their married names." He sighed and looked over at Isabelle. "We've gone far enough down memory lane. I'm ready to watch a movie."

"That sounds good to me."

"Which shall we watch first; a movie called "A Mad, Mad, Mad, Mad World" or a video of the Red Skelton Shows..."

"Red who?" she piped up.

"Skelton. I guess he was before your time." He paused. "Believe it or not, he was before my time too. But mother and daddy liked him so I ended up with all his shows. Which shall it be?"

"I want to see what I missed out on, so how about the Red Skelton Show?"

He slipped the video in the VCR and they sat back to watch.

"I don't know when I've laughed so much," Isabelle commented when they had finished watching the second movie. "This was just what I needed."

"Me too," he said, looking at his watch. "It's almost midnight," he gasped. "I've got to get you home before your parents send out a search party."

"Remember we're celebrating my eighteenth birthday so I'm officially an adult. Mama and Daddy can't set curfews for me any longer."

"Yeah, but I don't want them to think I'm the kind of guy who would take advantage of a young girl, especially on her eighteenth birthday." He helped her to her feet and they walked to the car.

They were quiet on the way to the ranch, each absorbed in their own thoughts.

Did Isabelle really have a good time tonight or was she just pretending in order to spare my feelings? Brock still wasn't sure he'd made the best decision by eating at home.

Was this a real date and if so, will he ask me out again, or was this a one time thing and only a gift for my birthday? Isabelle's thoughts were troubled too.

He drove into the driveway at the ranch and stopped the car. He walked around to her side and helped her out. They walked arm in arm to the door.

"I wanted to get you home before your birthday ended so I could give you the rest of your gift," he said, taking her in his arms and kissing her casually. "Happy Birthday again," he said. "And, I hope you didn't mind that kiss."

"I didn't mind it at all. It was the perfect ending to a perfect birthday gift," she assured him. "I did have a happy birthday, and a lot of it was because of you. Thanks for a great time tonight."

"The pleasure was mine," he said. "I'd like to see you again. Would it be okay if I pick you up for church Sunday morning?"

"Mama and Daddy and the boys are going home on Sunday. I'll have to check and see what time they will be leaving," she explained. "I'll let you know. Goodnight and thanks again."

The light was on when she stepped inside. She walked into the den to see if someone was waiting up for her. "Daddy," she scolded, "what are you doing up at this hour?"

"I'm going over some papers for the meeting tomorrow with Harriet and I guess the time got away from me." He looked at his watch. "It's midnight," he said. "I could ask you what you're doing up at this hour."

"Daddy."

"I know you're eighteen and officially an adult, but you'll always be my little girl and I will always worry about you."

"Well, you don't have to worry about tonight," she told him. "Brock was a perfect gentleman and I had a great time." She told him all about her evening. "I felt like a princess right out of a fairy tale."

"So, you like him?"

"Yes, Daddy, I do like him, and he asked about picking me up for church on Sunday, but I told him I'd have to check with you and see what time you're planning to leave."

"We're staying for church Sunday morning and leaving for the airport straight from the church. Rex is driving us there and Ellie and Mimi are coming along. I thought we'd stop and have dinner somewhere before we get on the plane. Why don't you invite your young man to come with us?"

"She laughed. "He's not exactly a young man and he's certainly not mine, but I will call tomorrow and invite him."

"How old is he?" Brad raised his eyebrows. He was definitely interested in the age of this man whom had caught Isabelle's attention.

She laughed again. "Daddy, can you believe he was a senior in high school when you and I were stranded on that island, and he knew all about it?"

Brad mentally ran figures through his head. "That makes him at least thirty. Don't you think he's a little old for you?"

"Daddy, he just took me out to dinner for my birthday; he didn't propose marriage. But I did enjoy his company and I'm looking forward to seeing him again. I hardly thought of Bo at all when I was with Brock. I'd say that's a big plus in his favor."

"I agree, but I'm still concerned about you getting involved with someone who is only a few years younger than your mother and me."

"He's not *that* old," she teased grinning. "Just kidding, Daddy."

He shook his head and gave her a big hug. "Seriously, sweetheart, Bo hurt you very badly so be careful that you don't turn to someone else on the rebound. Give yourself time to heal."

"Don't worry, Daddy, it will be a long time before I get interested in another man. The hurt that Bo did is too fresh in my mind and it will take a while to get over what he did to me. But I will get over him. There will be life after Bo."

"Good for you," Brad said. "Now, I think it's time we both get to bed.

She leaned over and kissed him on the cheek. "Goodnight, Daddy. I love you."

"I love you too, sweetheart," he said, giving her a big hug.

Isabelle lay in bed thinking back over the day. What had started out to be a horrible day had turned into a great one. She had hardly thought of Bo at all tonight when she was with Brock. She wasn't sure what it meant but she was happy they had a date for Sunday, even if he was thirty years old.

Chapter 5

The next few weeks bounced between smiles and tears for Isabelle. It wasn't easy getting over Bo. The love she felt for him was real and was supposed to last a lifetime. Her heart hadn't gotten the message that it was over between them; it just kept loving him and longing for him. When she was with Brock, she could forget her feelings for Bo and laugh and have fun, but when she was alone those feelings came rushing back to haunt her.

Like tonight. She had drenched her pillow with tears. "Bo, where are you," she cried out into the darkness that not only shrouded the room but her heart as well. "Are you living it up somewhere, or, are your mother's fears well founded? Could J.T. Prince reach out from that federal prison and get vengeance on you for the part you played in bringing his drug empire down." She wiped tears that ran down her face. "Bo, I pray you're alive and well somewhere for I could never want anything bad to happen to you, but I hope I never have to see you again." She tossed and turned as memories of Bo tore her apart. "Oh, God, help me," she prayed, knowing it would take an inner healing to forget the love she felt for Bo.

"Isabelle, did you sleep at all last night," Mimi asked, when she walked into the kitchen the next morning, yawning and rubbing her bloodshot eyes.

"Not much," she replied. "I can't go on like this. I'm so tired I can hardly get through the day. I haven't had a good night's sleep since all this started."

"And you don't eat enough to keep a bird alive," Mimi added. "I think you need to go to a doctor and…"

"I agree," Isabelle said, interrupting Mimi. "I'm going home and let Aunt Angelina check me over. She will know how to get my body back on track. And I'm going today."

"Good for you," Mimi said, embracing the young girl. "Angelina will make sure you get the best treatment around."

Isabelle picked up the phone and dialed.

"Roseanna, Inc."

"Harriet. You're just the person I want to talk to."

"Hi Isabelle," Harriet replied. "What can I do for you?"

"I want to go home for the weekend," she explained. "Is the company jet available?"

"It's gone right now, but will be back here late this afternoon. Will that be soon enough?"

"That will be fine."

"Okay, I'll tell the pilot to have it fueled and ready to go by five p.m."

"I'll be there, and, thanks Harriet."

"Don't mention it hon," she replied. "Give your folks my regards."

Isabelle dialed Angelina's clinic as soon she hung up the phone. "Angelina, I'm coming home tonight," she explained when her aunt answered. "I'm feeling under the weather and I'd like for you to check me over. I hate to ask you to work on Saturday, but I can't get there until late tonight."

"That won't be a problem," Angelina assured her. "I'll be happy to help one of my favorite nieces." She hesitated momentarily, then, asked, "Is it serious?" There was a note of worry in her voice.

"No, I'm just run down, that's all," Isabelle told her. "I haven't been able to eat or sleep much lately and I need to get my system back on track."

"Okay, I'll fix you up," Angelina promised. "How about ten o'clock in the morning?"

"That will be great. I'll see you then, and, thanks."

Isabelle awoke the next morning and looked around. It felt good being in her room again, among all her things. She picked up Pooh Bear and held him close. "We've been through a lot together, you and me," she said, as if he could hear her. "I've told you my deepest secrets through the years and you've always been there to listen to my tales of woe. Thanks for listening last night as I went on and on about Bo and the way he hurt me." She paused, looking him over. He was a little frayed around the edges but that didn't matter. "You're still my favorite," she said, giving him a big hug. "It's nine o'clock," she gasped, looking at her watch. "I've got to get out of here." She tossed Pooh Bear gently down on the bed, grabbed her robe and headed for the bathroom.

"Are you feeling any better?" Angelina asked, as Isabelle walked into the clinic about an hour later.

"A little," Isabelle answered. "I slept better last night; being in my own bed made all the difference."

"That's great. Now, let's see if we can't figure out a way to help you sleep better every night, and maybe, even get your appetite back."

Angelina ran several tests, then, ran some twice. She came back into the room where Isabelle was waiting. "I need to run this test again," she stated with a worried look on her face. "I'll be right back."

Isabelle had a queasy feeling in her stomach. Why so many tests? What was her aunt looking for? What had she found?

Angelina walked back into the room, sat down opposite Isabelle, and took hold of her hand. "Hon, I have to ask you this question just to rule out the possibility. Is there any way you could be pregnant?"

A gasp of horror came from Isabelle's lips. "No," she cried out. "Not that, please, not that. I can't be. I just can't be. This can't be happening to me."

"Bo?"

Isabelle nodded and fell into Angelina's arm sobbing violently.

Angelina held her close and comforted her. She was beginning to understand their sudden break-up, the canceled wedding. "Did he force you?"

"No, not really," Isabelle sobbed.

"Can you tell me about it?"

"Yeah," Isabelle answered trying to compose herself. "The day I arrived in Nashville Bo suggested we elope that night and I agreed. He made some phone calls and set it up and we went to the preacher's house and..."

"He married you, slept with you and then left you?"

"Not exactly," she explained. "You see the ceremony was a fake. The preacher was not a real minister; the marriage license wasn't real either. Bo's friend promised to give him a thousand dollars if he could get me to marry him that night. It didn't have to be a real wedding. I just had to think it was. Bo was supposed to explain it to me afterward, but he didn't, and when I woke up the next morning he was gone and no one has seen or heard from him since."

"And, now you're pregnant." Angelina felt anger like she'd never felt rise up inside her. "Just wait 'til your daddy hears about this."

"No, you can't tell him, or Mama," Isabelle cried. "They must never find out."

"Sweetheart, this is not something you can keep hidden," Angelina said, gently, lovingly. "You're about six weeks pregnant and pretty soon you're gonna start showing. We've got to tell Brad and Roseanna now." She dialed the phone.

"Hello."

"Brad, can you come right now," she said. "Isabelle needs you."

He dropped the phone and raced out the door. He jumped into his car and in a couple of minutes was racing through the door of the clinic. "What's wrong with

Isabelle?" His heart was racing as he asked that question, afraid of the answer.

"Calm down, Brad," Angelina coaxed. "Isabelle is fine physically, but, there is something wrong. Now, before we go in there I want you to promise that you're going to keep your cool and not go off the deep end."

"You're scaring me and I won't promise anything," he said, walking into the room where Isabelle sat waiting. He rushed over and took her in his arms. "I'm here, baby. Everything's gonna be all right."

She burst into tears and clung to him. "Nothing will ever be right again, Daddy. My life is over."

He looked at Angelina. "Will someone please tell me what's going on here?"

Angelina looked at Isabelle. "Do you want me to tell him?"

Isabelle nodded.

"She's pregnant."

He let go of Isabelle and looked at her in disbelief. "Pregnant? How…"

"Brad, listen," Angelina interrupted, and told him the whole story.

Brad's jaw twitched as it did when he was extremely angry. "He let you believe you were married and spent the night with you, then, left without so much as a goodbye or explanation…wait 'til I get my hands on that boy."

"Oh, Daddy, help me," she pleaded. "I don't want to be pregnant. I don't want a baby. I'm too young to be a mother. You always made things right for me when I was growing up. Can you make this go away, Daddy?"

He shook his head as a tear ran down his face. His little girl was in trouble and this time he couldn't make it go away. He pulled her close. "No, sweetheart, I can't make it go away but I can promise you that everything will be okay."

"Nothing will ever be right again," she cried. "My whole life is ruined and I wish I were dead."

"Baby, don't say that. We'll get through this together," he promised just as Roseanna walked in.

The color drained from her face when she saw the tears and the worried looks on their faces. "What's wrong?" she gasped.

"Mama, help me," Isabelle cried, running into her arms.

"Of course I'll help you baby," Roseanna said, holding her close. "Tell me what's wrong."

"She's pregnant," Brad blurted out.

Roseanna couldn't believe what she had just heard. "Isabelle?"

"It's not what you're thinking," Brad quickly explained and told her the story of the fake wedding ceremony.

Roseanna pulled her daughter into her arms again. "Oh, my sweet baby girl," she cried.

"Mama, I don't want a baby," Isabelle cried. "I'm just a kid myself. Please help me."

Roseanna was too choked up to speak so she held her daughter close and cried along with her.

Brad dialed his cell phone. "You need to get here as soon as possible," he said, when Kent answered.

"What's up?" Kent asked, puzzled by the harshness in his voice.

"Isabelle's pregnant."

"Bo?"

"Of course it's Bo," Brad snapped. "What kind of girl do you think she is?"

"I'm sorry, Brad. I didn't mean that the way it sounded. I'm just surprised, that's all," Kent quickly explained. "I'll be there as soon as possible."

"I'll have the company jet waiting at the airport and a rental car will be waiting when you land in New Orleans."

"Thanks, I'll see you in a bit."

The next call was to Belle and Jesse. After a quick explanation, they promised to be there as soon as possible. They got there in record time and tried to console Isabelle, but she was beyond consoling.

Kent arrived late that afternoon. He rushed in and took Isabelle in his arms, and not knowing what to say to her, he held her close. Finally he spoke. "Hon, I'm so sorry. I'll do anything to help."

"I don't want this baby Uncle Kent," she sobbed. "Can you make it go away?"

A look of pain crossed his face. "No, I can't do anything about the baby, but I can track that son of mine down and bring him back to marry you."

"No! I don't want to marry him."

"But Isabelle, he's the baby's father. He has responsibilities."

Brad spoke up. "Sweetheart, maybe you should think about this."

"No! I hate Bo and I'll never marry him," she screamed. "Just leave me alone!" She ran, sobbing, out the door.

Brad, Roseanna and Kent started after her. Jesse stopped them.

"Let me go," he said. "I've dealt with things like this before. Maybe she will listen to me."

They nodded and he hurried out after her and followed her to the gazebo in the back yard. He sat down on the swing beside her and put his arm around her.

She clung to him. "Uncle Jesse, why can't they leave me alone?"

"Honey, they just want what's best for you."

"Well, they don't know what's best for me," she cried. "I hate Bo and if they try to force me to marry him, I'll leave and never come back!"

"Honey, let's talk about this."

"There's nothing to talk about," she cried. "I never want to see him again and that's final."

"Have you ever considered that maybe Bo still loves you?"

"No, he doesn't love me, maybe he never did," she answered. "He couldn't have betrayed me like that if he loved me."

"He was drinking that night, right?"

"That's what a friend of his told me, but what difference does that make?"

"It could make all the difference in the world. People do things when they are drunk that they would never do otherwise."

"I don't believe someone would betray the one they love no matter how drunk they were."

He thought carefully before going on. Did he dare tell her the truth about what he had done all those years ago? Was she mature enough to hear it, and how would it affect her feelings for him. But she needed to hear it so he decided to tell her. "Sweetheart, do you remember when Belle and I were getting a divorce?"

"Yes," she answered, "but what does that have to do with this? I'm sure you would never betray Aunt Belle the way Bo betrayed me."

"You're right, I love Belle with all my heart and under normal circumstances I would never hurt her in any way, but one night I got drunk and..."

"You got drunk? I didn't know you drank, Uncle Jesse."

"That was my first time ever to drink and it threw me for a loop and..." He hesitated. "Isabelle, I slept with another woman that night because I was so drunk I didn't know what I was doing. When I woke up the next morning and realized what I had done, I wanted to die. I loved Belle with all of my heart but yet I had broken the vows I made to her on our wedding day, because I was drunk and couldn't think straight. My only hope was that Belle would never find out."

"Did she? Was that the reason for the divorce?"

"Yeah, she found out and the next day she threw me out of the house and started divorce proceedings. It was only the grace of God that got us back together." He took Isabelle's hand and continued. "I'm not proud of what I did and I don't like to talk about that part of my life, but I told you in hopes it might make you understand that when a person is drunk they do things they would never do otherwise. Belle is the most precious thing on earth to me, but even though I loved her more than life itself, I betrayed her because I was drunk. So, honey, maybe Bo was so drunk that night he wasn't thinking straight. When he comes back maybe you should at least hear him out before passing final judgment on him."

"Uncle Jesse, you didn't plot ahead of time to betray Aunt Belle. Bo did plot to trick me into marrying him because of the thousand dollar bet. I love you for wanting to help me but nothing has changed. I hate Bo and I'll never forgive him. I'd rather die than marry him. The subject is closed so let's go back inside." She stood up and walked toward the house.

"Sweetheart, we're sorry we jumped on you like that," Brad said when she walked in the door.

"I'm truly sorry," Kent added. "After I heard what Bo did that night, I wouldn't even think of suggesting that you marry him. Please forgive me."

She nodded, then, spoke calmly but firmly. "I've made a decision. I don't want this baby so I'm putting it up for adoption..."

"Honey, we'll take the baby and raise it as our own..."

"No, Mama, you won't," Isabelle stated flatly. "I never want to see this baby so I'm giving it to strangers. Don't try to stop me. I'm eighteen, and legally that makes me an adult, so I can make my own decisions, and you will have to accept the one I've made concerning the baby." With that she turned and walked down the hall, into the bedroom and shut the door behind her.

They looked over at Jesse. "Can we stop her?"

"I don't think so," he replied. "She's old enough, legally, to decide what she wants to do. All we can do is to hope and pray that she will change her mind before the baby gets here."

"I can't let her give our grandchild to strangers," Roseanna said. "I'm going to have a talk with that daughter of mine." She walked down the hallway and opened the door to Isabelle's bedroom. Her heart broke at what she saw. Isabelle was lying across the bed clutching Pooh Bear in her arms and sobbing uncontrollably. She sat down on the bed and put her arms around her.

"Mama, please don't hate me," Isabelle pleaded, throwing herself into her mother's arms. "I can't stand it if you and daddy hate me."

"Oh baby, we could never hate you," Roseanna said softly, fighting back the tears. "Don't you know how much we love you? We will always love you no matter what."

Talking to Isabelle could wait. She needed nurturing now and Roseanna was going to nurture her. She held her close and stroked her hair gently. She planted kisses on her face and wept along with her.

Chapter 6

Isabelle and Kent arrived home late Sunday afternoon. Mimi was waiting for her with open arms and insisted on staying home with her instead of going to church.

"I think you need me more than the folks at church do," she said and the subject was closed even though Isabelle assured her she would be fine.

Now, Isabelle sat on the couch in the den pondering the situation she was in. "Why Lord," she questioned aloud as tears rolled down her face. She was deep in thought and didn't hear the doorbell.

"I'll get it," Mimi called from the kitchen and hurried to open the door.

"I haven't heard from Isabelle. Is she all right?"

"Brock, thank God you're here," Mimi said. "She's in the den and she's really down. I think you're just what she needs."

He rushed into the den and sat down beside her. "Hi Isabelle," he said, taking her hand in his.

"I'm sorry Brock, but I'm not up to entertaining company right now."

"I don't consider myself company; and I'm not here to be entertained. When you didn't call or show up at church I got concerned about you, and I'm not leaving until I know you're okay."

"I'll never be okay again."

"You got a bad report?"

"I got the worse report I could possibly get."

"Oh no," he gasped. "What's wrong?"

"I'm pregnant."

"Pregnant? I-I don't know what to say."

"There's nothing to say," she told him.

He put his arm around her. "Everyone makes mistakes and..."

"Yeah, I made a big one when I let Bo talk me into eloping that night."

He pulled away from her. "You're married?" He couldn't believe it. He had gone out with a married woman. He had even kissed her. "Why didn't you tell me?"

"I didn't tell anyone except Mimi, but I'll tell you all about it now," she said and told him about the fake ceremony and the thousand dollar bet.

Again he was shocked by what he heard. "Bo did that to you?" He took hold of her hands and shook his head. "What you must have gone through. Why didn't you confide in me? I would have helped you."

"I was ashamed," she answered. "I didn't want anyone to know."

"Isabelle, there's no reason for you to be ashamed," he said. "You believed you and Bo were married. There's no shame in that, so stop beating up on yourself. You've got to be strong in the months ahead, and especially when the baby is born."

"I'm getting rid of the baby," she blurted out.

"Isabelle, you can't be thinking of having..."

"An abortion," she said before he could finish his sentence. "Of course not. I would never kill this baby; but I don't want it, so I'm putting it up for adoption."

"Are you sure that's the answer? What if you regret it later?"

"That's not going to happen," she assured him. "I don't want anything around to remind me of Bo. And if I kept this baby or allowed my family to adopt it, I would be reminded of him every time I saw the baby, and I'm not going to let that happen. I'm giving it to complete strangers." She paused a moment, then added, "My mind is made up so don't try to change it."

"I wouldn't think of trying to change your mind," he said defensively. "I just want what's best for you."

"Okay, now that that's settled, I'm glad you're here," she said taking hold of his hand. "But you had better think long and hard before you decide to keep seeing me. It could ruin your ministry. I won't blame you if you go away right now and never come back."

"I'm not going anywhere," he stated firmly. "If my ministry can be ruined by keeping company with you, then it is not strong enough to begin with."

"You don't realize how bad it will get," she said. "When the media gets wind of the fact that I'm pregnant and not married, they will have a heyday. They will drag my reputation through the mud as well as anyone close to me. So if you're not absolutely sure…"

He put his hand over her mouth. "I'm sure."

"Okay," she said, "fasten your seatbelt 'cause you're in for a bumpy ride." She leaned up and kissed him on the cheek.

"Now, that we've decided I'm here to stay, let's change the subject to food," he said. "I didn't eat before church and I'm starving. Do you think Mimi would mind if I raided the fridge?"

Isabelle laughed. "Of course she wouldn't mind. Go rummage to your heart's content."

"You caught me red-handed," Brock said playfully when Mimi walked into the kitchen just as he was about to take a bowl of potato salad from the refrigerator." After a brief pause he added, "I sure hope there's some fried chicken in here to go along with this."

Mimi laughed. "There's plenty of left-over chicken as well as baked beans, slaw and yeast rolls, and I believe I can find a big piece of your favorite chocolate cake."

"Mimi, you're a darling," he said, kissing her on the cheek. "What can I ever do to repay you?"

"Try to coax Isabelle into eating something," she said, a worried frown knitting her brow. "She wouldn't touch a bite of this food at supper time and I don't think she's eaten at all today."

"We'll have to do something about that, and I think I know just the thing," he said, setting the potato salad back into the refrigerator. "I'm going to take her to her favorite drive-in. She loves their hamburgers and I don't believe she can resist a hamburger and a big thick chocolate milkshake."

"You may have something there," Mimi said. "But getting her to go may not be so easy. She's determined to stay right here."

"Just leave that to me. I'll talk her into going," he said. "And, Mimi, save me a big piece of that chocolate cake," he called as he walked out of the kitchen.

He took Isabelle's hand and lifted her to her feet. "Come," he said. "We're going out."

"You've eaten already?"

"No, I have a better idea. You and I are going out to eat."

"I'm not hungry."

"Not even for a hamburger and chocolate shake at your favorite drive-in?"

"No, and I don't want..."

"I won't take no for an answer," he said, leading her toward the front door. "I'm starving and I don't want to eat alone, so at least come and keep me company. We'll be in the car so no one will recognize you."

"Okay," she agreed reluctantly, "as long as no one sees me."

A little later they pulled into the drive-in. Brock parked the car and pushed the button for service. "We'll have two number one dinners and two large chocolate milkshakes," he said when a waitress asked for his order.

"Why did you order two dinners," Isabelle asked, a bit tartly. "I told you I'm not hungry."

He grinned. "I know how much you like these hamburgers and I'm too hungry to fight you off when you get a whiff of my burger and shake."

She grinned but didn't comment.

In a few minutes a teenage girl brought their food to them. Brock gave her a twenty dollar bill. "Keep the change," he said.

"Thank you," the girl said happily as she turned to walk back inside.

"That's probably the biggest tip she's ever gotten," Isabelle commented.

He nodded as he opened the bag and pulled out one of the hamburgers. He unwrapped it slowly, making sure the aroma would drift over to Isabelle. "You sure you don't want one?"

"Well, maybe I could eat a bite or two of the burger and drink a sip of the milkshake."

"What about fries?"

"Yeah, I'll take a few of them," she said, wolfing down a big bite of hamburger followed by a big gulp of chocolate milkshake.

He placed the fries on her lap along with several packets of ketchup, chuckling to himself. He took a few bites of the burger and fries and washed them down with the shake. "This is good. I'm sure glad we came here, aren't you?"

Her mouth was too full to answer so she nodded her head. "Thanks for making me come with you," she mumbled, swallowing hard.

"It's still early and I'm not ready to go home," he commented when they had finished eating, "How about a ride in the country?"

"I'm not really up for a ride in the country. I'd rather just go back to the ranch."

"Okay," he said, "as long as you don't send me home early."

"I promise," she said, laughingly. "You can stay until Mimi runs you off."

"I'm not sure if that is good or bad, but we'll give it a try," he said, pulling the car out on the highway and heading toward the ranch.

"Mimi," he called a few minutes later when they walked into the den. "How about some of that cake you promised to save for me? And, make it a big piece."

"I'll take some too," Isabelle added.

"Coming right up," Mimi yelled from the kitchen. In a few minutes she walked into the den, carrying a tray with two pieces of chocolate cake topped with vanilla ice cream along with a cup of freshly brewed coffee and a glass of milk. She handed the cake and ice cream to them, and the cup of coffee to Brock. "Drink all of it," she told Isabelle handing the milk to her.

Isabelle made a face but took the glass of milk and nodded.

"Brock, were you able to coax Isabelle into eating something?"

"Coax her?" he teased. "It was a good thing I ordered two meals or I would have had a fight on my hands to keep her from taking my dinner away from me."

Mimi laughed at the picture that flashed in her mind. "You did eat then," she said putting her hand on Isabelle's shoulder.

"Yes, Mimi, I ate all of my meal and I still have room for this cake and ice cream."

"Thank the Lord you got your appetite back," Mimi exclaimed.

"You may not be so thankful when I eat you out of house and home."

Mimi hugged her. "It's past my bedtime so I'll go and leave you two young folks alone," she said yawning. "And Brock, don't keep her up too late."

"I'll be leaving soon," he replied.

"Well goodnight, you two."

"Goodnight, Mimi," they said.

After finishing the cake and ice cream, Brock took hold of Isabelle's hand. "Are you going to be all right?" he asked a worried look on his face.

"Yeah, I think everything is going to work out okay now," she answered. "I've got three concerts scheduled for next month, then, I won't do anymore concerts or personal appearances until after the baby is born. That way, neither my fans, nor the media will know that I'm pregnant."

"Are you moving back home after you've finished the concerts?"

"No," she answered quickly. "Mama and Daddy and my other relatives will try to pressure me into keeping the baby or letting one of them adopt it, and that's not going to happen; so I'm going to have my baby here and put it up for adoption."

"Isabelle, before you do anything, let me check around," he said thoughtfully. "I've heard of a Christian adoption agency where all the potential parents are screened closely and only Christian families are allowed to adopt the babies."

"That would be great," she said. "Even though I don't want this baby, I do want it to have a family who will love it and give it a Christian upbringing."

Okay, I'll look into it," he promised. "I've got to be going," he added looking at his watch. "How about taking that ride in the country tomorrow?"

"That sounds good," she answered. "What time should I expect you?"

"I'll take the day off so why don't we pack a picnic lunch and make a day of it? I'll pick you up around ten o'clock in the morning."

"I'll be ready."

He stood and pulled her to her feet. He took her in his arms and kissed her. "Good night," he said. "I'll see you tomorrow."

Chapter 7

Brock arrived at the ranch sharply at ten the next morning. He started to ring the doorbell just as Isabelle opened the door.

"That was quick," he said.

"I can always depend on you to be on time so I was waiting at the door," she commented. "I'm all set to go, and Mimi has fixed a picnic basket overflowing with all kinds of goodies."

"That sounds great, but can I ask a favor of you?"

"Sure, what is it?"

"Will you bring your guitar along?"

"Of course I will, but may I ask why?"

"I want you to teach me to play..."

"The guitar?"

"Yeah, does that seem so incredible?" he asked. "I've wanted to play ever since I was a kid."

"Okay." She went to the closet and picked up her guitar. "I've never tried to teach anyone to play before so don't expect too much."

"At least it will be a start," he said. He poked his head in the kitchen. "Bye, Mimi," he called. "We'll see you later, and thanks for the picnic basket."

Mimi came out of the kitchen wiping her hands on her apron. "I was happy to do it," she said. "You kids have fun today."

"We will," he said giving her a big hug.

They walked to the car. Brock put the picnic basket and the guitar in the back seat and then helped Isabelle into the front seat. He got into the car and they were on their way.

"Where are we going for our picnic?"

"I'm taking you somewhere special."

"Is that all you're going to tell me?"

He nodded, but said nothing. He didn't want her to know where they were going until they got there. He felt sure she wouldn't agree to go if she knew. He prayed she would understand and forgive him. He was doing this for her good, but he wasn't sure she would see it that way.

They rode along in silence for a few minutes. Then Brock asked, "When is your next concert, Isabelle?"

"In a couple of weeks," she replied. "Are you coming?"

"Of course," he said. "I've never seen you perform before an audience.

"I've sung at church."

"I mean a really big audience, and actually the folks at church don't count; they're like family."

"You're right about that."

"It won't make you nervous if I'm there, will it?"

"Of course not," she assured him. "I'll feel better just knowing you're sitting out there cheering me on."

They had driven for about thirty minutes when he turned onto a narrow winding road that led to the top of a mountain. "Hold on," he said, "this might be a bumpy ride."

He drove for a few minutes before coming to a stop under a big shade tree. He turned the motor off, got out, ran around to the other side and opened the car door. He took her hand and helped her out. "Come this way," he said, leading her over to a path that led to the place for the picnic.

Isabelle looked around at familiar sights. She had been here before. Suddenly she stopped. "Why did you bring me here?" she demanded. "This is the place where Bo proposed to me." There was hurt and anger in her voice.

"I know," he said softly. "That's why I brought you here."

"How could you do that knowing this place is filled with so many painful memories for me?"

"Isabelle, come sit down. Let me explain why I chose this place." He led her over to the wrought iron bench.

"No, I won't sit there! Take me home now!"

"Please, listen to me," he pleaded. "I have a good reason for coming here."

"I can't imagine what it is," she snapped. "When I told you about this place, I didn't dream that you would trick me into coming here, and you still haven't told me why."

He sat down on the bench and motioned for her to sit down beside him. When she refused he said, "Isabelle, this is just a plain ole wrought iron bench. It has no special powers. Please, just sit down and let's talk."

Reluctantly she sat down. Bo's words rang in her ears. *"I love you with all my heart...Isabelle, will you marry me?"*

"No, no, I can't," she cried jumping to her feet.

Brock pulled her back down on the bench. "Isabelle, I'm sorry, but I think you must sit here and talk this out. You need to get rid of the bad feelings that you have concerning this place."

"Tell me, how do I do that?"

"The best way to get rid of bad memories is to replace them with good ones," he answered, not letting on that he noticed the sarcasm in her question. "So, let's give it a try, okay?"

"I don't know." She was not at all convinced that anything good would come from being here.

"Isabelle, I promise we're going to have so much fun here today, that when you think of this place again, it will just be pleasant memories." He put his arms around her and drew her close. "Just look around at all the beauty here. It would be a shame if those bad memories kept us away from this place."

"Okay, I'll give it a try," she said, snuggling in his arms and for the first time since they got there, relaxing a bit. They sat for awhile, content to be there, then, he broke the silence.

"Isabelle, I told you a lot about me when I was growing up, but I know hardly anything about your childhood, except, for the time you and your daddy were stranded on that island."

"What would you like to know?"

He thought a moment before he answered. "I picture you as a perfect child, so I don't imagine you ever got into any real trouble."

She laughed. "I got into a lot of trouble when I was a kid, and there was this one time when I was fifteen that I got into major trouble. I thought I would be grounded for the rest of my life."

"Sounds interesting," he said. "Tell me about it."

"There were these two boys, Troy and Todd. They were brothers and very good looking. They were both in college and were home for a visit. Every girl in school wanted to date them, so when they asked Brianna and me for a date, we were thrilled, to say the least. We knew our parents would never let us go out with college guys, so we made plans to sneak out and meet them."

"You didn't," he gasped.

"Yeah, we did," she said. "We had it planned perfectly. We would go to bed early, around seven, then, we would sneak out the window and meet the boys a little distance from our houses. They would pick up Brianna first, then come by and get me; and that part went off without a hitch."

"But you did get caught."

"Did we ever," she replied. "We thought we were old enough that our parents wouldn't come into our rooms to say goodnight; but my mama did. When she realized I was nowhere around she told daddy, and they got on the phone with Lance and Sara to see if Brianna knew where I was. Needless to say, when they went to check with Brianna, she was gone too."

"And the two of you were in big trouble."

"Yeah, but we didn't know it, and we had the best time we'd ever had up to that point in our lives. We went to the movies in town and then stopped at Earl's Drive-In for burgers and shakes, so by the time we got home it was after midnight. I was dropped off first and as I climbed in the window to my room I was feeling pretty proud that we had pulled it off. I soon found out different. Mama and Daddy were sitting on my bed waiting for me. They scared me out of my wits when they turned on the light."

"What happened?"

"They had figured out that Brianna and I were together, so first they called Lance and Sara to let them know that she would be home soon, then, they started in on me. My parents don't usually scream and yell, but that night was an exception. When they found out I was missing all kind of thoughts went through their minds of the terrible things that could have happened to me."

"I can imagine how scared they must have been."

"I explained to them that we had been on a date with two really nice boys, whom they both had known most of their lives, thinking that would take some of the pressure off, but boy was I wrong. They hit the ceiling when they learned that we were out with college boys, yelling that boys that age expect more from a date then just a movie and burgers. I told them that Troy and Todd were perfect gentlemen, but it didn't calm them down a bit. After what seemed like hours of yelling and screaming at me about the dangers that face young girls who act foolishly the way Brianna and I did, they told me what my punishment would be."

"And, what was it?"

"I was grounded for a month, and when they said grounded, they meant grounded. I couldn't go anywhere except to school and to church. They took my cell phone and my laptop away from me, and I was not allowed to talk on the phone to anyone except relatives; and every last one of my relatives preached me a sermon on the dangers that young girls face by sneaking out of the house like that."

"What happened to Brianna?"

"Evidently our parents decided together on our punishment cause she got the same thing that I did. She fared better than me because she only had her parents and grandmother to preach to her. I think Uncle Andy gave her a sermon too. He's the youth minister at our church and felt it was his duty to talk to her."

"How did you handle being grounded for a month?"

"I thought I'd go crazy. I wasn't even allowed to ride my horse. I could go to the barn and feed him, but that was all. I loved riding Chocolate Drop and rode every day after school, so I really missed that." She sighed. "Another thing that I missed was talking to Bo. As teenagers we were always there for each other. Even though we were hundreds of miles apart, when one of us was in trouble we'd call the other one and talk until things got better. I needed him then so much but my cell phone and our home phone were off limits, so I had to come up with another way to call him."

"What did you do?"

"I coaxed my little brother, Will, into letting me use his cell phone to talk to Bo. He agreed, but knowing if mama and daddy caught him he would pay the piper too, I had to make it worth his while. I had to give him my allowance for a whole month."

"Was it worth it?"

"Well, at first it was. I did get to talk to Bo a couple of times and that helped, but Will thought mama and daddy were getting suspicious, so he wouldn't let me use it anymore. But the little rat made me pay him my allowance just the same."

"Well, you really didn't need an allowance if you couldn't go anywhere."

"Yeah, but they had taken away my allowance for that month so I had to give Will my next months allowance," she said. "So, even when I was free to go places and do things I didn't have any money to spend. Mama and Daddy gave us a generous allowance so I couldn't ask them for more money without explaining why I needed it."

"What did you do?"

"My uncle Jesse is a Counselor so I went to his office, laid a quarter on his desk, and told him I was in need of counseling and I was hiring him. He grinned and picked up the quarter and asked how he could help me. I reminded him, since I was a paying patient that anything I told him had to be kept a secret between the two of us. When he agreed not to say anything I told him the whole story and that I needed a job in order to make some spending money. Then I told him I wanted to work for him on Saturdays. He thought a moment and said that could be arranged. He said I could come in each Saturday for the next month and help him straighten his office and he would pay me more than enough to make up for my allowance. I don't think his office really needed straightening. Uncle Jesse is very particular with his business affairs, so I feel certain he created work just to help me out."

"He sounds like a really nice guy."

"He's the best," she said. "He never mentioned a thing to Mama and Daddy. I don't think he even told Aunt Belle in fear that she might let it slip to Mama."

"I can't imagine your parents being that strict on you."

"Well, Daddy is usually a push-over and I think he would have let me off after the first week, but not Mama. She's tough when it comes to discipline. She doesn't bend an inch. When she said grounded for one month she meant it. When I got into trouble I always hoped that Daddy would be the one to punish me 'cause I could wrap him around my little finger so to speak, but not Mama."

"I've heard that daughters and fathers have a very special relationship, but since I was an only child, I never witnessed it first hand."

"Well maybe someday you will have a daughter and you'll find out," Isabelle said. "I've always been daddy's little girl and I can get almost anything out of him. The only exception is Mama; if she says no then he says no. He will never go against her decisions."

It sounds like they have a good strong marriage," he commented. "I hope to have a marriage like that one day, but right now I'm starving. What say we tackle that picnic basket?"

"Sounds good to me," she said.

He got the basket from the car along with the guitar. They walked over to the picnic table. He spread a red-checkered cloth on the table and she set the food out. "Hmm, fried chicken and potato salad," she said. "Looks like Mimi cleaned out the fridge."

"It's a feast fit for a king," he added. "There's nothing better than Mimi's cold fried chicken and potato salad."

"Not to mention hot corn on the cob, green beans, and homemade rolls," Isabelle said, taking several thermal dishes from the basket. "She's determined that I'm going to eat healthy even on a picnic."

"That's Mimi for you," he said, "but she did put in a couple of slices of that chocolate cake."

They settled down to eating and after they finished they put everything back into the picnic basket. "Now to my lessons," he said, picking up the guitar.

"I hope you're not expecting too much," she told him. "It takes a long time to learn how to play a guitar."

"I'm a fast learner," he said.

"Okay," she said laughing to herself. She knew it would take months of lessons and practice before he could play the guitar, and after he struggled with the lessons today, he would know it too.

"We'll try "Amazing Grace," she said and played it on the guitar while she sang the words. "Okay, now I'll show you how to play that song." She placed his fingers on the strings teaching him the different chords. She showed him how to strum to make the melody.

He had trouble remembering the chords and also pressing the strings hard enough to make it sound right. After an hour, she shook her head.

"School's over for today," she said, reaching for the guitar.

He held on to it. "Let me try it on my own," he suggested. "That way we can tell how much I have learned."

"You don't even know how to chord."

"I just want to try."

"Okay," she said, teasingly. "Take it away, Maestro."

Awkwardly he put his hands on the chord and played a few notes. Then he strummed hard and loud before he started playing "Amazing Grace" so perfectly that each word sounded out fluently.

Isabelle's mouth flew open in disbelief. She had never heard it played more beautifully, but she was not at all pleased. He finished and took a bow.

"Cute, real cute," she snapped. "Take me home now!"

"Please, don't be offended, Isabelle, it was just a little joke."

"Do I look amused?" She flung those words at him then walked off in a huff.

He called after her but she paid no attention, so he put the guitar back into the case, picked up the picnic basket and followed her to the car. He winched when she got into the car and slammed the door so hard that the windows rattled. He tried talking to her on the way home but she sat like a statue staring straight ahead and not saying a word.

"Isabelle, I'm sorry," he said when he pulled into the driveway at the ranch. "Please forgive me."

His pleas fell on deaf ears. She jumped out of the car, grabbed her guitar and the picnic basket, slammed the door shut, rattling the windows again, and ran into the house without saying a word.

"I hope I never have to see that man again," she exclaimed when Mimi walked into the den.

"Brock?" Mimi shook her head. "That must have been a doozey of a fight the two of you had."

"He made me so mad," Isabelle fumed. "You wouldn't believe what he did."

"What did he do?" Mimi asked, not able to believe that Brock could ever do anything really bad.

"He asked me to teach him how to play the guitar so I spent an hour teaching him the basics. Then he wanted to play a tune to see how much he had learned. He played "Amazing Grace' and played it to perfection. Chet Atkins doesn't have a thing on him."

"Brock plays the guitar?"

"Yeah, and he made a fool out of me."

Mimi put her arm around Isabelle. "Honey, I'm sure he didn't mean to. He just wanted to surprise you."

"Well, he surprised me all right," she fumed. "I doubt if I'll ever speak to him again." She walked to her room and slammed the door behind her.

"Poor Brock," Mimi whispered. Isabelle had inherited her mother's temper, and this was the first time he was on the receiving end of her anger.

A couple of days later, Brock's phone rang. "Hello," he said, picking it up.

"You're forgiven, but it's going to cost you."

"Isabelle," he exclaimed joyfully. "Just tell me what you want me to do." He didn't care what it cost him. She was speaking to him again.

"You're going to be the lead guitarist at my next concert."

"No, I'll do anything, but not that."

"Okay," she said. "I guess this is goodbye then."

"No, don't hang up," he pleaded. "Let's talk about this."

"There's nothing to talk about. Either you play at the concert or…"

"I'm coming right over," he said and hung up the phone before she had a chance to answer.

Isabelle grinned. She had him over a barrel and he knew it. She felt sure he would give in to her wishes.

Chapter 8

Isabelle scampered out on stage, waving and throwing kisses. "Thank you! Thank you!" she called over the noise of the crowd. "It's good to be back in Nashville and to see all of you again. I'm going to start with one of my favorite songs. It's called "Standing Out" and I wrote it for a very important person in my life, my daddy. Daddy has always been my hero and I know that if I follow in his footsteps, I'll never fall, for he is the best example of a Christian that I know. He's always been there for me. So, Daddy, even though you're not here tonight, this is for you."

Applause thundered throughout the auditorium when she finished and took a bow. "I'm going to sing some new songs tonight as well as some old ones. I hope you enjoy them. She sang a couple of new songs that she had written, some of Roseanna's songs, as well as some oldies that the audience joined in and sang along.

"Now, before my last song, would you help me thank the guys in the band as I introduce each one? You already know most of them," she said, introducing each amid a great round of applause. "Now, give a hand for the newest member, our lead guitarist, and my friend, Brock Mitchell."

He took a bow, blushing deeply, when young ladies all across the auditorium whistled and shouted remarks of admiration to him, some not too flattering for a minister's ears to hear.

Isabelle noticed his embarrassment and quickly spoke up. "For my last song tonight we're going to sing a song that is familiar to all of you…"Amazing Grace". Please join in and worship the Lord in your own way." The audience lifted their voices in singing. After the first two verses, Isabelle turned and nodded to Brock to pick it out on the guitar. He did, a bit reluctantly, amid applause, and, screams from his female admirers. He breathed a sigh of relief when the concert ended and Isabelle took her final bow.

"I'm glad that's over," he remarked later in the car on the way home. "At least that's behind me and I will never have to perform at a concert again."

"Wrong. I have two more concerts and I want you to play at both of them," she informed him. "But, maybe I'd better keep a close eye on you with all those ladies in the audience whistling at you." She grinned. "Do I need to be worried?"

"No," he answered quickly. "And some of those 'ladies' need their mouths washed out with soap."

She giggled mischievously. "Next time I will introduce you as Reverend Mitchell. Maybe that will help."

"Isabelle, I really don't want to do that again," he stated seriously. "Please don't ask me to."

"Brock Mitchell, besides my grandpa, you're the best guitarist I've ever heard, so don't try to wiggle out of our three concert agreement."

"I didn't sign anything."

"Yeah, but you gave your word."

She had him there. He had agreed to do it, but under unfair pressure from her. It was either agree to it or she would never speak to him again. "Okay, I'll do it, but under great protest."

"Thank you," she said sweetly, snuggling close to him and laying her head on his shoulder.

He pulled over to a roadside park and stopped the car. "Is it all right if we stop here for awhile? I need to talk to you."

She raised her head from off his shoulder. "I'm listening," she said wondering what was so important that he had to stop the car and park here.

He took her hands in his. "Isabelle, I'm falling in love with you, and I want to know if there's a chance of you loving me back."

She put her fingers to his lips. "I can't talk about that yet," she said. "I care about you, a lot, but I can't give you an answer now. I don't want to make any long term commitments until this ordeal with the baby is over. And besides, the hurt I suffered over Bo's betrayal is still too fresh, and I can't trust my feelings when it comes to matters of the heart. But, I hope you won't give up on me."

"That will never happen, and it was insensitive of me to bring up the subject when I knew you are still hurting."

"Bring it up again in a few months, please, because you are the kind of man that I want to fall in love with one day; the kind of man I want to marry."

He didn't answer but instead pulled her into his arms and kissed her.

The next two concerts went well. "Well, I got safely through the first hurdle," Isabelle said, breathing a sigh of relief when the third concert had ended and she was in the car beside Brock on their way to the ranch. "No one even suspects that I am pregnant, and with any luck at all, it will stay that way. When the baby is born it will given to the adoptive parents and no one will be the wiser. My reputation will be intact and I can resume my career."

Brock didn't answer but he was plenty worried. Things had a way of backfiring. He hoped and prayed that didn't happen to Isabelle. He didn't think she could handle any bad publicity. He reached over and squeezed her hand.

True to Isabelle's prediction, everything went fine for the next few weeks. She had gotten over morning sickness and was feeling good about the situation but she didn't go out in public now that she was far enough along in her pregnancy for folks to notice.

Brock had been at the ranch since early that morning. He spent every free moment with her to keep her from being lonely. "Isabelle, I've either got to go to the grocery store or starve," he announced standing up.

She stood up. "I'm going with you," she told him. "It's cold enough outside for a coat so no one can tell that I'm pregnant." She got her coat and put her arm through his as they walked outside.

"Are you sure you're up to this?" he asked pulling into the parking lot.

She nodded her head. "It feels so good to be out in public again," she said as they walked hand in hand into the store, got a shopping cart and started up the first aisle.

They had gone all the way through the store and were at the fruit and vegetable aisle when Brock spoke up. "I forgot to get milk. It's all the way over on aisle one. Wait here and I'll be right back."

Isabelle was humming a song when a woman walked up to her.

"You're Isabelle, the singer, aren't you?"

"Yes, I am."

The woman yanked Isabelle's coat open. "You hypocrite," she shouted. "You *are* pregnant," then she slapped Isabelle across the face so hard that it sent her reeling backwards.

Brock had only gone a few feet when he heard the commotion and ran to Isabelle's side. He grabbed the woman's hand before she could strike her again. "You better be glad that I'm a gentleman or they'd be picking you up off the floor," he said angrily. He pulled Isabelle close just as the flash of a camera went off practically in his face. He saw the photographer out of the corner of his eye but he couldn't worry about that now. He had to get Isabelle out of there. He picked her up in his arms and ran out of the store, just as the camera flashed again.

"I'm sorry Reverend," the store manager said following them outside. "I've never seen that woman before, but I will get her license number in case you want to press charges against her for assaulting Isabelle."

"Thanks," Brock said. "We'll talk later. I need to get her home now."

On the way home Isabelle sat trembling, staring straight ahead. She pulled her coat snugly around her trying to shut out the cold that enveloped her.

"Isabelle, I'm so sorry. I shouldn't have brought you here," Brock said, but she didn't hear him. She was too stunned to hear or to speak. He pulled her close and held her until they arrived at the ranch. Then he ran around to her side of the car, opened the door and helped her out. She walked aimlessly in front of him into the house, right past Mimi, without saying a word. Then she walked down the hall to her bedroom, went in and shut the door.

"Brock, what happened?"

"It was horrible," he said and told her the whole story of how the woman assaulted Isabelle in the grocery store.

"That poor child," Mimi said, fighting back the tears that welled up in her eyes as anger filled her heart. "We've got to do something about this."

Brock nodded in agreement. "There was a reporter there, taking pictures, and I'm certain he got it all on film."

"It will be splashed all over tomorrow's headlines," Mimi said. "I don't know what that will do to Isabelle." Then as an afterthought she added, "I'm going to call Brad and Roseanna. They need to know about this."

"She could sure use her parents right now," Brock said. "Maybe they will know how to handle the press."

"Roseanna has had enough bad publicity over the years so they are used to dealing with reporters." She picked up the phone and dialed their number.

"Hello," Brad said in his usual jovial manner.

"Brad, you and Roseanna need to come here right away," Mimi said, getting right to the point. "Something terrible has happened."

"Isabelle." He felt his knees go weak and his heart skip a beat.

"No, Brad, she's okay," Mimi replied and then told him what happened.

"We'll be there as soon as possible," he said, hanging up the phone. "Roseanna, throw some things into a suitcase. We're going to Nashville."

"What's wrong?"

"I'll tell you on the way to the airport," he said, dialing Harriet's phone number. "We're coming to Nashville," he said when she answered. "Can you send the plane right away?"

"Yes, it will be waiting when you get to the airport."

Brad and Roseanna arrived at the ranch a few hours later. Isabelle was asleep so they quizzed Brock.

"Did you get a good look at the reporter?" Brad asked.

"No, but now that I think about it, there were two men there; one was holding a microphone and the other was snapping pictures."

Roseanna spoke up. "Doesn't it seem a little strange that a reporter and photographer would just happen to be on the scene when that lady confronted Isabelle."

"Yeah, what's the chance of that happening?" Brad asked. "About one in a million," he added, answering his own question.

"You think she was set up?"

"I'd just about stake my life on it, Brock," Roseanna answered. "And, if that's the case then they had to go to great lengths to pull it off. First, they had to hire that woman and have her standing by; then they had to know Isabelle would be at that store at that particular time. My guess is they were staking out the ranch and followed you to the store. Then, they contacted the woman and told her where you were, and got everything on tape and film so they can use it in the article. And, I'm pretty sure I know who is behind it."

"Who would do that to a sweet girl like Isabelle?"

"Mimi, I don't think that Isabelle is the real target," Roseanna answered. "I think they are trying to smear my daughter's name to get back at me."

"Sweetheart, tell me the name of the newspaper who would print malicious gossip like this." There was anger in Brad's voice.

"Honey, I told you about this seedy paper called 'The Voice of Truth'. Their motto is: 'The paper that is not afraid to print the truth no matter who it offends.' Of course their opinion of the truth is usually far from the real truth. They print just enough of the truth so they can't be held libel, and then they build on that with a lot of speculation, which unfortunately their readers believe. They printed a few articles like that about me when I came to Nashville the first time, but fortunately for me, J.T. Prince was powerful enough to squash most of them, and he even sued them and almost put them out of business; and because of that, the editor of the paper hates me and will do anything to smear my name, even if it means hurting our daughter in the process."

"I've a good mind to buy that newspaper and fire everyone there," Brad blurted out angrily.

"That's a great idea, honey," Roseanna said eagerly. "We'll wait and see if the article comes out tomorrow and if so, we'll go to the owner and make him an offer he can't refuse."

"Do you think he will sell the paper to you?"

"Yes Brock, I'm sure of it," Roseanna answered. "He's a sleazebag who would do anything for money. He doesn't care who gets hurt as long as the money comes in. He'd sell his own mother if the price was right."

The next morning Brock arrived at the ranch early. He had picked up a paper from the local newsstand. He hurried to the door and rang the doorbell.

Brad opened the door. "I was just on my way out to buy this," he said when Brock handed him the paper. They hurried to the den and opened it. The article covered the front page.

Brad read the headlines aloud: "YES, SHE'S PREGNANT BUT WHO IS THE FATHER?" There was a big picture of Isabelle as the woman opened her coat revealing the fact that she was pregnant, then a smaller picture of the woman slapping her across the face. There was another big picture of Brock holding her in his arms racing from the store. Brad sucked in his breath and handed the paper to Brock. "You read the rest."

Brock took the paper and began to read. "What popular young gospel singer is with child without the benefit of a wedding band on her finger? You might not believe me if I told you, but the pictures say it all. Isabelle would have us believe that she is that pure innocent little girl who sings so sweetly; but the facts speak for themselves...she is pregnant and she is not married. Isabelle, will you come forward and tell us the name of the father of your baby? Is it your former fiancée who skipped town right before your wedding day, or, is it the handsome preacher who so gallantly came to your defense when that lady assaulted you in the store, or, do you even know the identity of the father? These are questions that this reporter wants answered and I'm certain your fans will want to know the truth too."

Tears misted Brad's eyes as he thought of the pain this would cause Isabelle. "God forgive me, but I'd like to have a few minutes alone with the low-life who wrote this article. When I got through with him he would rue the day he was born."

"I know how you feel," Brock piped up. "Preacher or not, I'd beat him within an inch of his life."

"Is the article in there?" Roseanna asked walking in and seeing them with the paper.

Neither one of them answered. Instead Brock handed the paper to her. She read the article silently then shook her head and clenched her teeth as her dark eyes flashed with rage. "Come on, Brad, let's go."

"It's barely daylight," he pointed out. "Where are we going this early?"

"We're going to buy a Newspaper," she replied, picking up the phone book as she walked out the door.

"Honey, the bank won't open for hours…"

"Remember Charles told us to call him at home day or night in case of an emergency, and I'd say this qualifies as one," Roseanna said. Charles Hightower was the president of the bank where they did their banking in Nashville and she felt sure he would be happy to assist them in this. Roseanna dialed his home phone. "I hope I didn't wake you," she said when he answered, "but we have a problem and we need your help."

"No, you didn't wake me and I'll be happy to help in any way I can. Just tell me what you need."

Roseanna told him about the article and of their plans to buy the Newspaper and fire the editor and also the reporter who wrote the article.

"That newspaper is a disgrace to Nashville," he said. "They've hurt a lot of good people in this town and it's time someone put a stop to it. I'll go to the bank right now and have a cashier's check all ready to be filled out when you call; and Roseanna, tell your daughter not to worry about that article because most of the folks here in Nashville won't be influenced by it."

"Thanks, Charles," she said, turning off her cell phone. She picked up the phone book and scanned the pages eagerly. "Here it is," she mumbled writing down an address and handing it to Brad. "This is where the owner of that sleazy paper lives, so turn this car around and let's go pay him a visit."

Brad made a right turn at the next intersection and proceeded in the direction of the address Roseanna had given him. Meanwhile she made a few more phone calls. In about twenty minutes they pulled into the driveway of a big red brick house.

"This is it," he commented getting out of the car. He opened the door for Roseanna and helped her out. They walked up to the house and Brad picked up a paper from the porch; then he rang the doorbell.

A short stout disgruntled man jerked the door open and yelled, "What do ya mean ringing my doorbell this early?"

"We're here to offer you a deal that you can't refuse," Roseanna replied, stepping inside.

"Wait, I didn't invite you in."

"You won't be sorry after you hear what we have to say," Brad said, following Roseanna inside.

"Just who are you?"

"I'm Bradley Leflourche and this is my wife Rosanna."

"You're the singer," he said, obviously pleased. "But why are you here?"

"We want to buy your Newspaper Company and we're ready to make you a generous offer," Brad said, getting right to the point.

"And what makes you think my Paper is for sale?"

Brad handed him the paper he had picked up from the front porch. "Page one," he said.

The man opened the paper and scanned the article. He shrugged his shoulders. "So?"

"So, that girl is our daughter and we don't take too kindly to her name being dragged through the mud," Roseanna snapped.

77

The man reached for his glasses and read the article slowly. "Is your daughter pregnant? Is she married?"

Brad felt himself getting angry but he tried to speak as calmly as possible. "She is pregnant and she is not married."

"Then it seems to me that the problem is yours, not the Papers. I can't help if your daughter has low morals. You should have taught her better."

Roseanna could see the vein on Brad's neck jumping and she knew he was about to lose it, so she stepped between him and the man. "Sir," she fumed getting right in his face, "your reporter should have checked out his story and got all the facts before he wrote that article. And, besides that, it's unethical to hire someone to publicly assault another person in order to get a story, and I also believe it's against the law."

"Are you accusing my reporter of doing that?"

"I have the proof," she informed him. "I talked to Kent Abbott of the police department. They found the woman who assaulted Isabelle and she admitted she was hired by your paper to do so, and she is willing to testify to it. If you want to check it out just call the station, they'll be happy to give you the details."

The man cleared his throat nervously. "I didn't know about this article and besides I can't be held liable for what a reporter does."

"We'll see what a court of law thinks about that," Brad said threateningly. "Come on, sweetheart, let's get out of here." He took her hand and walked toward the door.

"Wait," the man said. "Can't we work something out?"

"There is one way to keep this from going to court," Brad answered. "Sell us your Paper."

"How would that keep us out of court?"

"Because we plan to fire that sleazebag reporter as well as the editor who allowed the article to be printed, and to put an end to the trashy gossip that the paper publishes," Roseanna told him. "Now do we have a deal or not?"

"What kind of deal are we talking about?"

"Name your price and we'll go from there," Brad answered.

"Well, the newspaper is worth a lot of money," the man said, smacking his lips greedily thinking of the big bucks he could get from them. "A couple of million dollars should be a fair price."

Brad rubbed his chin as if thinking it over. "Maybe we should consider what it will be worth after we take you to court," he suggested.

"No, that won't be necessary," the man blurted out. "Why don't you make me an offer?"

"One million dollars, with the understanding that you personally print a retraction of the article in tomorrow's paper; and you, the editor, and the reporter will publicly apologize to Isabelle."

"Done," he said.

"Call your lawyer and the two of you meet us at my lawyer's office in an hour, and bring all the necessary paperwork," Roseanna told him. "Here's the address," she added, handing him one of Ross's business cards.

"Sweetheart, what in the world are we going to do with a Newspaper Company?" Brad asked on the way to the bank.

"I've taken care of that," she told him. "I called a reporter friend of mine, Art Clancey. He's an excellent newsman and knows everything there is to know about running a newspaper. I offered him a job as editor of the paper, that is, with your approval."

"If you think he is the man for the job then it's okay with me," Brad answered. "You've had more dealings with the media than I have, so I trust your judgment completely."

They picked up the cashier's check at the bank then hurried to the lawyer's office. Things went smoothly and in less than an hour they had the documents in hand making them the new owners of the Newspaper. They hurried over to the newspaper office. Art Clancey was waiting in the parking lot. Roseanna walked over to him. "Come on," she said. "Let's go make their day."

The three of them walked through the front door of the office and headed straight for the door marked Editor.

A pretty young receptionist ran after them. "Excuse me, but you can't go in there without an appointment."

"Oh, I think we can," Brad answered and kept on walking toward the office. He opened the door and they went in.

The receptionist was right on their heels. "I'm sorry, Mr. Varner," she explained. "I tried to stop them."

"That's okay, Stephanie. I'll handle it." The tall frail looking man in the editor's chair held the stub of a cigar in his mouth. He looked at the three intruders. "What is the meaning of this," he demanded gruffly, grinding his cigar in a dirty ashtray on his desk.

Roseanna laid the newspaper down on the desk and pointed to the article. "In case you don't remember me, I'm Roseanna, the country singer whose reputation you've tried to drag through the mud all these years. This is my husband Brad and Isabelle is our daughter. But of course you already know that, don't you? That's why you went after her; to get back at me for what J.T. Prince did to you way back then."

"That article is true," he said. "Your daughter is pregnant and she's not married, so how dare you come here making accusations against me and my paper."

"What about the fact that you hired that woman to assault Isabelle," Brad said, getting right in the editor's face.

"You—you can't prove that." Mr. Varner's voice was not as confident as before.

"We already have," Brad said. "So, I suggest you get up out of that chair and get out of this office---right now."

"You've got some nerve telling me to get out of my own office. I'm going to call my boss..."

"You're talking to him," Brad informed him, laying the documents down on the desk. "Roseanna and I are the new owners of this paper and that makes us your boss."

Mr. Varner paled as he read the papers stating that they did in fact own the paper. He cleared his throat. "Well, er, I-ah-what can I do for you?"

"First get the reporter who wrote that article in here."

"Yes sir, Mr. Lefourche, right away, sir." He pushed the intercom button. "Tell Rodney to get in here on the double."

A couple of minutes later a young man walked into the room. His tousled blonde hair and his clear blue eyes, along with his ready smile gave the appearance of innocence and trust.

Roseanna took one look at him. "Looks can sure be deceiving," she muttered to herself.

"You wanted to see me, boss?" the young reporter asked.

"Yes, Rodney, it's about that article you wrote in today's paper."

"It's causing a big stir. The phones haven't stopped ringing," he bragged. "I guess we put that little tramp in her place. We showed..."

Brad grabbed him by the collar and held on tight. "I ought to put my fist in your face, right now," he said, drawing back to hit him.

"Honey, don't," Roseanna pleaded, grabbing his arm. "That's not the way to settle this."

Mr. Varner cleared his throat loudly. "Rodney, this is Brad and Roseanna Lefourche. They are Isabelle's parents and..."

"I reported the truth and you can't touch me legally."

"Rodney, shut up and listen!" The editor's voice was stern. "Not only are they Isabelle's parents; they are also the new owners of this Paper."

"Yes, Rodney, maybe we can't touch you legally but we can touch you where it hurts most---in your pocketbook. You're fired. Now, clear out your desk and get out right now." Brad's words were harsh and final.

"But before you go, you're going to write a public apology to our daughter which will be printed in tomorrow's paper," Roseanna told him firmly.

"Why should I?" he sneered.

"If you ever want to work again as a reporter anywhere in this country I suggest you do it." Roseanna shoved a sheet of paper into his hands.

He sat down and wrote the apology. After Brad and Roseanna approved it, he went to clear out his desk.

"I want to add my apologies, too," Mr. Varner nervously offered.

"I think that's a good idea," Brad said, handing him a pen. "And, make it good."

"There that's done," he said, as he finished writing. "Now, is there something else I can do for you?"

"As a matter of fact, there is," Brad told him. "You can get up out of that chair and let the new editor sit down." He motioned to Art.

"You can't fire me," he stormed. "This paper can't survive without me."

"We don't want this paper to survive the way it is," Brad replied. "We're going to clean it up until every bit of the stink that you left behind is gone. You have 'til the middle of the afternoon to clear your things out. Goodbye and good riddance."

Roseanna turned to Art as soon as they walked out of the office. "We need to discuss the financial arrangements. We don't want any of the profits from the paper, so we've come up with a plan, that is, if you will agree to it," she said. "You will be paid a yearly salary of fifty thousand dollars and also one-half of the profits will be yours. The other half will be spilt equally between the Home for Girls that Jake and Sam operate, and the Center for kids that Andy Winslow owns. Does that sound fair?"

"It's more than fair, it's fantastic," he replied. "Thank you both for giving me this opportunity and I promise to do everything within my power to make this a newspaper that you will be proud of."

"We're certain you will do just that," Brad said, shaking his hand. He took Roseanna's hand. "Come on, sweetheart let's get back to the ranch. I'm sure Isabelle has read that article and she will need us."

"Keep us informed," Roseanna told Art as she gave him a kiss on the cheek.

Brad and Roseanna arrived at the ranch before noon. Isabelle rushed into their arms and burst into tears.

"It's okay, sweetheart," Brad said. "We've taken care of everything,"

"We now own a newspaper," Roseanna added and told them the whole story.

"And, that's the end of the bad publicity," Brad said.

Roseanna shook her head. "I'm afraid that's not the end of it," she said. "I believe some of the other tabloids will pick up on the story and keep it going. Unless I miss my guess we're in for a few more bad days before this dies down."

"Do you think we need to hang around for a while?"

"Yes, honey, I think we do," she answered. "I've had my share of bad publicity over the years and I know how to cope with it. I don't want Isabelle to go though this alone."

"Thank you," Isabelle said, hugging them. "I feel better already, knowing the two of you are here.

Chapter Nine

The next four months crept slowly by. Isabelle was anxious for the baby to be born so she could get on with her life. Now it was only two weeks away and she was sitting in the den thinking how good it would be to get all this behind her, marry Brock, and begin their life together. Her thoughts were interrupted when she saw his car drive up. She met him at the door.

"Hi," she said, opening the door, then leaning up and kissing him.

"Wow, that was some welcome," he said, taking her in his arms and giving her a big kiss. Then arm in arm they walked into the den and sat down on the couch. He turned to her with a serious look on his face. "Are you sure it's okay for me to go to this seminar? I don't have to go."

"Of course you have to go," she answered. "You're teaching a class and I promise you I'll be fine. I'll miss you, but I'll be perfectly okay. My due date is still two weeks away, and it's not like I don't know the date I got pregnant, so there's nothing to worry about."

"Well, if you're certain," he said, a bit hesitantly. "I am excited about teaching this class and I have studied for weeks on the lesson, so since you're positive that you will be all right, I will go, but I'll miss you too."

They talked on for a while then it was time for him to leave.

"I'll be home late Saturday night, so I'll see you first thing Sunday morning," he said, giving her a goodbye kiss as he headed out the door.

Isabelle sighed as she walked back into the den. She was missing him already. He had been her strength these past months; she had become accustomed to leaning on him.

He would only be gone a couple of days, but right now that felt like forever. Mimi was gone on a weekend trip to the Smoky Mountains with Rex and Ellie and also Kent, Mavis and Beth; so she was alone in the house, and having nothing else to do she went to her room to take a nap. She was just drifting off to sleep when the doorbell rang. "Who could that be," she mumbled sleepily as she dragged herself to the front door and opened it. "Bo," she whispered when she saw him standing there in the doorway.

"Issy, I've got to talk to you," he announced, walking past her into the den.

Anger rose up in her. "You don't have anything to say that I want to hear," she snapped. "And don't call me Issy. I hate that name."

"Please Isabelle, let me explain," he pleaded. "Our future depends on it."

"*We* don't have a future."

"You can't mean that," he said. "I know I made a big mistake and I'll regret it as long as I live, but I'm here to try to make it up to you. Please forgive me and give me a chance to make things right between us."

The anger she felt turned to rage. "Bo Abbott, how dare you come here and ask me to give you another chance!" Her voice was sharp and piercing as she screamed louder and louder. "Forgive you---Never! I hate you for what you did to me. Get away from me and stay out of my life! I never want to see you again!" She erupted into violent uncontrollable sobs that shook her body.

He pulled her into his arms and kissed her. "Issy, I'm so sorry..."

She shoved him away and slapped him with a force so fierce that it twisted her body around. She screamed and grabbed her stomach. "The baby," she gasped. "The baby..."

"Baby?" Bo had not noticed that she was pregnant until now. "Isabelle, I didn't know. I'm sorry." Then regaining his wits he picked her up and hurried out to his car. He set her down in the front seat and buckled her in, then jumped in the other side and sped away. "Don't worry Issy, I'll get you to the hospital in record time. Why didn't you tell me about the baby? I would never have pressured you to hear me out." He looked over at her. When she didn't say anything, he continued. "This is my fault. If anything happens to you or the baby, I'll never forgive myself."

He reached over and took her hand; she quickly snatched it out of his grasp.

"I am the baby's father, right?"

Anger flashed in her eyes. "It's true, you fathered him, but you will never be his father." She grabbed her stomach and doubled over. "Hurry, Bo!"

He got quiet and pushed on the gas pedal. He must concentrate on his driving now. He had to get her to the hospital quickly, but safely. He didn't say another word until he drove up to the emergency entrance and stopped the car. He jumped out and ran around to her side. He picked her up in his arms. "We're having a baby," he yelled as he carried her through the front door.

"Put me down, Bo!" Isabelle ordered as nurses rushed to her aid. "I'm perfectly capable of walking."

"Oh, no you're not," the head nurse remarked, walking up just then, pushing a wheel chair. "Get in this chair and I'll take you to maternity."

Bo followed close behind them as they made their way through the halls of the hospital. Finally the nurse stopped. She pushed Isabelle into a room and helped her into bed. "You rest now and a nurse will be in shortly to take care of you."

The nurse had barely gotten out of the room when the door opened and Bo walked in. He walked over and sat down in the chair beside her bed.

"Bo, get out of my room. I don't want you here," Isabelle stormed.

"I won't let you go though this alone," he said firmly. "I'm staying right here."

"We'll see about that," she said, pushing the button to summon help.

In a moment a voice answered. "Do you need something?"

"Yes, I need this man to get out of my room and leave me alone," Isabelle said, looking at Bo defiantly. "He is making me very nervous by being here."

"Young man, I must ask you to leave immediately," the head nurse said, a few moments later when she walked into Isabelle's room.

"But I'm the baby's father."

"Is that right?" She looked at Isabelle.

"Yes, he is the biological father, but I hate him, and I don't want him anywhere near me."

The nurse looked at Bo. "I believe it would be better if you leave. She needs to relax and it's obvious that you're making her nervous." She stood there until Bo left the room. "Hon, you try to rest now," she said, pulling the covers up around Isabelle. "I don't think he'll bother you again."

Bo sat in the waiting room watching the door. He saw the nurse from Isabelle's room walk by. He waited a few more minutes then quietly got up and walked to her room. He opened the door and looked in. Isabelle had her face turned away from him so he tiptoed over to the bed. He picked up the summons button and held it out of her reach, then, he reached out and touched her.

"Issy, I've got to talk to you."

She reached to grab the button but it was gone.

He held it where she could see it. "You've got to listen to me," he said softly. "I can't let you believe that I left because I didn't love you. I loved you with all my heart and I still do. Please let me explain, then, afterwards if you still want me to leave, I'll go peacefully."

When she didn't object he continued. "Isabelle, I'm so sorry I tricked you into that fake wedding ceremony. I would never have done that if I had been in my right mind, but I was drinking that night and I couldn't think straight. I had started drinking after my graduation ceremony ended and continued all that night and the next day and…"

"What about the thousand dollar bet; don't tell me that didn't sway your decision," she blurted out. "It really hurt me, knowing that you would betray me for a thousand dollars---knowing that the money meant more to you than I did."

"Isabelle, please don't think that," he pleaded. "Let me try to explain why I made that bet. As you know I had to do a lot of community service because of the drug stuff, and that took a lot of my time. Between that and trying to keep my grades up enough to graduate, there wasn't much time left over for me to work at my job; so my funds were meager to say the least. Our wedding day was getting close, so when Jeff said he would give me a thousand dollars if I could talk you into marrying me that night, it seemed like a good idea. I wanted to take you on a honeymoon you would never forget and that's why I agreed to do it."

"Bo, you didn't know me very well. I didn't care about a fancy honeymoon. Anywhere, as long as you were there, would have been okay with me."

"I know that I made a horrible mistake," he said, as if she had not interrupted. "I was supposed to tell you after the ceremony that it was a trick, but as God is my witness, I was so drunk, that before the ceremony was over, I believed it was real and that we were actually married." He wiped a tear away. "The next morning when I woke up I had sobered a little and I realized what I had done. I had betrayed you in the worst way and I wanted to die. I couldn't stand to see the hurt in those big blue eyes when you found out what I had done, so I took the coward's way out. I jumped in my car and drove. It didn't matter where I went. I just had to get out of there. I drove until I almost ran out of gas. I stopped at a gas station and right across the street was a rehab for alcoholics. I knew that was for me, so I went over and told them I needed help, and that I was willing to work for my rehabilitation. I had the thousand dollars, but it felt dirty and I wouldn't touch any of it. The next few months I scrubbed toilets, cleaned up other people's vomit and did anything else that needed to be done. It wasn't pleasant, but knowing that I was getting clear of alcohol so I would be worthy to come back to you, kept me going. I was dismissed late yesterday and I started home. I didn't stop until I reached the ranch and you."

"You didn't sleep?"

"No, I was so excited about seeing you again that I couldn't have slept even if I had tried."

"Bo, you were gone almost nine months and you didn't call one time."

"I wanted to call you, especially on your birthday. Oh how I wanted to hear your voice on the day we were supposed to become man and wife, but I couldn't do it. I felt too ashamed for hurting you and running away like I did."

"You should have called your mother. She thinks you're dead."

A look of pain crossed his face. "God forgive me," he whispered. "I didn't mean to hurt her but I should have realized she would be worried sick. I'll call her now." He dialed but there was no answer.

"Oh," Isabelle said, "they went on a trip to the Smoky Mountains, but they will be back on Sunday."

"Isabelle," he said, "I didn't call you because I knew if I heard your voice, I couldn't stay away from you; and I had to stay there until I was completely clear of my addiction. I couldn't come back to you until I was sure I would never take another drink."

"You think you're cured?" There was sarcasm in her voice. "I've heard it's very hard to cure an alcoholic. That he almost always goes back to drinking."

"There's another reason I know that I will never again use alcohol; I found the Lord while I was gone. The Lord forgave me, Issy, and now I'm begging you to forgive me and give our love another chance."

Her anger had subsided somewhat and the hatred she felt for him had lessened, but she knew she could never give him what he wanted---another chance. She spoke kindly but firmly. "Bo, I'm happy that you are alive and well, and I'm thankful that you have accepted the Lord, but as for the second chance; it's not gonna happen. When you left, I was devastated and it took me a long time to get over you, but I did. I have a wonderful man in my life now and I love him with all my heart. We plan to get married soon. I don't know if I can ever truly forgive you but even if I do, there will never be anything between us again."

"But Isabelle..."

"If you'll excuse me, I'm going to rest now, at least 'til the next pain hits."

He heard the finality in her voice and he knew he had lost her forever. He walked out of the room and back to the waiting room. Even if there was no hope left for the two of them, he would stay until the baby was born. He couldn't let her go through that alone. He walked over to the desk and spoke to the lady sitting there. "Keep me informed on how Isabelle Lefourche is coming along, please."

She nodded and he sat down in one of the chairs close to her desk.

"Mr. Abbott. Mr. Abbott," the lady said, shaking him slightly.

He opened his eyes and sat up. "I must have dozed off," he mumbled. "What time is it anyway?"

"It's almost seven o'clock and Miss Lefourche just gave birth to a baby boy."

"A boy," he said, smiling proudly. "I have a son. Can I see them?"

"You can go in to see her shortly. She can explain things to you."

A few minutes later, Bo walked into Isabelle's room only to find her crying.

"Issy, what's wrong? Has something happened to the baby?"

"Oh, Bo, I want to see my baby. Make them bring him to me."

"They will bring him to you as soon as they finish with him."

"No, no they won't," she cried. "I'll never get to see my baby."

"What are you talking about," he said, puzzled. "They can't keep your baby from you."

"That's just it, Bo," she explained. "He's not legally my baby. I put him up for adoption and he belongs to someone else."

"They can't take your baby against your will."

"I signed papers."

"You gave our baby away?"

"I didn't think I was ready to be a mother and I couldn't bear the thought of having him around to remind me of you. But now I know I love him no matter what and I want to be his mother. But it's too late."

"Maybe not," Bo said. "Why not call a lawyer and see if there is anyway to stop the adoption."

"It's after office hours."

"But this is an emergency," Bo said. "Aren't lawyers the same as doctors; you know that oath they take to always be available when people need them?"

"I hope you're right," she said, checking the phone book and dialing. "I'm calling Mama's lawyer, he'll know what to do," she explained while the phone was ringing. "Mr. Turner, I'm sorry to bother you at home," she said when he answered. "This is Isabelle, Roseanna's daughter, and I need your help." She explained things to him.

Ross was familiar with the situation between Isabelle and Bo. "Give me a moment to think about this," he said. After a pause he asked, "Did Bo sign the papers?"

"No, he didn't sign them. Is that important?"

"That depends," the lawyer answered. "Can you get in touch with him?"

"He's right here," she said. "Will that make a difference?"

"It will certainly make things a lot easier," he told her. "I'll be right over." He got there a few minutes later. He went over and gave Isabelle a kiss. "It's going to be all right," he assured her. He turned to Bo. "Come with me."

They walked to the nurse's station. "Miss Lefourche in room 165 would like to see her baby," Ross informed the lady behind the desk.

"I'm sorry," the lady said. "Miss Lefourche put her baby up for adoption and part of the agreement was that she would not see the baby, so we're not allowed to let her see him."

"Well, we have a new development that overrides any former agreement," Ross informed her. "This is the baby's father and he didn't sign anything, so there won't be an adoption. Now, take the baby to his mother."

"We'll do it right away," the lady said, and went to make sure it was done.

Ross went back to Isabelle's room. "Everything is okay," he said. "The baby will be here soon."

"Thank you," Isabelle said, taking hold of Ross's hand. "You don't know how much it means to me to get to see my baby and hold him in my arms. At least I will always remember what he looks like..."

"You won't have to remember anything since you will be taking care of him each day."

She looked at him with a puzzled look. "What do you mean?"

"There is not going to be an adoption today or any other day and you've got Bo to thank for that."

"Bo?"

"Yeah, since he's the baby's father and he had not agreed to the adoption, he had the power to stop it and he did, so the baby is yours to keep."

"Thank you," she said, tears of joy running down her face. "How can I ever repay you?"

"Just take good care of that little boy," he answered as Bo walked in followed by a nurse with the baby in her arms.

"Here, mommy, here's your little boy," she said, placing the baby in Isabelle's arms.

"Thank you," Isabelle said, moving the blue blanket so she could see his face.

Ross leaned over and kissed her. "That's a fine young man you've got there," he said, admiring the baby. "I've got to go now. Call me if a problem arises over the adoption."

"I will and thanks again."

"I'd like to add my thanks to that too," Bo said shaking his hand. He pulled a chair close to the bed and looked adoringly at his baby son. "He's so perfect," he said, removing the little blue cap from off his head. "Hey, he's got blonde hair like me, and I believe he has my eyes too."

"The color of his hair and eyes will probably change, and, I have blue eyes too," Isabelle informed him. The last thing in the world she wanted was for the baby to look like Bo.

"It would be better if he got his looks from you," Bo said. "To have a beautiful mother like you and end up looking like me would be such a waste."

Isabelle had almost forgotten how charming Bo could be. She couldn't let him get to her. She had to stay focused. "He will be the most beautiful baby in the world no matter who he looks like." She didn't want to dwell on his looks so she removed the blanket from around him and they looked him over carefully. They counted his fingers and toes. They planted kisses on his tiny face. All too soon the nurse came in to take him back to the nursery.

"Can't he stay in here with me tonight?"

"No," the nurse answered. "Since he was born a couple of weeks early he needs to be where we can watch him closely."

"Is something wrong with my baby?" Isabelle was on the verge of panic.

"He seems to be in perfect health, but because he is a little premature we want to keep a close eye on him."

Isabelle held him close and kissed him. "Bye, bye, mommy's little man," she said and handed him to Bo.

He held him a moment, then kissed him. "Take good care of our baby," he said as he handed him back to the nurse.

"We will," she said, turning to Bo. "Isabelle's had a rough day and needs to sleep now, so you should go and let her rest."

"I'm on my way out," he promised. Then he took Isabelle by the hand. "Issy, I'm going to a nearby hotel and I'll be back tomorrow. You rest now." He leaned down and kissed her on the forehead, then walked out of the room.

Isabelle didn't go to sleep right away. She tossed and turned as troubling thoughts went through her head. Had Bo gotten the wrong idea about the baby; about her? She had told him that there was no way they would ever be together but did her actions prove otherwise; at least to him. She felt an uncertainty go through her. "Oh, Brock, I wish you were here," she whispered. "I need you to hold me. I need your strength."

She felt strong arms lift her up as a tender kiss touched her lips. "Sweetheart, I'm here."

"Brock---but how?"

"The pastor's wife called and told me that you were in the hospital and I left right away."

"But your class..."

"Nothing is more important to me than you and I would have come regardless, but everything worked out okay. I gave the pastor my notes and he is going to teach the class."

"I'm glad you're here," she said, clinging to him. "I need you so much."

"Is it the baby? Is he okay?"

"He's small, but he's okay..."

"You had the baby?"

"Yeah, and we need to talk about that."

"Honey, you need to rest. The nurse gave me permission to come see you but only for a few minutes; she said you needed to sleep."

"I can't sleep until we talk."

"Okay, as long as she doesn't come and toss me out. So what do you want to talk about?"

"You remember when you told me you were falling in love with me but I wasn't ready to talk about it then. Well, I'm ready now, but first there's something I need to tell you." She took his hand. "I've made a decision that affects both of us and after you hear me out I won't blame you if you want to take it all back."

"Isabelle, the day I told you I was falling in love with you, I meant it and I still mean it. I love you and nothing you say will change my feelings for you."

"Hear me out first, then, decide," she said. "My baby is a beautiful little boy and when I saw him, I knew what I had to do. I'm going to keep him. I love him and I want to be his mother. I know when you said you loved me, it was going to be just the two of us and I don't know how you feel now that there is a baby involved. I will understand if you don't want to raise another man's child."

He didn't answer right away. When he did his voice was slow and deliberate. "What if I tell you that it does make a difference and I don't want to raise Bo's son."

Isabelle's lips quivered as tears filled her eyes. "I love you, Brock, and I'd do almost anything to have you in my life, but I won't give my baby up for anyone, not even you, so I guess this conversation is over." She turned away from him.

He reached out and pulled her to him. "Honey, I didn't mean that. I only wanted to see if this decision of yours to keep the baby was a whim, or if you truly love him and want to be a mother to him. I'm glad to see that your love for him is genuine. I'll be proud to be his father and I will love him as if he were my own son."

"You could do that?"

"My darling, that little boy is a part of you and that makes me love him already," he said. "Now that that's settled, let's make it official." He took her hands and looked into her eyes. "Isabelle, I love you. You're the one I want to spend the rest of my life with; the person I want to wake up beside each morning; the one I want to love for all my days on earth; the..."

"Get on with it---I can't say yes until you ask me."

"Isabelle will you marry me?"

"Yes, yes, with all my heart, I will marry you."

They sealed their engagement with a kiss. "I have to pinch myself to make sure this is real," he said, kissing her again. "A beautiful young girl like you falling in love with someone like me---that only happens in dreams."

"I feel the same way about you loving me; but if I'm dreaming don't you dare wake me, for I want this dream to go on forever."

"I've got to get out of here," he said with a sigh. "I'm not sure what that nurse would do if she came in and I'm still here."

"Can't you stay a while longer?" She took his hand. "Please sit beside me and hold my hand 'til I fall asleep. That chair over there reclines so you can be comfortable while you wait for me to go to sleep."

He pulled the chair over, reclined back in it, and took her hand.

The nurse came in a while later. Brock was sitting in the chair holding onto Isabelle's hand and they were both sound asleep. She got a pillow and blanket from the closet. She put the pillow under his head and spread the blanket over him. "There's no need to disturb them," she said, softly. "Isabelle doesn't need a pill tonight. He's the best medicine she could have." She turned off the light, tiptoed out of the room and shut the door quietly behind her.

Chapter 10

Excitement ran rampant at the ranch on Monday. Isabelle and the baby were coming home from the hospital today. A host of family and friends were gathered there to welcome them home. Brad and Roseanna had flown in late last night on the company jet. Kent and Mavis were there. Big Jake and Sam had hurried over this morning to join in the celebration and Ellie and Rex rounded out the happy group.

"They're here! They're here," Roseanna exclaimed, glancing out the window and seeing Brock's car coming down the lane that led to the ranch. Everyone except Brad and Roseanna had gone to the hospital over the weekend and had seen the baby, so when Brock and Isabelle walked into the den, they stepped back and let the two proud grandparents have their first look at him.

"Daddy, he's named after you," Isabelle said, placing the baby in his arms. "I figured there were enough William's and Bradley's in this family so I named him Brady, you know like the Brady Bunch on TV."

Brad smiled as he got the first look at his grandson; his name sake. He lifted the baby up and kissed him gently on his tiny little face.

"Okay, grandpa, you've had him long enough, it's my turn now," Roseanna stated a few minutes later taking the baby from Brad.

Just then the doorbell rang. Brad opened the door. "What are you doing here," he demanded crossly when he saw Bo standing there.

"Why shouldn't I be here? I'm the reason Isabelle has the baby."

Brad grabbed him by the collar. "How dare you mention that? Now get out of here before I…"

"No, Daddy, he's not talking about that," Isabelle cried. "I wouldn't have the baby if it weren't for him. As you know I signed papers giving my baby to strangers; so legally he didn't belong to me. I was not even supposed to see him. But I caught a glimpse of him when they were taking him from the room and I realized that I wanted to hold him and tell him how much I loved him. Bo was at the hospital with me and suggested we call a lawyer. I called Ross Turner and he came right over. Because Bo is the biological father and he had not agreed to the adoption, he could stop it, and he did, so thanks to Bo we have this beautiful little baby boy to love and to keep for the rest of our lives."

Brad cleared his throat and let go of Bo. "Son, I'm sorry I jumped on you like that. Please accept my apology." He held out his hand. "Our family will forever be grateful."

Bo shook his hand. "You have every right to hate me for what I did to Isabelle. I hate myself more than you could ever know, and I want to apologize to all of you for the pain I've caused."

"I think I speak for all of us when I say you're forgiven," Roseanna said, giving him a hug. "Every time we look at Brady or hold him; on his birthdays or Christmas or any special occasion, we will silently thank you for making it all possible. Now come on, let's get back to admiring this beautiful grandson of mine."

After lots of 'ohs and ahs' and about a jillion pictures of Brady, at least one with every person there, as well as by himself, they settled down to a lunch of sandwiches, chips, soft drinks and dozens of Mimi's famous homemade cookies.

"Isabelle, you must be exhausted," Mavis said when they finished eating. "We're going so you can get some rest." Then after another hug and kiss for their grandson, Mavis and Kent left. The others followed soon and only Brad, Roseanna, Brock and Bo were left.

Sweetheart, we're going to the office to do some work," Brad said, giving Isabelle a big kiss. "That is, if we may borrow your van, Mimi."

"Of course, you can borrow the van provided that you will drop me off at the mall. I want to do some shopping."

"That sounds great, Mimi," Roseanna said. "I think I'll go with you, that is, if you can get along without me at the office." She looked over at Brad.

"We'll manage somehow," he said. "I know you're anxious to buy things for Brady." He leaned over and kissed her. "Buy him something special for me."

"With all this talking about shopping we've completely forgotten about Isabelle," Mimi said. "She can't stay here alone."

"I'm not going anywhere, so go and shop 'til you drop," Brock said.

"Okay, I guess we're off then," Brad said. He put his arm around Isabelle. "You try to get some rest and we'll see you in a few hours."

"Okay, Daddy." She lay down on the couch and closed her eyes, but she couldn't rest. "Brock, would you push the baby's bassinet over here by me?"

"Honey, you've been through a lot these past couple of days. You need to rest," he told her.

"I know, but I can rest better if he is close to me. You can sit here with us and that will make me rest even better."

He pulled the bassinet close to Isabelle then sat down beside her. She laid her head in his lap. He leaned down and kissed her. "I love you sweetheart," he whispered.

"I love you, too."

Bo was feeling somewhat uncomfortable and started looking nonchalantly around the room. He spied the copy of the baby's birth certificate and picked it up. He began to read it under his breath. "Brady Lee Lefourche?" He checked it again, then, spoke aloud. "Isabelle, you put the baby's last name as Lefourche."

"Yes, but that's only temporary," she explained. "After Brock and I are married, he's going to adopt him legally and his name will be changed to Mitchell."

"Over my dead body," Bo stormed. "He's an Abbott and no one is going to take that away from him."

Isabelle sat up and looked at Bo. "Surely you can't expect me to give him your last name."

"Well, you're sure not going to give him that man's last name."

"Bo, be reasonable," she pleaded. "I don't want my son going through life with a last name that's different from mine. What will that do to him? He's bound to ask questions."

"He won't if he knows the truth from the beginning," Bo reasoned. "Just tell him I'm his father."

"And what about when he wants to know why his father and mother are not together? What do I tell him, Bo? Do I explain to him the circumstances of the night he was conceived---how you tricked me into thinking we were married so you could win a thousand dollar bet. Then instead of telling me the truth you slept with me, then left me, like I was a worthless piece of junk. Do you want your son to know that he was conceived under such ugly circumstances? Well, I don't want him to know that. I want him to think that he was conceived in pure love by a mother and father who truly loved each other."

"We did love each other..."

"You didn't love me," she blurted out. "I loved you but you never loved me. Love doesn't do what you did to me."

There were tears in his eyes. "Issy, if you believe that, then I know you can never forgive me. I don't deserve your forgiveness, but I do love you and our son with all my heart. I know that I've lost you, but I won't lose my son. I'll never give up on him."

"Bo, please, if you won't do this for me, then do it for Brady. He doesn't deserve to be shuffled between two fathers. I don't know why it matters to you anyway."

"Isabelle, you don't know what it means to a man to have a son; someone to carry on his name down through generations to come. Brady is an Abbott. That's his heritage and you're asking me to take that away from him. He has a right to know who he is, and I'm gonna see that he gets that right."

Isabelle started crying and hid her face on Brock's shoulder. He pulled her close before he spoke. "Bo, this discussion is over. Isabelle is in no shape to handle it right now. Nothing can be settled today. We have a couple of months before a decision has to be made. That gives us plenty of time to think this over and to pray about it. I'm sure God will show us the best solution to this problem." He hesitated momentarily. "Now, it's time for you to leave. Isabelle needs to rest."

Bo stormed out and slammed the door behind him."

Isabelle jumped to her feet. "I hate him," she screamed. "He hasn't changed a bit, and I almost fell for his line. I almost trusted him again."

"Isabelle, please calm down," Brock coaxed leading her over to the couch. "You've just had a baby. You don't need to get upset."

"I can't help it," she said, sitting down on the couch. "He's going to ruin my life again. Brock, what are we going to do?"

"We'll put it in the Lord's hands and let Him work it out," he said. "Now, stop fretting and get some rest young lady---Doctor Mitchell's orders."

She laid her head back down in his lap and he stroked her hair until she drifted off to sleep. Then he eased her head down on the couch and stood up. He pushed the bassinet into the kitchen, got all the stuff the baby would need and picked up the portable phone from the table in the den. He turned the ring signal down, then, walked into the kitchen and shut the door. Isabelle needed to sleep and he was well able to take care of the baby until she woke up. She was still asleep hours later when Brad, Roseanna and Mimi got home.

"Come help me, please," Brad laughingly told Brock as he walked into the kitchen. "We needed a big rig to carry all the packages these two ladies bought, but not having one available, we managed to squeeze them all into Mimi's van."

"Brad, I need to talk to you," Brock remarked on the way to the van. "Bo and Isabelle had a run-in after you left and it left her all stressed out."

"What was it about this time?"

"He found out that I'm planning to adopt Brady and give him my name, and he hit the ceiling. He said it's not going to happen. He wants the baby to have the Abbott name."

"Do you think he can stop you?"

Brock thought a moment. "Well, he stopped the other adoption because he's Brady's biological father so that may be enough to stop me from adopting him."

"How's Isabelle holding up?"

"She finally went to sleep," he answered. "But I believe she's about at the breaking point."

"I'll speak to Bo," Brad said. "I'll tell him how fragile Isabelle is right now. I'll go over right after supper."

"Thanks, that takes a load off my mind," Brock said. "He'll listen to you."

It took several trips to get the packages in the house.

"Did you ladies completely clean out the mall?" Brock asked jokingly.

"Just the baby stores," Brad replied laughing.

"Brady needed everything," Roseanna spoke up in defense of her and Mimi's shopping spree.

"Well, it looks like you got everything, sweetheart," Brad said teasingly.

Isabelle leaned up and looked around. "What's all this?"

Roseanna rushed over to her. "Oh, baby, I'm glad you're awake. Now we can show you the stuff we got for Brady."

"Please, can we eat first," Brad begged in a famished voice. "I don't relish the thought of eating at midnight, and that's how long it will take if you show her everything; my stomach can't wait that long."

"Oh you," Roseanna said, hitting him on the arm. "But since we don't want you starving right before our eyes, we will eat first. Gentlemen, please follow me into the kitchen where supper will be served in about five minutes."

"Five minutes---right," Brad teased.

"Eat your words, baby," Roseanna teased back, as they walked into the kitchen where the table was filled with dishes of fried chicken and all the trimmings.

Not to be outdone Brad felt of the dishes. "The food is hot," he commented, a little taken back. "How did you do all this in just a few minutes?"

"It's a trade secret," Mimi said, grinning, hoping they didn't see the thermal boxes from the chicken place downtown. "Women just know how to get things done."

Brad nodded knowingly. "I thought I smelled fried chicken on the way home; but I thought I was hallucinating because I was on the verge of starvation. Now, I know you two women stopped at our favorite chicken place and bought supper."

"Like I said, women know how to get things done," Mimi said braggingly.

Brock was taking all this in. He could hardly wait to be a part of this wonderful family who made even simple things fun.

Chapter 11

"Honey, I've got some bad news," Brock said arriving at the ranch a few days later. "I got word this morning that my Aunt Elizabeth is sick and they don't think she will make it."

"I'm so sorry," Isabelle said, putting her arms around him. "She's your only living relative, isn't she?"

He nodded. "Mom was an only child and Dad only had the one sister," he said. "Aunt Lizzie and Uncle Carl never had children, so that only leaves me."

"I can't imagine being the only one left in our family," she commented. "How sad that must be."

"Yeah, knowing I will be the only one left in our family does leave an empty feeling in me."

"When we get married we'll have lots of kids and start your family tree all over again; and 'til then you can share my big family with me."

"I can hardly wait." He looked at his watch. "It's time for me to get going."

"I'm going with you," Isabelle said. "I can be ready in a few minutes."

"Honey, you can't go," he said. "You've just had a baby and you're not strong enough to make that long trip."

"But I don't want you to go through this alone."

He kissed her. "I love you for caring about me but I may be gone a couple of weeks and there's just no way you can come with me."

She knew he was right so she submitted. "I'll miss you so much and I'll call you every day."

"I'll miss you too," he said. "But let me call you. My schedule will be hectic so it will be better if I call when I'm free."

"Okay, I'll be waiting by the phone."

"Oh, before I forget it how are things going with Bo?"

"I haven't heard from him since the day we brought the baby home. I don't know if that's good or bad. I have no way of knowing what he's thinking."

"I think it's a good sign," he said. "Your dad had a talk with him before they left to go home and I guess it worked."

"It looks that way," she said. "Bo respects Daddy a lot. I just hope he don't start coming around when he finds out that you are gone."

"If he gives you trouble just let me know," Brock told her. "Now, I've really got to get going. Give Brady a kiss for me and I love you."

"I hope and pray that everything turns out well with your aunt and I'll be anxiously waiting here for you to get back."

They walked arm and arm to the door and after several long lingering kisses he said goodbye, walked to his car and drove away.

Isabelle waved 'til he was out of sight, then, walked back inside. Sighing deeply she sank down on the couch. There was a sick feeling in the pit of her stomach, but she had to put her feelings aside and think of him. He had a rough time ahead and there would be no one there to help him through it. "No one, but You, Lord," she whispered. "Be with him and let him feel your love and also my love and all the other people who love him." Tears misted her eyes as she thought of Brock being alone and facing losing his aunt whom he loved dearly.

The funeral was over and Brock lingered by the gravesite. It had been a hard week. Aunt Lizzie had gone down fast and he only had a few days with her before she died. He thanked God for those precious days. They had talked about the good times they'd had together when he was growing up; he'd told her about Isabelle and promised to bring her to visit after they were married; she had talked to him about her will, and said that he would inherit everything. She told him where all her important papers were and gave him her lawyer's name and address. They shared many wonderful moments, but those moments were cut much too short. As he sat by her bedside, holding her hand, she died peacefully in her sleep.

Now, standing here by her gravesite he wiped the last tear from his eyes and laying his hand on top of the casket, he said his final goodbye.

"I love you, Aunt Lizzie and I'll miss you, but I know you are in a much better place, and I can only imagine the joy and bliss you're feeling right now being reunited with Uncle Carl and the rest of the family. I know you will be happy in that wonderful place; but maybe you can look down on me ever now and then. I'm getting ready to embark on a brand new experience, being a husband and father all at once, and I'm sure I'll need lots of help. I'll say goodbye now. I'm going to miss you." He kissed the tips of his fingers and rubbed them lovingly over the coffin as tears streamed down his face.

"Brock."

He felt a hand gently touch his shoulder. His heart leaped inside him. That familiar voice... He whirled around. "Susan," he whispered. He grabbed her and held her close.

"Oh, Brock, I'm so sorry about Aunt Lizzie," she cried. "I tried to get here for the visitation but I didn't know about it in time. I took an early flight this morning and got here in time for the funeral."

"You were at the funeral? I didn't see you."

"I didn't want you to know I was here so I sat in the back. I wanted to see you alone first, in case it was awkward seeing each other again."

"It could never be awkward seeing you."

"I feel that way too but I wasn't sure how you would feel."

"We've got so much to talk about," he said, giving her another hug. "Can you stay awhile or do you have to go right back?"

"I can stay for a little while."

"Good," he said, handing her a set of keys. "Here are the keys to Aunt Lizzie's house. You go on ahead and I'll be there as soon as I settle up with the funeral home."

About an hour later he walked into the house where Susan was waiting. "Is that coffee I smell?"

"Yes," she said walking out of the kitchen. "I rummaged around in the fridge and fixed something to eat. I imagine you must be hungry after the day you've had."

"I'm starved," he replied. "The folks at church prepared a big meal before the funeral but I was too nervous to eat much, so my stomach is grateful to you," he added as they sat down at the table to eat.

"There were so many people at the funeral," Susan said. "They had to put extra chairs in the aisles."

Yes, everyone who knew Aunt Lizzie loved her, and, they all showed up to pay their last respects."

"She would have been proud."

"Yeah," he said. "But I think she would have been most proud to know that you were here. You were one of her favorite people. Sometimes I think she loved you more than she loved me."

"Remember when we were kids how we played at her house and she never seemed to grow tired of us being around."

"I think we made up for the kids she and Uncle Carl wanted, but never had," he said. "I believe they enjoyed having us around. There was no place in this house that was off limits to the two of us."

"We had a lot of good times here and I'm going to miss her so much," she said, tears welling up in her eyes.

He put his arm around her. "Aunt Lizzie wouldn't want us to be sad, so dry those tears and let's get caught up on all the years we've been apart."

"You're alone here so does that mean you're not married?"

"I'm not married but I am engaged. How about you? Is there a husband---kids?"

"No, I've never met the right guy, but tell me about your fiancée---this girl who was lucky enough to win your heart."

"You're never going to believe this," he answered with a big smile. "You remember Roseanna..."

"The singer?"

He nodded. "Do you remember when her husband and little girl, Isabelle, supposedly drown, then showed up months later alive and well? Isabelle is the girl I'm going to marry."

"But she's a child."

"Not anymore. She's eighteen now and a very lovely woman," he said. "She has a baby whom I hope to adopt as soon as we are married. It's not what it sounds like," he quickly explained and told her all about the night that Bo tricked Isabelle into believing they were married.

"It sounds like she's had a lot of hurt in her life," Susan said.

"She has," he said, "but I hope to change all that as soon as we're married. I'm going to dedicate my life to making her happy."

"Tell me all about her," Susan said.

"I met her at her eighteenth birthday party. It was supposed to be her wedding day to Bo and it was a very sad day for her. Her family and some friends came from Louisiana and since I was the new youth minister at the church I was invited too. As a birthday gift to her I invited her to have dinner with me. She accepted and we had a special catered dinner at my house and afterward we talked.

She asked me if I had ever been in love, so of course I told her about you."

"Did you tell her about graduation night?"

"No, of course not," he answered rather abruptly. "I had just met her so of course I wouldn't mention something like that. And besides that was personal between you and me."

"And our friends---remember?"

"I'll never forget that. You confided in your friend Darlene, and she told some others and before it was over they all knew our secret plans," he said. "Susan, it's a little late in coming but I want to apologize to you for that night."

"You have nothing to apologize for."

"Yes I do. When we were making plans on how to celebrate our graduation I'm the big mouth who suggested spending the night together; so it is my fault."

"I didn't have to agree to it, but I did, so the fault is equally mine."

"When Isabelle told me about the fake wedding I almost flipped out, thinking back to graduation night when practically the same thing happened to us."

"Yeah, our friends insisted that we go through a mock ceremony so it would seem like we were really married, and that way we wouldn't feel so guilty about sleeping together."

"The big difference was that both of us knew the ceremony was a fake; and we did feel guilty. Even though we had strayed far away from God, we still knew what we did was wrong."

"And we both were in the altar on Sunday morning praying until we knew we were forgiven," she said.

"And you left for Boston on Monday without me making things right. I'm so sorry about that."

Susan burst into tears. "Oh, Brock, I'm the one who is sorry," she blurted out. "There are some things about that night that you don't know. I've got to tell you, and when I do, it's going to turn your world upside down."

"Susan what can you possibly tell me that will turn my world upside down?"

"That night---graduation night---I got pregnant."

"You---pregnant---a baby?" He couldn't believe what he'd heard. "I didn't know. I'm so sorry---I didn't know. What about the baby?" Tears misted his eyes.

"It was a girl. Her name is Victoria and she's twelve now."

"Victoria---you named her Victoria?"

"Yes, and I call her Torie---you used to say if you ever had a daughter you wanted to name her Victoria and call her Torie, so that's what I did. I figured that way she would always have a part of you with her.

"Thank you for doing that," he said, through tears in his eyes. "You're an amazing woman, Susan Madison. But why didn't you tell me? I would have been there for you, for our daughter."

"I didn't know I was pregnant for about three months."

"Why didn't you tell me when you found out?"

"Do you remember the last letter you wrote me?"

"No," he said, shaking his head. "I don't even remember who wrote last."

"You did. I never answered your letter," she said. "I had gone to the doctor that morning and he told me I was three months pregnant. I could hardly wait to tell you. I was going to call and tell you that I was flying home for a visit. When I got there I was going to tell you in person that you were going to be a father; but when I got home, your letter was waiting. You wrote about getting the call into the ministry and how excited you were. You said that your life had taken a turn for the better and how you were always going to do your best to be a good example to those you ministered to, so that you would never be a stumbling block to anyone. I couldn't take the chance of ruining your ministry if I came forward and told you. How would it look for a man of God to be presented with a baby born out of wedlock? I just couldn't mess up your life."

He wiped tears from her eyes and pulled her into his arms. "Oh, Susan, it would not have mattered; I would have been there. Talk about ruining someone's life---look what I have done to yours---the hurt you must have felt all these years."

"My life is okay," she said. "It was my choice not to tell you so there's nothing to forgive."

"Susan, the money," he cried out. Did you have enough money to live on? I would have sent money. I would have supported you and our daughter."

She put her arms around him. "Our life has been fine," she assured him. "It was rough at first, but I found a young woman who needed a place to live and she moved in. I gave her free room and board in exchange for baby sitting. We arranged our schedules so that she would be home during the hours I was in school and she watched the baby 'til I got home. I had an internet business which I worked at night after the baby went to sleep. It was very successful, so I had plenty of money for me and our daughter."

"Does she know about me?"

"She doesn't know your name. I told her that her father is a wonderful, caring man; that you didn't know you had a child, and if you knew you would be there with her."

"I'd like to meet her, that is, if it's okay."

"I'm sure it's okay," she said, "but first there's something else I need to tell you about that night."

"Okay, I'm listening."

"It's about the wedding ceremony---it wasn't a fake, it was real. The minister was real and so was the marriage license. We've been legally married for almost thirteen years."

"Are you sure?" he asked. "How did our friends manage to pull it off---how could they get a real marriage license?"

"I don't know how they did it, but I do know that it was real, and we are legally married. I checked it out. Darlene saw your wedding announcement in the local paper here and panicked. She called and told me. I called the license bureau and they confirmed it. The minister registered the license the next week after the ceremony so that made it legal in sight of the law. I'm so sorry about this but I feel certain that it can be taken care of. We may have to get a regular divorce and I don't know how long that will take but..."

He put his hand over her mouth. "This is all too overwhelming for me to digest at once. I've just found out that I am a father and that you and I are legally married. I'm going to need time to think this through." Pain showed in his face as he realized what this could mean for him---for Isabelle, and their plans for the future.

"Brock, I'm sorry I had to tell you this, but I couldn't let you marry someone else while we are legally married. I'll do what ever it takes to make you a free man as soon as possible so you can go ahead with your plans to marry Isabelle."

"There are things to be considered here so let's not make a hasty decision," he said. "Let's take off to Boston right now and after I meet my daughter and see her reaction to all of this, then we can decide what to do."

"But you don't have a plane ticket."

"We'll drive through in my car," he suggested. "I'll drive back here on Sunday afternoon and finish taking care of Aunt Lizzie's business affairs."

"But we won't get far tonight," she said. "Are you sure you don't want to get a good night's sleep and head out early tomorrow."

"No, I can't sleep anyway and I want to see my daughter as soon as possible."

"Okay, I'll call and let her know that you are coming."

"No, I want to surprise her. That way I'll see her true expression."

The next afternoon Brock stood in the living room of Susan's lavish brick house, waiting for Victoria to get home from school. His muscles tensed when he heard a car door slam outside and he knew it was her.

"I'm home," she shouted, rushing into the room and throwing her books down on a chair. She saw Brock standing there. "Hello," she said politely. "Are you here to see my mother?"

He looked at the young girl standing there. She was blonde like Susan, but she had his brown eyes. He felt a love like he had never known swell up in his heart. He finally composed himself enough to answer her. "No, Torie, I'm here to see you," he told her. "I'm your dad."

"You're my real daddy?"

"Yes I am, and I'm sorry that I haven't been here for you all these years."

"Mom said you didn't know about me."

"That's right. I only found out last night that I have a daughter. I wanted to come and meet you and tell you that I love you, and I want to be a part of your life if you will have me."

"You really want me?"

"I want you with all my heart and I hope you will let me be a real father to you."

"You're going to always be here with me? You won't leave me?"

"Honey, I promise you I'll be here, and, there's nothing on earth that can ever make me leave you."

"Daddy," she cried running into his arms. "I always dreamed that someday you would come and want to be my father." She clung to him.

Brock held her in his arms while tears of joy ran down his face. It felt good holding his little girl like this, and he knew that from now on he would be a part of her life, no matter what it cost him.

He kissed her and looked into her big brown eyes. "Let's get your mom in here and go on a shopping spree. I've got twelve years to make up---twelve birthdays and twelve Christmas's. I'm not too good at this shopping stuff, but between the three of us, surely we can come up with some pretty awesome gifts."

"Okay, Daddy." Her eyes were dancing with glee. "Come on, Mom, we're going shopping," she shouted excitedly, taking his hand and skipping out of the room.

Chapter 12

Brock arrived in Nashville late Monday night. It was too late to see Isabelle so he drove to his house. He would try to get a few hours sleep before going out to the ranch. He knew sleep wouldn't come easy with all the things sloshing around in his head; things that had to be resolved. "Oh, God, help me," he prayed as he tossed and turned trying to decide the best way to handle the situation. His thoughts ran rampart as he struggled with the reality of what must be done. "How can I give her up when I love her so much?" he cried aloud. "How can I hurt her this way?"

He couldn't sleep so he got out of bed, made a pot of coffee, and paced the floor, drinking cup after cup of black coffee, trying to find an answer; but the answer wouldn't come.

He drove out to the ranch about mid-morning the next day. His legs felt like lead as he walked up to the door. His hands shaking, he rang the doorbell.

"Brock, you're home," she cried happily, when she opened the door and saw him standing there. She threw her arms around him and gave him a big welcome home kiss. "I missed you so much," she added and kissed him again.

"Is Mimi around?"

"No, she's off on a big day of shopping with a friend," Isabelle explained. "She won't be home until tonight, so that gives us a whole day alone here, and we've got a lot to talk about; a lot of plans to make."

"Let's sit down," he said, frowning because she was here alone and he felt sure she would need someone with her when she heard what he had to say. He took her hand and walked over to the couch. "Honey, there are some things I need to talk to you about and I need you to listen closely."

"I'm all ears," she said, snuggling close to him.

He gently pushed her aside and stood to his feet. "Isabelle, you know how much I love you…"

"Yes, I know you love me," she said, puzzled by the way this conversation was going.

"Please don't ever doubt my love for you." Tears ran down his face as he pulled her into his arms and held her close. "Baby, I don't think I've ever loved you more than I do right at this moment. Oh, Isabelle, I'm so sorry."

She stepped out of his arms and looked up at him. "Brock, what's going on? You're scaring me."

"Please forgive me," he cried. "I didn't mean for it to happen…"

"What happened? Why do I need to forgive you?"

"Susan came to the funeral and we--we…"

Isabelle's knee's felt like water. "Are you trying to tell me that you cheated on me this weekend---you slept with Susan---is that why you didn't call me?" Her voice was raised in anger.

"I wish it were that simple," he said sadly. "I didn't cheat on you, but something did happen, and I need to tell you about it starting from the beginning." He slumped down on the couch.

"By all means tell me the whole story," she snapped sitting down beside him.

"Remember the night I told you about Susan and me---well I didn't tell you everything about us." He hesitated, searching for the right words to say. "This is going to seem strange when you hear it and you may wonder why I didn't mention it sooner, but it just didn't seem important before."

"But it is now?"

He nodded. "It was a few days before we graduated and Susan and I were discussing how to celebrate our graduation. We wanted to do something special; something we had never done before. I suggested we spend the night together in a motel. I expected to get my face slapped for even suggesting such a thing, but to my surprise, she agreed. She told her friend, Darlene, who passed it on to others and before we realized it all our friends knew about it and they made plans of their own. They planned a fake wedding ceremony for us so we wouldn't feel so guilty about spending the night together; it would be like we were sorta married; but it didn't work. Even though we had strayed a long way from the Lord, we knew what we were doing was wrong and we felt plenty of guilt. We both prayed for God's forgiveness on Sunday. Then on Monday she left for Boston to start college and a few weeks later I got the call into the ministry and you know the rest of the story."

"That happened a long time ago, what does it have to do with us?"

"Well, you know how folks say your past always comes back to haunt you. That's so true; at least in this case. Susan didn't come home just for the funeral. Her friend, Darlene, had read about our upcoming wedding and she called Susan with a confession. Our so called wedding that night was not fake; it was real. The minister was real, the marriage license was real, and we've been legally married all these years."

"You're married to Susan?" Isabelle's lips quivered as tears misted her eyes. "Are you sure this is not just another prank?"

"Susan checked it out and it's for real," he said. "It seems the minister was not in on the prank and he recorded the license and that made it official."

"If this weren't so serious it'd almost be funny," she said. "I thought my wedding to Bo was real but it was a fake. You thought your wedding to Susan was a fake and it was real."

"I'm sorry, honey," he said. "I wish this had never happened but it did and, we've got to deal with it."

"You'll get a divorce, of course," she said. "I know this means we will have to postpone our wedding but that can be arranged. I'll call Mama now..."

"No, wait," he said, "there's more."

"Don't tell me anything else. I don't want to hear it," she said putting her hands over her ears.

"I've got to tell you and you've got to listen." He took her hands and held them tightly. "The two wedding ceremonies were right the opposite, but the rest of it was not. For you see, just like you, Susan got pregnant that night."

"Susan had a baby---why didn't you tell me you have a child."

"I didn't know. Susan didn't tell me until after the funeral." He told her the reason why Susan had kept the baby a secret from him. "When I found out that I have a twelve year old daughter I was shocked to say the least."

"I understand how you must feel," she said. "But honey this won't be a problem. Your daughter will be welcome in our home anytime. I will love her like she is my daughter too. She can spend holidays and summer vacations with us. I promise I will make sure she knows that she is a part of our family."

"It's not that simple," he said, a look of pain in his eyes. "I don't want to be just a holiday or vacation kind of father. I want to be there for her every day. I want her to know she can depend on me."

Isabelle was quiet for a moment before speaking. "Then we'll move to Boston, get a house close to where she lives, and you can see her on a daily basis. You will always be close by in case she needs you."

He shook his head. "Isabelle, that's still not what I'm talking about. When I say I want to be there for her, I mean I want to be there when she goes to bed at night and when she wakes up in the morning. I want us to be a real family."

Isabelle looked at him with hurt and disbelief in her eyes. "Is this goodbye Brock? Are you leaving me?"

A tear ran down his face. "Isabelle, I'm sorry. If there was any other way..."

"No," she cried. "It can't end like this. You made promises to me."

"I know, but I've got to ask you to release me from those promises. You've got to let me go, Isabelle. I've got responsibilities that I can't run away from. My daughter needs me. She's been without a father for twelve years. I made her a promise that I will be a father to her and that I will never leave her, and that promise outweighs any other promises."

"But you love me."

"Yes, I do love you, but I can't think of myself now or even you; my daughter is my first priority. I love her, Isabelle, just as you love Brady. You understand that kind of love. You were willing to give me up if I wouldn't accept your son and that's how I feel about Torie. It's tearing me apart to walk away from you, but I'll choose my daughter over anything or anyone."

"What about Susan? Won't you be a hypocrite pretending to be a husband to her when you're in love with me? How can you go through life with someone you don't love?"

"I do love Susan; not in the same way I love you, but my love for her is real and I'm sure it will grow deeper each day I spend with her."

"How is she going to feel if she finds out that you love me?"

"She already knows. We talked about it at length. She feels as strongly as I do about the three of us becoming a family, and she is willing to bear with me until I can put my love for you in the past. We both feel certain that day will come, and when it does I will be free to fall in love with her all over again; the way I loved her when we were young."

"What if that day doesn't come---what if you never get over me? Will you leave her and come back to me?"

He sighed. This was harder than he thought it would be. He had to make her understand as gently and lovingly as possible that there were no options here. He was leaving and there would be no turning back. There could never be anything between them again. He reached out and took her hands. "Isabelle, I've resigned my position as youth minister here, I've packed up all my things and when I walk out that door, I'm going straight to Boston. As soon as I get there Susan and I are going to her pastor's house and we're going to repeat our marriage vows to each other, and I'll never break those sacred vows. When I pledge myself to her it will be a total commitment; and it will be forever. I can never again dwell on the love you and I shared. So put me out of your heart and go with your life. I need to know that you are happy before I can be totally happy."

With tears streaming down her face she slid his ring off her finger and put it in his hand. "Go," she said, "but don't ask me to put you out of my heart---I can't do that. I'll never forget you; you are the love of my life and you always will be. Just go now and leave me alone."

"Isabelle, I don't want to leave you like this..."

"Go, get out of my sight," she ordered, pushing him toward the door.

He hurried out the door with tears running down his face, and, without looking back he ran to his car just as Bo drove into the driveway.

"Brock, you're home," Bo said, then noticing the tears he asked, "What's wrong."

"Go to Isabelle," Brock told him. "She needs you."

"Has something happened to the baby?"

"Just get in there Bo. Help Isabelle," Brock said, jumping in his car and speeding off.

Bo's heart was pounding wildly as he rushed into the house. He panicked even more when he saw Isabelle standing there as if in a trance. He put his arms around her and held her close. "Issy, what's wrong. Is it the baby?"

Isabelle clung to him. It was as if they were kids again and Bo was there for her; making things right as he had done when they were growing up. "He's gone, Bo, he's gone."

"No, no," Bo cried, thinking of Brady. "Our baby can't be gone."

Isabelle shook her head. "No, not the baby; Brock is gone. He left me Bo, just like you did."

Bo wondered what had happened but he wouldn't press her for an answer. She needed comforting now and he would comfort her. He led her over to the couch and sat down, then, he took her in his arms again. "I'm here, Issy," he whispered. "I'm not going to leave you. Just let it all out."

She wept until there were no tears left. A lump, the size of a baseball, made it impossible for her to speak so she laid her head on his shoulder and relaxed in his arms, her heart crying inside her. "Bo," she finally called out faintly.

"Don't try to talk, Issy," he said seeing the effort it took for her just to whisper his name. "Lie down on the couch and I'll get you something to drink." He came back in a few minutes with a tray which held a cup of hot herbal tea and a cup of coffee. "Here drink this," he said, handing her the tea.

"Thanks, Bo," she said sitting up and taking the cup of tea.

He sat down beside her with the cup of coffee in his hand. "Do you want to talk about what happened?"

She nodded and told him the whole story.

He set his coffee cup down and put his arms around her. "I'm so sorry, Isabelle. I don't know what to say about the decision he made, but I do know you don't deserve that kind of treatment. I don't know if I can help in any way but I'll always be here if you need me."

Brady's cries interrupted before she could comment. "Excuse me," she said and went to tend to the baby. She came back several minutes later carrying him and a bottle.

"I'll do that," Bo said, taking the bottle and reaching for the baby.

She felt too drained to argue so she put Brady in his arms. "You'll need to burp him half way through his bottle."

"Look at him go," Bo exclaimed. "You'd think he was starving."

"He slept right through his last scheduled feeding so he probably feels like he is starving," she commented. "Anyway, he sure seems to be enjoying that bottle."

"That's because he knows his daddy is feeding him."

Isabelle started to protest but didn't. She was too tired to get into it with Bo. She would set him straight later.

Brady went back to sleep almost as soon as he finished his bottle. Isabelle laid him back in his bed. As she walked back into the den the happenings of the day hit her like a ton of bricks. She broke down and started crying again.

Bo rushed over and took her in his arms. He couldn't bear to see her hurting like this so he pulled her close and held her.

"Oh, Bo, what's wrong with me," she cried. "Why is it that no man wants to marry me?"

"Isabelle, there's nothing wrong with you," he said, as a pang of guilt hit him knowing that he was at least partly to blame for the way she was feeling. "You're the most vibrant woman in the world and any man would give all he owns just for the chance to marry you…"

"What about you, Bo? You didn't want to marry me; now Brock doesn't want to marry me, so there must be something wrong with me."

"I was a fool to treat you the way I did and if only I could go back and live that night over..." He leaned down and kissed her, gently at first, then, when she returned his kiss, he kissed her with all the passion in his heart.

Suddenly she shoved him away and slapped him across the face with all the strength she had left. "Bo Abbott, how dare you!" Her eyes dark with anger was matched only by the fury she felt inside. "You know I'm vulnerable now and you try to take advantage of me..."

"I-I didn't," he stammered. "You kissed me back..."

"If I did, it was a mistake. I didn't mean it!" She was screaming now. "I hate you, Bo! Every bad thing that's happened to me this past year is your fault! Now get out of my house and out of my life for good. Get out now. I never want to see you again!"

"No, Isabelle, I won't leave you here by yourself. I'm staying until Mimi gets home, then I will go; and I promise I'll never bother you again." His words were cold and blunt.

"See that you don't," she screamed and ran to her room and slammed the door shut.

Bo sat with his face in his hands. He felt so alone; like the bottom had dropped out of his world. Why did he kiss her? He should have known that would make things worse between them. He loved her so much, but he was always doing things that made her hate him even more. He didn't blame her for hating him; he deserved it. And she was right; all of this was his fault. If only he had not betrayed her...they would be married now and she would never have fallen in love with Brock, and she wouldn't be hurting like this. "I promise I won't mess up your life again, Issy," he muttered aloud. He picked up the newspaper and turned to the ad section. He wrote down some numbers and made a few calls. Then he settled down to wait for Mimi to get home.

Mimi got home around nine o'clock. "What are you doing here, Bo?" she asked when she walked in the den and saw him lying on the couch.

He told her the whole story. "This hit her hard, Mimi," he said. "I hope you can help her get through it."

"She needs all of us to help her, Bo."

"Not me," he said, shaking his head. "She made it very clear that she doesn't want me around so I'm getting out of her life for good. I'm moving first thing tomorrow."

"Where are you going?"

"I'm moving across town close to the Center," he told her. "Andy called this morning and made me manager of the Center; and that means more money, so I can afford an apartment of my own."

"Do your parents know this?"

"No, I'll tell them as soon as I get home, which is where I'm headed now." He leaned over and kissed Mimi. "I don't know when I'll see you again," he said. "Take care of yourself, and Isabelle and Brady." He walked out the door before she could see the tears that were flooding his eyes.

"God help us all," Mimi prayed, looking in on Isabelle and the baby. They were both sleeping. "Poor little thing," Mimi whispered as she gently stroked Isabelle's face. Then she walked over and lifted Brady out of his crib. She laid him in his bassinet and rolled him to her room. "Your mommy needs to sleep through the night," she said to the baby as if he understood. "She'll have plenty of time tomorrow to remember all this and try to deal with it."

Chapter 13

"Mama, I don't think I can do this," Isabelle said as she stood in Roseanna's dressing room waiting for the concert to begin. "I'm not ready to sing yet."

"Baby, I think you must sing tonight," Roseanna said, putting her arm around her daughter. "Your fans know the pain you've gone through this year and they are worried about you. They need to see you on stage, singing, so they will know you are okay."

"But I'm not okay, Mama, I'm a basket case," she said. "You know what tomorrow is, but yet you insist that I get out on that stage and perform. I just can't do it."

"I'm sorry the concert is the night before your wedding to Brock was supposed to take place, but that's the only open date they had; and I believed the Home for Girls and Andy's Kid's Club needed the money we will raise here tonight, so I went ahead and scheduled it. I know you're hurting, sweetheart, but I believe singing tonight will help you break the ice on getting back out in public again," Roseanna said. "Won't you just sing one song?"

"I'll try, Mama," she conceded. "I have written a new song about the way I feel, but I'm not sure I can do it justice."

"Thanks, Baby," Roseanna said, planting a kiss on her daughter's forehead. She heard Travis Houston introduce her so she scampered out on stage and burst into singing, "It's A Matter of Dreams." That was the song that had launched her career all those years ago and it was still a favorite among her fans.

She sang song after song and was coming close to the end of the concert. "I have a special treat for you," she announced. "My daughter has written a new song and she is going to sing it for us now. As you know it's been a while since she sang on stage, so let's give a big Nashville welcome to Isabelle!"

Applause thundered throughout the auditorium as fans paid honor to the young girl whom they loved; the girl who had gone through so much hurt since her last appearance on stage.

Isabelle ran out on stage and bowed to the audience. "Thank you," she called over the noise of the crowd. "It's a privilege to be here tonight. I wrote this song a couple of weeks ago. It's called "Where Is My Mountain" and I hope you like it."

> Lord, I gave you my life; heart, body and soul,
> And I promised to work for you, anywhere you said go;
> And Lord I've been faithful; I've done all that you said,
> Still all I see Dear Lord, is a valley ahead.
>
> Lord, where is my mountain, that I've heard of so long,
> I've been in the valley, 'til my hope's almost gone;
> Lord, show me my mountain, and give me strength to climb,
> For I've been in the valley, for such a long time.
>
> I know you've been with me, each long weary mile,
> And that you'll stand by me, through each heartache and trial;
> So I'll keep pressing on Lord, 'til I gain victory,
> Over things by the roadside, that try to stop me.
>
> Lord, where is my mountain, that I've heard of so long,

I've been in the valley, 'til my hope's almost gone;
Lord, show me my mountain, and give me strength to climb,
For I've been in the valley, for such a long time.
Lord, I've been in this valley, for such a long time."

She finished the song and with tears streaming down her face she took a bow and ran off stage amid thunderous applause. Brad had sensed that she was having a struggle so he quietly got up out of his seat and walked back stage. He was waiting there and took her in his arms. "It's okay, sweetheart," he said holding her close.

"Oh, Daddy," she cried, "when will it all end---when will I have peace again?"

"Honey, it may not end today or tomorrow or even next week, but I promise you, you will reach your mountain someday; and then you will look back on all of this as a growing experience; and life will be good for you again."

"You promise, Daddy?"

"I promise sweetheart."

Roseanna walked back to the microphone. "She's okay, folks," she said, noting the audiences' concern for Isabelle. "Her daddy is with her backstage and he can always make things right for her." She paused a moment pondering what to do next. "I've never done this before, and I apologize to the guys in the band, but I'm going to sing a song that wasn't on the list for tonight's concert." She turned around. "Daddy, could you play a few stanzas of the song we were singing on the plane coming here, so the band can get familiar with it." She talked while he played softly. "I wrote this song a couple of days ago and now I know why. It's for you, Isabelle. It's as if God is sending a message to you through the words of this song. It's entitled, "He'll Calm Your Storm," and if anyone else is going through a storm right now; He will calm your storm too. While I sing this song, just lean on Him; and, as surely as he spoke the words, 'Peace be Still' to the raging waters and they obeyed Him; He can calm the winds of your storm." The band started playing and she sang with feeling and might.

> "Once I wandered in darkness, on life's ship at sea,
> And Satan's dark waters held bondage on me;
> Then Jesus reached down with His almighty arm,
> He said I love you and I'll calm your storm.
>
> And He will calm your storm,
> The storms of life that's left you battered and torn;
> He's the strength for the weak when they're hopeless,
> Child, He loves you and He'll calm your storm.
>
> It won't matter whatever your problem might be,
> It won't matter if it's too big for you or me;
> For my Lord is ready, He's able and waiting,
> He will calm the winds of your soul.
>
> And He will calm your storm,
> The storms of life that's left you battered and torn;
> He's the strength for the weak when they're hopeless,
> Child, He loves you and He'll calm your storm.
> Oh, child, He loves you and He'll calm your storm."

Roseanna took a bow and ran off stage to Isabelle. She put her arms around her and held her close. "It will be alright, baby," she told her, taking her hand and walking back on stage. "It's been great being with you tonight," she said, as she and Isabelle took a final bow. They walked off stage amid a thunderous applause.

People from the audience flocked to Isabelle, telling her how much they enjoyed her song; that they loved her and were praying for her. Isabelle was so busy talking to them and signing autographs, that for a while at least, her problems were forgotten and she was able to smile and be happy.

"Honey, I'm sorry we have to leave right away," Roseanna said, as the last of the folks left the auditorium. "Your daddy has that speaking engagement in town tomorrow at noon. Harriet has our plane waiting at the airport. So we'll go straight there from here."

"But you'll be all night getting home," Isabelle pointed out. "Wouldn't it be better to get a good night's sleep and leave out early in the morning?"

"We have reservations at our favorite hotel in New Orleans," Roseanna answered. "We will spend the night there and drive to Belle and Jesse's tomorrow morning. Brad and Jesse will go to the meeting and Belle and I will spend the afternoon shopping."

"That sounds great. I wish I were going with you," Isabelle said. "Give Aunt Belle and Uncle Jesse a big hug for me and have a great time shopping." Isabelle kissed Brad then Roseanna. "Give everyone back home my love." She turned away before they could see the tears misting her eyes.

"Goodbye sweetheart," they said waving to her.

The next morning Isabelle checked the clock on the nightstand. It was almost noon and she was still in bed. She hadn't slept that late; she had gotten up and dressed, but found that there was nothing to do, so she laid back down. Mimi had taken the baby over to Kent and Mavis before she went shopping. They wanted to keep him for the day. Now, lying here alone, her thoughts turned to Brock.

Almost two months had passed since he left her and Isabelle was no closer to forgetting him than the day it happened. Instead of turning to God for help to forget him; she had turned away from God. Thoughts of Susan and him filled her mind. Dark, hateful thoughts consumed her as she envisioned the two of them together. It's not fair," she cried aloud. "I should be sharing his life not her. I hate her! I wish she were dead. Oh God, please let her die." She knew God would never do what she was asking, but in her heart she wanted Susan dead.

"Oh, Brock, do you remember what today is?" she whispered. "Are you thinking of me or have you already forgotten me?" Tears rolled down her face as thoughts of him and his new family flashed through her mind. What was he doing right now at this moment? Was he kissing his wife or laughing with his daughter. "Oh, Brock I miss you so much," she cried out. "If only I could hear your voice and talk to you one more time."

Her thoughts were interrupted by the ringing of the phone.

"Hello," she said halfheartedly, not really wanting to talk to anyone.

"Isabelle."

Isabelle couldn't speak for a moment. That familiar voice, the one she longed to hear. Could it be possible? "Brock... is that really you?"

"Yes and please don't hang up. I need to talk to you."

Isabelle's heart skipped a beat. Did he remember today and was he thinking of her. "I'm listening," she said.

"I don't know what to say to you. I just needed to hear your voice today of all days; the day we were supposed to become man and wife."

"You did remember."

"Of course I remember. How could I forget our wedding day?"

"Our wedding day---that's almost funny," she said wiping away the tears. "This is my second wedding day in less than a year and both times the grooms ran out on me before the ceremony."

"Isabelle, I hurt you and I'm sorry; if there had been any other way..."

"Is it worth it," she asked. "Are you hurting today the way I'm hurting. Is that why you called? I have to wonder how you're doing on our wedding day; do you really care how I am, or, are you just trying to soothe your guilty conscience?"

He detected the hurt and bitterness in her voice. "Maybe, a little bit of both," he answered truthfully. "I am truly concerned about you, and I know that you are hurting because of me, so I do feel guilty. But I don't regret how things turned out. I wouldn't trade the time spent with my daughter for anything on earth."

"And what about your wife; do you feel the same way about her?"

"I love my wife and I'm happy with our life together. I wouldn't change things even if I could. Susan is pregnant and we're both very happy about that."

Isabelle slammed the phone down and fell across the bed weeping. The phone rang and she answered it, trying to get control of her emotions.

"Isabelle, we got cut off…"

"No, we didn't get cut off," she blurted out angrily. "I hung up because I didn't want to listen to you talk about how happy you are." Her breath was coming in short gasps now. "You go ahead and have a happy life with Susan, and have your kids with her too, but don't ever call me again."

She slammed the phone down again. "It's not fair, God! I should be the mother of his children, not her. She had no right showing up in his life after all these years and spoiling things between us. It's just not fair," she cried. "I hate her!" She fell across the bed and wept bitterly over today and the emptiness she felt inside.

She didn't know how long she had lain there when the doorbell rang. She got up, wiped the tears away as best she could and answered the door. "What are you doing here with my baby?" she demanded when she saw Bo standing there holding Brady in his arms.

"We were at the mall and Mom got a phone call from one of the ladies that works in the store; it seems there was a problem that none of them could handle so she had to rush down there, and Dad had to go to work so they asked me to bring the baby home."

"You were at the mall with them?"

"Yeah, they called me and told me they were bringing Brady to the mall and asked me if I wanted to join them..."

"I told you to stay away from my baby," she snapped, grabbing him from Bo's arms. "Where did this shirt come from," she demanded angrily as she read the words, I love my Dad, printed on the front of the shirt.

"I saw it in the mall and I bought it."

"Why is he wearing it?"

"He spit up on his other shirt and I put this one on him," Bo answered. "What's the big deal anyway; it's just a shirt."

"It's what it implies," she said. "You are not his daddy and you never will be. I want you to hear this, Bo, and I want you to hear it good. I will never allow you to ruin my baby's life the way you ruined mine, so I'm warning you, stay away from him and away from me. Do you understand?"

"Oh, yeah, I understand completely," he replied angrily. "And it will be my great pleasure to stay as far away from you as I possibly can, but, as for Brady; that's another matter. He's my son and I will be a part of his life; and I want you to understand that!" He walked out and slammed the door behind him.

Isabelle stood there shaking like a leaf as fury, like a fire, raged through her. Brady's cries jolted her back to her senses. "I'm sorry, baby," she whispered as she realized her anger was affecting him. "Mommy will calm down, I promise," she whispered again, holding him close and kissing him. She sat down and rocked him, singing a lullaby to him in a soft calm voice. She would not allow Bo to upset her to the point where it jeopardized Brady's well being. She had just laid the baby in his crib when Mimi came home.

Mimi took one look at her and gasped. "Isabelle, what's wrong?"

Isabelle ran into her arms. "Everything is wrong," she cried.

"Let's sit down," Mimi said, leading her over to the couch. "Now, tell me what's got you so upset."

"Bo brought Brady home from the mall and we got into it," she said. "I was so mad that I ordered him to stay away from the baby and from me."

"How did he take that?"

"He said he'd be happy to stay away from me, but that Brady is his son and he's going to be a part of his life and warned me not to try to stop him."

"That doesn't sound good," Mimi said. "Do you think he can cause trouble for you?"

"Maybe," she answered. "I did sign papers giving the baby up, so I don't know what legal rights Bo has, especially since he's the one who stopped the adoption from going through. I'm going to call mama's lawyer first thing Monday morning to find out if Bo has any rights where Brady is concerned."

At exactly one o'clock Monday afternoon Isabelle walked into Ross's office. He had been in court all morning so this was the earliest he could see her. "I'm Isabelle Lefourche," she told the pretty young lady behind the desk.

"Come right this way," the receptionist said, picking up a file and walking down the hall. "The trial is lasting longer than expected but you are to wait in here and he will be here shortly. I'm just filling in for the regular secretary," she explained, "so I don't know my way around the office. But here's your file in case you need it." She laid the file on the desk and walked out.

Isabelle picked up the file and flipped through it aimlessly. "This must be Mama's file," she muttered and started to close it when her glance fell on the word, divorce. "Divorce?" Isabelle looked at the front of the file to make sure it belonged to Roseanna. Roseanna Lefourche was typed in big letters. "It is her file," Isabelle whispered in disbelief. She flipped through it again until she came to the page where Ross had written comments about the divorce. She read it aloud. "Roseanna is divorcing Brad on grounds of adultery. No! That can't be true!" There had to be a mistake somewhere so she read further. "Brad is having an affair with his co-worker, Dori, and plans to marry her as soon as the divorce from Roseanna is final." Isabelle struggled to breathe. "No! No! That's not true. Not my daddy---he wouldn't. He's a good man. He would never cheat on Mama. He would never commit adultery." She read it over again. There it was in black and white. Daddy had committed adultery with Dori---he had cheated on Mama. She jumped up and ran out of the office, tears flowing down her face. She didn't hear the young lady behind the desk call out to her.

She jumped in her car and spun out of the parking lot. "I've got to talk to Mama," she said and dialed Roseanna's cell phone.

"Hello."

"You hypocrite," she screamed when Brad answered instead of Roseanna. "How could you do that to Mama? How dare you tell me how to live when you were having an affair with Dori? I hate you!" She turned off her cell phone and tears blinded her as she drove aimlessly through the streets of Nashville.

Brad stood there horrified. "Roseanna," he yelled. "Isabelle knows! She knows!"

"Isabelle knows what?" Roseanna asked, rushing into the room.

"She knows about Dori and me and she hates me. She called me a hypocrite. What am I going to do?"

"We're going to Nashville and we're going to set her straight about you."

Roseanna called her mother and asked her to pick up the boys from school and keep them overnight. She didn't explain why. Then she called Harriet and finding out that the company jet was available she told her to send it immediately. She didn't tell her the reason either.

It was dark already when Brad and Roseanna arrived at the ranch. They didn't have their keys with them so Brad rang the doorbell.

Isabelle opened the door and tried to shut it when she saw him standing there.

He put his foot in the doorway. "I've got to talk to you sweetheart," he said, walking into the foyer.

"I won't listen to a word you have to say, you hypocrite."

"Well, you will listen to me, young lady and you will do it now," Roseanna stormed, walking in, anger flashing in her eyes. "How dare you talk to your daddy that way?"

"Mama, I don't understand how you can take up for this man who cheated on you over and over again."

"I don't know where you got your information, young lady, but I'm here to set the record straight about your daddy."

"The where doesn't matter; all that matters is whether or not my information is correct." She looked at Roseanna in defiance. "Did daddy sleep with Dori; did you catch them in bed together in South Africa; did you see them kissing at the hospital there; and, did you file for divorce on grounds of adultery?"

A look of pain shrouded Roseanna's face. Where did her daughter learn those things, and how can she explain it to her without making Brad seem guilty? "I did not file for divorce on grounds of adultery," she answered truthfully. "Where did you hear all this stuff?"

"It was all in your file at your lawyer's office..."

"You read my private file?"

"Yes, I did, Mama, and I'm glad," she retorted. "Otherwise, I would have never known that my daddy is a liar and a cheat."

"Don't you dare call your daddy a liar and a cheat!"

"Then those things in the file are not true," she said coyly. "Did Ross get the facts wrong?"

Roseanna sat there unable to answer right away.

"Tell me, Mama, did daddy sleep with Dori?"

Roseanna looked over at Brad with a look of panic in her eyes. He could see the pain she was going through so he spoke up.

"It's true, Isabelle, I did sleep with Dori when we were in Africa, but there were circumstances..."

"What circumstances! Was it because she was a beautiful woman and you were a lonely man?" She was screaming now. "And what about those other things, Mama; did you catch him in bed with Dori and did you see him kissing her?"

"I jumped to a lot of bad conclusions back then..."

"Answer my question, Mama, are the accusations true?"

"Yes, Isabelle, they are true but..."

"There are no buts," she blurted out. "Either he did or he didn't. I don't know how you can be so naïve, Mama. How can you believe anything this man says? I will never believe a word he tells me again."

"I believe him because I know him. He is the most wonderful husband in the world and the best daddy ever, and, as for you young lady, you need to remember this kind gentle man who has been your father all these years; how he has given of himself to you and the boys over and over, with no limitations on his love. When you remember those things then you will beg his forgiveness."

"I will never forgive him, much less ask for his forgiveness," she lashed out. "As far as I'm concerned, I don't have a daddy any more."

Anger boiled up inside Roseanna. "Well, if you don't have a daddy, young lady, then you don't have a mama either! Come on Brad, let's get out of here."

"But sweetheart, let's think about this," he pleaded.

"There is nothing to think about," she said. Then she turned to Isabelle. "I expect you to call your father and apologize to him, and also beg his forgiveness. Until that day comes I'm not home for you, so don't bother to call."

Isabelle burst into tears as Roseanna and Brad stormed out the door. "Please, Mama, don't leave me. I need you. Please, come back. Don't shut me out of your life. Mama, I love you. Please, Mama, I need you. I can't make it on my own. Mama, please come back." But her pleas fell on deaf ears. Roseanna kept walking toward the car not realizing the long term effect that what just happened would have on her family.

Brad looked back at Isabelle and she was sure she saw tears in his eyes. But she didn't want him; she wanted her mother. She ran to her room, fell across the bed and wept as her heart broke inside her.

"Mama, I need you," she whispered over and over as tears ran down her face and soaked her pillow. Finally Brady's cries snapped her out of it. She got up from the bed and wiped her tear stained face. There were no more tears, just a cold empty feeling inside her. "If that's the way you want it, Mama, then that's the way it will be. I'll never forgive Daddy for being a hypocrite all these years and if that means I won't have you in my life, so be it." She picked up Brady and held him close. "It's just you and me now, sweetheart, but don't worry, we're gonna make it. We don't need anyone else."

Chapter 14

Roseanna awoke with a start the next morning to the ringing of the telephone. "Hello," she said sleepily, picking up the phone and shaking herself trying to get her mind focused.

"Did I wake you?" Jesse sounded surprised.

"Yeah," she answered yawning. "What time is it anyway?"

"It's almost nine."

"Oh no, I didn't mean to sleep so late," she cried. "Brad is up already. I guess he didn't want to wake me."

"That's why I'm calling. Brad called and asked me to call you."

"He called? Where was he?"

"Yes, about an hour ago, and he asked me to call you, but I was with a patient and this is the first chance I've had to call," Jesse explained. "He wanted me to tell you that he is on his way to the cabin..."

"Our cabin in Mississippi?"

"Yeah," Jesse said. "He said he had some things to work out and he needed to be alone. He said not to worry, that he'd be okay and would call you later."

"I knew he was hurting, but I don't understand. Why would he not want me with him? He should have at least woke me up and told me what was going on. And, why did he call you instead of me?" Roseanna was confused. "What do you make of this, Jesse?"

"Something going on, that's for sure," Jesse answered. "Did the two of you have a fight?"

"No, but we flew to Nashville yesterday. Isabelle found out what happened in South Africa between Dori and Brad; and she was upset to say the least. She called him a hypocrite and told she hated him and never wanted to see him again. He was heartbroken and very despondent. He hardly said two words on the way home. I went right to bed when we got home and I don't know if he came to bed or not."

"That explains his mood when he talked to me," Jesse said. "But it doesn't explain why he went to the cabin without telling you."

"Do you think I should go there to be with him?"

"No, I'd wait for him to call," Jesse advised. "I believe he will realize he made a mistake and ask you to join him."

"Okay, I'll wait for his call."

Earlier that morning Brad was sitting in a restaurant in New Orleans drinking coffee when someone tapped him on the shoulder.

"May I join you?" the lady asked, pulling out a chair and sitting down.

"Dori?"

"I'm sure you didn't expect to see me in New Orleans, but I'm here for a meeting on new agricultural procedures," she explained. "There were classes last night, and again this morning. What brings you here this early?"

"I'm trying to sort things out," he said.

She poured coffee from the decanter into a cup and took a sip. Then she looked at him. "What things, Brad? Is it something I can help you with?"

He shook his head. "Aren't you going to be late for your class?" he asked, hoping she would go away.

"My class can wait," she said. "Something's wrong and I want to know what it is."

"I don't want to talk about it."

"I'm not leaving until I find out."

"Please, Dori, I want to be alone."

She shook her head. "I haven't seen that look of despair on your face since we were in South Africa when you thought you had lost Roseanna, and, you almost died that time. So don't ask me to leave. I'm staying right here until you tell me what's wrong."

He sighed heavily. "Okay, I'll tell you." He told her what had happened the day before with Isabelle, and Roseanna's reaction to it. "So, you see, because of what happened that night in South Africa between you and me, my wife and my daughter are at odds with each other."

"Brad," she said, "I think you need to go home and talk this out with Roseanna and…"

"I can't do that," he blurted out. "How can I tell my wife that I think she handled things wrong when she forbid Isabelle to call home unless or until she was ready to apologize for the way she treated me. It broke my heart when I saw the look on my little girl's face as she pleaded with her mother not to shut her out of her life, and Roseanna just walked away without looking back. How could she do that? I'm so angry with my wife 'til I can't stand to be in the same room with her, and for the first time in my life I don't like her very much. But, I can't tell her that, especially since she was defending my honor. So, it's best if I just get away from her for awhile."

"I can see your point," she said. "But, don't let this animosity you feel for Roseanna fester in your heart or the two of you will be in real trouble."

"I'm not going to let that happen," he told her. "I'm going to our cabin in Mississippi and stay there until I work it out. I just need some time alone…"

"Brad, you don't need to be alone. You need someone to talk to. I'm staying in this hotel and this is the key to my room," she said handing him a key. "I'm worried about you, so please promise me you'll go up to my room, and try to get some sleep, then, when my class is over we'll talk some more."

"I can't promise you anything," he said. "Now, go on to your class so you won't be late and I'll see you later."

Brad sat there a moment after she left pondering what to do. "Maybe a couple of hours sleep is just what I need before I go on to the cabin," he reasoned aloud, picking up the key and taking the elevator up to her room. He took his cell phone from his pocket and laid it on the table beside the bed. Then he fell across the bed and closed his eyes, hoping that sleep would come. But sleep didn't come, so after about thirty minutes he got up, splashed water on his face, left a note for Dori, and walked out of the hotel, got in his car and drove away.

Dori returned to the hotel shortly before noon. She went up to her room, hoping that Brad was there so they could talk about what was bothering him. But the room was empty. She spied the note and read it aloud. "Dori, I took you up on your offer to come here and rest, but I couldn't sleep, so I'm going on to the cabin. Don't worry about me, I'll be fine, but I could use your prayers. Thanks for your concern. Brad."

"The last thing you need is to be alone," she fretted. She dialed his cell number, then, frowned when she saw it lying on the table. She shook her head knowing Brad never went anywhere without his phone in case of an emergency. "I'll have to take this to him," she reasoned and threw her things into a suitcase and walked to the hotel garage, got in her car and headed for Mississippi.

Brad reached the cabin late that afternoon. It was bleak and lonely. He felt out of place here alone. He had never been to the cabin without Roseanna since their honeymoon. He was beginning to question the wisdom of coming here without her. He couldn't stand being in the cabin alone, so after he put away the supplies that he had bought, he went walking through the woods, trying to clear his head about the feelings he had against Roseanna. But no matter how far he walked, he couldn't come up with a solution. After an hour or so he gave up and went back to the cabin. "Coming here was a mistake," he muttered. "I can't even think straight without Roseanna here with me." He fixed a sandwich and poured a glass of milk, then sat down on the couch to eat. After he finished eating he laid down to rest a minute. He gave into the tiredness of his body and fell asleep.

Roseanna couldn't get her mind off Brad. Her thoughts were troubled. Why didn't he want her with him? Why didn't he tell her his plans to go to the cabin? Hours had passed since he talked to Jesse, yet he hadn't called her. What was going on in that mind of his? "I'm going to call him and tell him how much I love him and that I miss him so much, and I just need to hear his voice and know that he's okay." She picked up her cell phone and dialed his number.

"Hello." A woman's voice answered.

Roseanna stood there too stunned to speak.

"Hello. Is anyone there?" The woman's voice asked.

Roseanna quickly turned the phone off. "Dori," she whispered as her heart pounded within her. Panic consumed her as she remembered another time when Dori answered Brad's cell phone. She dialed Jesse's number. "Jesse," she cried when she heard his voice.

"Roseanna, what's wrong?"

"It's Dori. She's with Brad. They're at the cabin together."

"Why would you think that?"

"I called his cell phone and she answered."

"Are you sure you didn't call her number by mistake?"

"Yes, I'm sure," she said. "Brad's is the first number on my phone and Dori is the last one, so I couldn't have made a mistake."

"Roseanna, don't jump to conclusions in case there's a logical explanation."

"Give me another explanation; I don't like the thoughts that I'm having."

"I can't think of one off hand, but I do know Brad and I can't believe he would do this. He loves you with all his heart, Roseanna."

"I thought so, but now I'm not so sure," she said sadly. "Jesse, you remember the nightmare I had last year concerning Brad and Dori. What if it wasn't a dream at all? What if it was a premonition.? What if they really were involved then?"

"I'm leaving the office now and I'm coming to see you."

"No, Jesse, don't do that. You'd have to explain to Belle why you came all the way out here and I don't want anyone to know about this. I want everyone to think I'm with Brad."

"But, I'm worried about you, Roseanna."

"Don't worry, I'm not going off the deep end," she assured him. "I need time alone to think things through and decide how to handle this."

"Okay, if you're sure," he said. "Call me first thing tomorrow morning and let me know how things are going."

"I will," she promised before hanging up the phone.

Roseanna paced the floor, racking her brain, trying to come up with a way that Dori could have answered Brad's phone if she was not with him. "There just isn't any other explanation," she cried aloud. "Brad and Dori are together at the cabin." She fell to her knees weeping and praying. "Oh, God, help me. I loved Brad. I trusted him. How could he betray me like this? How could he pretend to be a minister of the gospel and commit adultery at the same time? Oh, God, help me understand." She lay on the floor crying as her heart broke into a million pieces and her world crumbled around her.

Dusk had fallen when Roseanna got up from the floor. She grabbed her head. The pain was so intense it was blinding her. She groped her way to the bathroom and got a bottle of pills from the medicine cabinet. Squinting to make sure they were pain pills, she poured a glass of water and swallowed two of them. She filled a pitcher with water, and holding the pills, the glass, and the pitcher in her hands, she walked into the den and set them on the coffee table, then, she collapsed on the couch. She put a pillow over her face to try to sooth her head, and finally drifted off into a troubled sleep. When she awoke later, her head was still hurting, so she took a couple more pills. This went on throughout the night.

Dori drove up to the cabin a few minutes before ten. It was dark inside, no lights anywhere, but Brad's car was parked in the yard, so he had to be here. "He's probably asleep, but I'll have to wake him," she said aloud. "I can't stay out here all night and I'm too tired to get back out on that highway." She knocked on the door, then, knocked again, a little louder.

Finally, Brad, looking tired and sleepy, opened the door. "Dori," he exclaimed. "What are you doing here?" It was obvious that he was both surprised and upset.

"I came to bring this," she answered, handing him the cell phone.

"You came all the way here just to bring my phone?"

"Well, I knew your parents are out of town and that you would need your phone in case of an emergency, but I was also worried about you. Brad, you're in no shape to be by yourself. You need someone to talk to, and…"

"This is not good," he snapped, shaking his head. "You shouldn't be here. How's it going to look, the two of us here together?"

"No one will know that I'm here," she said, trying to calm him down. "I called Mac and told him something had come up and I needed to stay a couple more days. He was fine with that."

"You lied to Mac!"

"I didn't exactly lie. I just didn't tell him the whole truth."

"I've got a bad feeling about this," Brad said. "I should make you get in your car and head home, but it's late, and it's not safe for a lady to be out on the highway this time of night. So, come on in. I'll figure something out."

She stepped inside and set her suitcase down. "You look like warmed over death," she commented and walked over and gave him a big hug and kiss.

"Dori, don't do that!" Brad said angrily. "Are you crazy? If you're gonna stay here there will be no more hugs or kisses. Do you understand?"

"Relax, Brad. I didn't come here with romantic notions on my mind. I'm worried about you and I want to make sure you're okay. I love Mac very much and I'd never cheat on him, so I promise I'll stick to the rules."

"Well, as long as that's settled I've got to figure out what to do," he said nervously. "I'll sleep on the couch and you can have the bed."

"No, I'm the intruder here so I'll take the couch."

"I'm used to the couch so there'll be no arguments," he said walking into the bedroom. "I'll be through in just a moment and then the bathroom is all yours."

Chapter 15

Brad awoke the next morning to the smell of bacon frying. He'd spent a miserable night on the couch, not only because it was full of lumps and broken springs, but also because of Dori being here with him. "Roseanna must never find out," he whispered, reaching for his bathrobe.

"Good morning. I have bacon and pancakes and a big pot of coffee ready," Dori commented handing him a mug of hot steaming coffee.

"Thanks," he said, sitting down at the table. "It sure smells good."

It was lunch time on Wednesday and Jesse was worried. He had been calling Roseanna all morning and since she didn't want anyone to know she was at home, she wouldn't chance being seen by going out; and since his number would come up on her phone, she would know it was him calling, so why was she not answering her phone? He jumped in his car and dialed a number on his cell phone. "Andy, go to Roseanna's and get in the house even if you have to break the door down," he said anxiously when Andy answered. "I'm on my way, but it will take me a while to get there, and I'm afraid we might not have time to spare."

"What's wrong?"

"I'll fill you in later, just go now."

There was urgency in his voice that frightened Andy. He jumped in the car and was at Roseanna's house in a couple of minutes. He grabbed the key from the special hiding place and ran to the front door. His hands trembled as he unlocked the door. He ran through the foyer into the den. "Oh no," he gasped. She was lying on the couch; her arm was limp and hanging down over the side; an empty pill bottle was lying on the floor, as if it had dropped from her hand. He quickly picked up the bottle and stuck it in his pocket, then, he picked her up and hurried to the car. He put her in the front seat, fastened the seatbelt around her, then, jumped in the car and raced to the clinic. "Angelina," he called pushing the door open, "Something is wrong with Roseanna."

Angelina rushed to meet him and cried out when she saw her sister. "Andy, what's wrong with her?"

He shook his head. "I found her on the couch and this empty bottle on the floor beside her. I think she took all of them." He handed the bottle to her.

"Thank God there's a faint pulse," Angelina said as she took Roseanna's vital signs. "We need to know how many pills she took. Get in touch with Brad, maybe he will know. Why isn't he here?" she asked as an afterthought.

Andy shook his head. "I haven't a clue to what's going on here. Jesse called me and told me to get to Roseanna's house quick and I found her like this."

"There's no way we can know how many pills were in this bottle, so we've got to assume that it was full and act accordingly." She turned to Cassie who was standing by, ready to assist in whatever needed to be done. "First, we've got to pump her stomach and then go from there."

Cassie rushed to get everything ready, saying a prayer as she worked.

"Andy, call Jesse back and tell him what's going on. Maybe he can shed some light on what happened."

Andy dialed Jesse's cell phone. "Roseanna's here in the clinic," he explained when Jesse answered. "It looks like she took an overdose of pain pills."

"I'm almost there," Jesse said.

"We need to find Brad. We need to know how many pills were in the bottle."

"I'll tend to that," Jesse answered and hung up. He immediately dialed Brad's cell phone. When there was no answer, he called Brad's mother. He quickly told her what was going on. "Brad is at the cabin and his cell phone is turned off. I want to warn you that Dori is probably with him and that's what caused all of this."

Janet Lefourche jumped in her car and headed for the cabin. She pounded on the door, anger rising up in her as she thought of what was going on here. When no one answered, she yanked the door open and stepped inside. "Bradley!" she yelled, giving way to the flood of tears that stung her eyes.

"Mom, you're home early," he said nervously, not wanting her to find Dori here. He wished he'd never agreed to let her stay.

"Brad, how could you do this," she cried without answering his question. "How could you bring that woman here?"

"Mom, it's not…"

"We'll talk about that later," she said. "Jesse called and Roseanna is—is…"

The color drained from his face. "What about Roseanna, Mom, tell me."

"She OD'd on pain pills and they don't know if…"

"Roseanna would never do that, Mom. There's got to be a mistake. Nothing could make her try to kill herself."

"What about knowing that you are here at the cabin with Dori---do you think that might drive her to do this?"

"Roseanna knows---but how?"

"That's not important now," his mother snapped. "Roseanna may be dying because you're here with that tramp."

"Oh, no," he groaned. "Roseanna, sweetheart, hold on, I'm coming," he whispered, bolting out the door. "Oh, God, help her. Don't let her die."

"Call Jesse," his mother yelled after him. "They need to know how many pills she took. And, Brad, if Roseanna dies it's your fault and I never want to see you again. As far as I'm concerned I won't have a son anymore."

He didn't reply but jumped in the car and sped away. He dialed Jesse's number. "There were at least forty pills in that bottle, Jesse. Did she take all of them?"

"Andy, tell Angelina there were at least forty pills in the bottle," Jesse said, before answering Brad. "It looks that way. The bottle was empty when Andy found her."

"How is she?"

"Angelina and Cassie are doing everything possible to get the pills out of her system. They're pumping her stomach right now and we're all hoping for the best and of course we're praying too."

"Tell her I'm on my way and I love her."

"I'm not sure that would help, even if she could hear me," Jesse replied. "I don't think she would believe that you love her." He hung up the phone before totally losing his temper and saying things that were better off left unsaid.

"Brad," Dori said, walking into the living room dressed in a bathrobe with a towel wrapped around her head. She'd been in the shower and had no idea what was going on.

"I'm sorry to disappoint you, but it's me, not Brad," Janet said angrily. "He's on his way home to his wife who's..."

"Oh no, this is not what you think," Dori blurted out. "Brad and I are not---nothing's going on between us."

"Don't insult my intelligence," Janet Lefourche snapped. "But right now I'm not concerned about that. Thanks to you and my son, Roseanna is fighting for her life and if she doesn't make it, I'll hold Brad and you responsible, and you will pay." With that she turned and walked out, got in her car and drove away.

Dori got dressed and threw her things into her suitcase and quickly loaded it into the car. She jumped in and sped away, fear tugging at her heart. She didn't know what was going on, but she did know her foolish actions might cause Roseanna her life, and if that happened, how could she live knowing it was her fault? "Oh, God, please don't let her die," she prayed as she started the long journey home.

Brad came rushing through the door of the clinic late that night. He barely noticed that the whole family was gathered in the waiting room. He ran toward the room where he thought Roseanna would be.

Andy jumped in front of the door. "You're not going in there!"

Brad glared at him, and, without a word, shoved him out of the way. Then he burst into the room, and over to the bed where Roseanna was lying. He fell to his knees beside her, pulled her into his arms and kissed her again and again.

Andy, momentarily stunned, regained his composure and stood to his feet. "He's not going to hurt her again," he declared, and started to go to Roseanna's aid.

Jesse put his hand on his arm. "He may be just what she needs right now. In spite of everything, she still loves him. He may get through to her when none of us can." He was remembering the time when Belle saw him kissing Pamela at the Inn and how it sent her into a stupor, and he was the only one who could bring her out of it.

"Well, I don't like it," Ellis stormed. "He hurt my little girl so much that she swallowed a whole bottle of pills, and now he acts like he's concerned about what happens to her." He stood up and turned toward Roseanna's room.

"Sit down, Ellis," Mama said firmly. "Angelina's in there with Roseanna. Let her handle this."

Brad held on to Roseanna, fear gnawing at his insides. "Sweetheart, I love you. Please believe that. Roseanna, if you can hear me, please know that I would never betray you. Baby, I'm so sorry. Please forgive me."

"Don't you think it's a little late for remorse, Brad," Angelina snapped. "How dare you come in here acting like you love her? You should've stayed at the cabin with your little playmate. Roseanna doesn't need you."

"I don't believe that," he replied. "She needs me and I'm staying, and no one had better try to make me leave. And, she didn't try to kill herself. Roseanna would never do that." He held her hands to his lips and kissed them.

"You may be right," Angelina said, taking Roseanna's vital signs. "I don't believe she took the pills all at once. But she did take them; and if Andy hadn't got to her when he did, I don't think she would have made it."

"How is she now?"

"She's going to make it, but the pills could have a lasting effect on her."

"In what way?"

"We don't know if any of her organs were affected," she explained. "We'll just have to wait and see."

"When can she go home?"

"We've done all we can do for her here," Angelina stated. "Her vital signs are good, and she is sleeping normally. She could go home now, Brad, but I'm not sure that would be wise."

"Because of me?"

"Well, you are the reason she took the pills."

"Can you stop me from taking her home?"

"No, I can't, but Andy and Daddy will certainly try to stop you."

He wrapped the blanket around Roseanna and picked her up in his arms. He walked out into the waiting room. "I'm taking her home," he announced.

"Over my dead body," Andy stormed and grabbed Brad.

"Mine too." Ellis Leblanc added, stepping between Brad and the door.

"She's my wife; I'm going to do what's best for her, so get out of my way."

"It's okay," Angelina said. "She's out of danger, her vital signs are stable and I think she would rest better in her own bed. And, Brad may be just what she needs right now. He can call me if anything goes wrong. So, let's all go home and let him take care of her."

"Thanks, Angelina," Brad said. "I'll call if I need you."

Later at home Brad laid Roseanna on the bed. Then he dressed for bed and lie down beside her. He took her in his arms. "Baby, I'm so sorry," he whispered. "This is my fault, and if you don't come out of it one hundred percent, I'll never forgive myself." The flood of tears that he had been holding back since the time his mother told him about Roseanna burst forth. He couldn't let go of them on the long drive home, nor at the clinic in front of her family, but now, lying here in bed beside her, he let go and wept over what he had done; but most of all he wept for Roseanna. "God, please help her," he prayed over and over. "Please help her mind and body to be free of all the effects of the medicine." Finally out of pure exhaustion, he fell asleep.

"Brad," Roseanna mumbled, the next morning, reaching out for him. "Brad," she said louder.

Brad roused up and opened his eyes. "Sweetheart, you're awake," he exclaimed, pulling her close and kissing her with all the love in his heart.

"What day is this?" she asked, leaning on her elbows and looking at him with a puzzled look on her face.

"This is Thursday."

"Thursday? What happened to the other days?" There was confusion in her voice. "My mind is all fuzzy, Brad. What's the matter with me?"

"Sweetheart, you spent yesterday in the clinic..."

"Angelina's clinic? Why?"

"You accidentally took an overdose of pain pills and..."

"I don't remember doing that," she muttered, shaking her head.

"Do you remember having a headache or anything like that?"

She racked her brain, trying hard to think. "No, I don't remember, Brad. I don't remember anything." She burst into tears. "Why can't I remember? I'm scared, Brad, hold me."

He sat up in bed and pulled her close. "It's okay, sweetheart, it will be all right, you'll see." A part of him was relieved that she couldn't remember the things that had gone on these past few days, but a bigger part of him was frightened, wondering if this memory lapse was permanent, and, if even worse damage had been done.

"Brad, I'm so weak," she mumbled, lying back on the bed.

He put his arms around her. "Honey, it's no wonder, after everything you went through yesterday. You must be starved. I'll fix you something to eat."

"I guess I am a little hungry. Would you help me to the couch? I don't want to stay in here by myself. I want to be close to you." She stood up and her legs buckled beneath her.

Brad reached out and grabbed her. He picked her up and carried her into the den and laid her on the couch. "What would you like to eat, sweetheart?"

"Whatever you want to fix is fine with me," she answered.

"Pancakes and bacon sounds good to me, but maybe I'd better check with Angelina first," he said, dialing the phone.

Meanwhile, at the Winslow house, a discussion was in progress. Andy was still fuming about Brad taking Roseanna home last night. "Angelina, I don't understand how you could let him do that," he groused. "After what he did to Roseanna, he's the last person who should be alone with her."

"So now you're questioning my medical judgment?" Anger flashed in her eyes. "I sometimes wonder if you're still in love with my sister and only married me so you could stay in the family and be close to her."

"Where did that come from?"

"Remember, I saw the two of you in the church that night, and the way you were kissing I thought you were going to commit adultery right there. And, it wasn't you who pulled away, it was Roseanna."

"Yeah, but I pulled away the next time..." He couldn't believe those words came out of his mouth. He braced himself for the fallout he knew was coming.

"The next time? What next time?" Her voice was raised in anger. "You didn't see her again until after we were married. Has there been a repeat of what I saw in the church that night?"

Andy stood there, not knowing what to say. A lie would work nicely now, but he couldn't lie, so while he was pondering how to answer her, she asked another question.

"Have you been with Roseanna since we've been married?"

"I've never been with Roseanna in the sense you're talking about."

"What exactly has gone on between the two of you? I want the truth."

The phone rang, giving Andy a welcome reprieve. "Hello," he said, thankful that he wouldn't have to answer Angelina's question, at least for the moment.

"I need to talk to Angelina," Brad said, a bit edgy, when he heard Andy's voice.

"Is Roseanna okay?" Andy asked anxiously.

"She's okay. Now, may I speak to Angelina, please?"

He handed the phone to her. "It's Brad."

"Hello, Brad, is something wrong?"

"No," he answered. "Roseanna's awake and she's hungry. We discussed having pancakes and bacon, but I thought I'd better check with you first."

"I will need to check her over," Angelina said. "I'll be right there."

"I'm coming too," Andy said, following her out the door.

"Why does that not surprise me?" Angelina grumbled under her breath.

Brad opened the door when they arrived a few minutes later. They walked into the den where Roseanna was sitting on the couch. Andy walked over and kissed her on the cheek.

"You can do better than that, Andy," she remarked, pulling his face close to hers. "Remember the night, sitting right here on this couch, when we kissed each other---now those were real kisses."

Pale and speechless, Andy looked first at Angelina, then, Brad. If looks could kill, he'd be dead now. Without a word he went into the kitchen and poured a cup of coffee. Brad walked in. "I'm helping myself to some of your coffee," he commented feebly.

"It looks like you've helped yourself to more than my coffee," Brad replied angrily. "It appears that you've helped yourself to my wife as well."

"Brad, let me explain…"

"What's to explain?" Brad snapped. "Did Roseanna get the facts wrong?"

"No, what she said was true, but there were circumstances, so please let me explain."

Brad folded his arms across his chest. "Go ahead and explain."

"Let's go outside," Andy suggested. "We wouldn't want the ladies to overhear." They walked outside. "First I want to tell you when it happened."

"I'm listening."

"It was the Christmas night when you were in South Africa. Roseanna had just learned that morning that you had slept with Dori and she was devastated. She put up a good front in front of the family that day but I could tell that something was wrong, so I followed her home that night to find out what was bothering her. At first she wouldn't tell me, but I told her I wasn't leaving until she told me. She started crying and told me that you had slept with Dori. I didn't believe it but she said you admitted it. I took her in my arms to comfort her. She said she felt safe in my arms and wished she could stay there forever. She said she wished that I was her husband because I would never betray her. Brad, she didn't mean that; it was the hurt talking. I looked into her eyes and reality slipped from our minds. It was as if we were transported back to the time when we were together and in love. I kissed her and told her I loved her and she said she loved me too, and kissed me. Things got out of hand, but I thought of Angelina and I jumped up and ran out the door."

"And, you didn't tell Angelina?"

"No, I couldn't. I knew it would hurt her so I kept quiet," Andy said. "Now, after all these years, I'll have to try to explain it to her."

Brad grinned impishly as thoughts of Andy trying to talk himself out of this, flashed through his mind. *I can understand why it happened but I feel certain that Angelina can't, and she will give Andy exactly what he has coming. I wish I could be there to see it.* Still grinning, he walked back inside.

"I've checked Roseanna over and I believe she had better just have fruit and cereal. I don't think her stomach is ready for bacon or pancakes. She can have coffee too." She leaned over and kissed her sister. "I'll be back later, but if you need me before then, have Brad to call."

"I'll walk you to the door," Brad said, wanting a chance to talk to her. "How is she?" he asked when they were out of earshot of Roseanna.

"She's still confused," Angelina replied. "The pills have affected her thinking as well as her memory. She never would have blurted that out about Andy and her kissing if she were thinking straight."

"Yeah, it's been a well-kept secret until now," he said. "Can you handle it?"

"Oh, I'll handle it, starting right now." She looked around. "Did Andy leave already?"

"He's probably waiting for you in the car. We had a little talk outside and I didn't see him come back into the house."

"Take good care of Roseanna and call if you need me."

Brad waved as she walked away, then he went back into the house to fix breakfast.

Andy sat quietly as Angelina turned the car around and headed home.

"Andy, talk to me."

"I don't know what to say, sweetheart, except I'm sorry."

"Well, that's not good enough," she snapped. "I want to know why you betrayed me with my sister. How could you do that?"

"I need to tell you everything right from the start, and that will take awhile."

"Well, I don't have much time. I've got to get to the clinic," she said, pulling into their driveway.

"Honey, couldn't you be late going in today. This is possibly the most important thing in our lives right now. Won't you please give me time to explain?"

"We'll talk when I get home tonight."

"The kids will be home from school by then, and I think we need to be alone when we discuss this."

"You're right, Andy," she conceded. "I'll call my secretary and tell her I'll be late coming in. I'm sure Cassie can handle things 'til I get there." She made the call and then sat down in a chair across from Andy and asked bluntly, "How many times did it happen?"

"Honey, as God is my witness, it only happened that one time."

"Why should I believe you?"

He shook his head. "You shouldn't believe me on my word only, but please listen closely while I tell you what happened, then, I hope that you will believe me."

"I promise to listen, but as to believing you, that's another matter."

Her voice was so cold. If only she would cry, he could hold her in his arms and comfort her, but he didn't know how to deal with this attitude.

"You remember the Christmas that Brad was in South Africa and the wreck where Jolee's baby was killed..."

"Of course I remember that," she snapped again. "What does that have to do with any of this?"

"It has everything to do with it," he said. "Please, honey, just let me finish."

"Go ahead."

"As you know, Brad came home for a couple of days to try to help Jolee cope with the death of the baby. Roseanna was happier than she had been in a long time. They celebrated the holiday on Christmas Eve before he left to go back. His Christmas present to her was to find a place over there for the kids and her to live so they could join him in a couple of weeks..."

Angelina sat patting her foot impatiently. "Andy, I don't have all day."

"Please honey," he said. "You've got to hear it all."

"Okay." Her voice was edgy.

"On Christmas morning she woke early and decided to call Brad and chat before the kids got up. He was away from his cell phone, so Dori answered it. When she found out it was Roseanna on the other end, thinking that Brad had told her all about the night they slept together, she blurted out the whole thing. Brad came up just in time to hear it; he grabbed the phone and begged Roseanna to let him explain, but she only wanted to know if it was true. When he admitted it, she hung up. Can you imagine the frame of mind she was in? Her whole world was shattered. Her dreams of moving there with him had turned into a nightmare. But she had to go through the day pretending everything was fine, in order that the family could have a good Christmas. She managed to fool the others, but I knew something was wrong. She went home early and I left a few minutes later so I could stop by her house and find out what had happened. She wouldn't tell me at first, but finally she burst into tears and told me everything. I took her in my arms to comfort her and she clung to me. Honey, when I looked into her eyes and saw the agonizing hurt there, I felt her pain. I kissed her and she kissed me and we spoke of loving each other. We stayed in each other's arms, kissing until I came to my senses and pulled away."

Angelina sat there, not saying a word. She looked at Andy in a way that tore him apart. He had never seen such hurt in those big brown eyes. Finally she spoke. "You say you didn't sleep with her, but did you want to, Andy?"

He hung his head. He couldn't lie to her. "Yes, sweetheart I did. But as much as I wanted her, I loved you more, and, that's why nothing else happened. I had lust in my heart that night for Roseanna, but I had love in my heart for you. A love so precious to me, that it kept me from breaking my marriage vows."

A tear rolled down her face. "I remember how happy I was that night as we celebrated our first Christmas in our new home. Later, you held me in your arms and told me how much you loved me, but little did I know that you were not even thinking about me, you were thinking about my sister. How could you do that to me? How could Roseanna do that to me?" She burst into tears.

Andy rushed over to her and took her in his arms. "Please don't blame Roseanna for this. She reached out to me because her world had crumbled around her. She had not only lost a husband whom she loved with all her heart, but she had also lost her spiritual guide. She was so confused." He hesitated momentarily, groping for the words to say to his wife. "Honey, she would never hurt you. In fact she would do anything on earth to keep from hurting you. That's why she moved to Nashville the next day and bought the ranch."

"That's why she moved to Nashville? She gave up the family and home she loved to keep me from being hurt. She loved me that much?" More tears ran down her face. "I could never blame her. But as for you, Andrew Winslow, that's a different matter. She was hurting; you weren't, so there's no excuse for what you did." She wiped the tears away. Then in a voice void of any love or understanding she said, "I'm going to work now and when I get home tonight, I want your belongings moved into one of the guest rooms." With that, she walked out and left him standing there, a look of disbelief on his face.

"She called me Andrew," he muttered. She had never called him Andrew before, not even when they first met and she hated him. The way she said it sent a message loud and clear. Forgiveness from her would be a long time coming, if it ever did. "I can't stay here under those conditions," he said aloud. He made a couple of phone calls, left a note for Angelina, threw some things into a suitcase, walked out the door, got into his car and drove away.

Angelina was late getting away from the clinic that night. She turned out the lights and locked the door. She walked the short distance from the clinic to the house.

There were no lights on when she opened the kitchen door. "Drew. Abby," she called, but no one answered. "Andy probably took them out to eat," she mused, kicking off her shoes and taking a bottle of water from the fridge. She went into the den and fell down on the couch. It had been a tiring day, both physically and mentally. "I'll rest a minute, then, I'll find something to eat," she said, then spied the note on the coffee table from Andy. She picked it up and read it. "Angelina, I'm leaving town. The kids are with Mama. I don't know how long I'll be gone. I'll be in touch. Andy."

"Oh, Andy," she cried. "What's happening to us? What are we doing to each other?" She walked through the house. It seemed big and empty without him. Would he ever come back? Could they resolve their differences? Could she forgive him for what happened with Roseanna? Could she ever trust him again? She didn't know the answer to those questions and since Andy had walked out on her, he obviously didn't care. She fell across the bed and wept for a love that had been so wonderful, so perfect, but now was marred by Andy's betrayal of that love. She sat up and wiped her tears. The kids must not see her like this. She picked up the phone and dialed.

"Mama, can the kids spend the night there?" she asked when her mother answered the phone.

"Of course they can. Is everything all right?"

"I don't know if anything will ever be right again," Angelina answered and burst into tears.

"Are you and Andy into it?"

"Not exactly. Andy is gone and I don't know if he will ever come back."

"I'm coming over."

"No, Mama. I don't feel up to talking."

"Okay, honey, but if you need me, just call."

"Thanks Mama," she said hanging up the phone. Then she fell down across the bed and wept 'til exhaustion took over and mercifully, she fell asleep.

Chapter 16

"Brad, what day is it?" Roseanna asked as they sat drinking a second cup of coffee.

"It's Sunday, sweetheart."

"Look at the time," she gasped. "You're going to be late for church."

"I'm got going to church today. I'm staying home with you."

"But, honey, you've got to go. You're the pastor."

"Andy is preaching today so I can stay home with you."

"Hurry, get the boys up or they will be late for Sunday school."

"Sweetheart, the boys are at Mama's, remember?"

"Oh, yeah," she said and a worried look crossed her face. "Brad, what's the matter with me? I can't remember anything. Did those pills fry my brain? Will I be like this for the rest of my life?"

"Oh, no, sweetheart," he assured her, taking her in his arms. "Don't even think that. It will take a while for the pills to get out of your system, but once they do, you'll be fine."

"Promise?"

"I promise, honey," he said. "With all the prayers that's going up for you, you'll be as good as new in no time." He was saying the right words; but there were nagging doubts in the back of his mind. What if she didn't get better; could he live with the guilt of knowing that he had done this to her? "Sweetheart would you like to go outside for a while?" he asked, trying to take her mind off her troubles. "It's such a nice day and the fresh air will do you good."

"Yes, I'd like that, Brad."

They dressed for the outdoors and were soon on their way to the stables. "Hello, Midnight Thunder," she said, putting her arms around the horse. She picked up a handful of oats and fed it to him.

"How would you like to go riding?" Brad asked.

"Could we?"

"I believe it will be all right if we both ride on the same horse," he answered. "Do you think your horse can hold both of us?"

"I'm sure of it," she said, with happiness in her voice that hadn't been there since she got home from the clinic. "We're going for a ride, boy," she said, patting Midnight Thunder on the neck and rubbing his mane.

Brad put the riding gear on the horse and then lifted Roseanna into the saddle. He pulled himself up behind her.

"Let's go, boy," Roseanna said and they took off across the meadow at a steady gait.

After riding for about an hour they rode back into the stable and Brad took the saddle and other gear off the horse. "I sure enjoyed that ride," Roseanna said, sighing happily, as they walked into the den. She sat down on the couch.

"Honey, it's so good to see you happy," Brad said, sitting down beside her. "We'll go riding again tomorrow."

"I'd like that," she said, leaning over and kissing him. "You always know exactly what to do to make me happy."

He took her in his arms and they sat there, contentedly, until the doorbell rang. "It's Mama," Brad stated, looking out the window. "She called before church this morning to say she was bringing Sunday dinner over." He opened the door and took the dishes out of her hands.

"How's Roseanna?"

"Come see for yourself," he said, motioning toward the den.

Roseanna looked up as she walked in. "Mama," she cried, happily.

Her mother embraced her warmly. "How are you, baby?"

"I'm feeling better, Mama. Brad and I went riding on Midnight Thunder and it did wonders for me."

"That's great, honey," she said. "I'll visit just for a moment. I've got some starving boys at my house to feed."

"How are the boys, besides being hungry, that is," Roseanna asked. "I miss them so much." She looked at Brad who had walked back into the den. "When do you think they can come see me?"

"If you keep getting better, it won't be too long before they'll be back home with us."

"Give them a big hug for Brad and me," Roseanna told her mother. "And, tell them we love them."

"I will, sweetie," her mother said and leaned over and kissed her. "Enjoy your dinner. Grandma helped fix it and she will be upset if you don't eat it, and, make a big fuss over it," she said getting up off the couch.

They laughed, knowing that she was right about Grandma. Brad walked her to the car. "How did things go at church today?" he asked, when they stepped outside.

"It was unusual," she answered. "We have three pastors but not one of them showed up today to preach, so Deacon LaPree let us out early."

"I don't understand," Brad said. "Andy was supposed to preach and it's not like him to neglect his obligations, especially to the ministry. What happened?"

"All I know is that Angelina called Friday night and said they'd had a big fight and he left. She hasn't heard from him since and has no idea where he is." There was concern in her voice. "Neither the twins nor her were at church today."

"That is my fault too," Brad said. "They fought because of this mess with Roseanna and me."

"Brad, about you and Roseanna, she seems happy now but what happens when she remembers that you were at the cabin with Dori? Do you think she's strong enough emotionally to handle it?"

"Angelina is hoping that she won't remember it for a few days. That will give her time to get stronger physically so she can be in better shape to cope with it."

"I'll pray that happens," she said. "And, Brad, don't be too hard on yourself. Don't try to shoulder the blame for everything bad that's happening in our family right now," she added giving him a kiss on the cheek.

"Thanks Mama," he said, waving as she walked to her car and drove away. Did Mama believe him? If anyone believed him, it would be her.

Late that afternoon Brad had gone out to empty the trash when the doorbell rang. Roseanna opened the door.

Dori walked past her and into the den.

Sharp pains went through Roseanna's head as she remembered that Brad and Dori were at the cabin together. "Get out of my house," she screamed.

"No, not before I apologize to you," Dori said. "I'm so sorry..."

"Get out of my house now!" Roseanna screamed again, grabbing a poker from the fireplace and raising it above her head.

"Roseanna, please I'm sorry. I didn't mean to hurt you..."

"Liar!" She aimed the poker at Dori's head and started to swing. "I'm going to kill you!"

"No, sweetheart," Brad yelled, grabbing her arm and holding it in mid-air. "Get out of here, Dori," he shouted angrily trying to hold Roseanna's arm so she couldn't bring the poker down on Dori's head.

"Let go of me, Brad! I'm going to kill her. I'm..."

"No, Roseanna," he said pulling her close to him and taking the poker out of her hand as Dori ran out the door. "Baby, I'm sorry. This is all my fault."

Roseanna pushed him away. "You---you took her to the cabin, Brad---our special place---how could you do that?"

"Sweetheart, it's not what you think..."

"Quit lying!" she screamed as a flood of anger swept through her. "You were there together. Don't deny it Brad." She grabbed her head and stumbled backward.

Brad reached out and caught her just as she fell. He laid her on the couch and dialed the phone. No one was home at Angelina's so he called Jesse's cell phone.

Jesse was in a meeting that Deacon LaPree had called that morning after church. He had asked each committee member to be at the church at three o'clock to discuss the matter concerning Brad and Dori. They would decide whether or not to keep him on as pastor. They had talked for about an hour when Jesse's phone rang. He answered it and Brad told him that Roseanna needed him.

"I'll be right there." He stood to his feet. "Excuse me," he said, breaking in on the discussion. "An emergency has come up and I've got to leave, but I vote to wait until we get all the facts before we take action in this matter." He ran out the door. In a few minutes he was at Brad's house.

"You got here fast," Brad commented, opening the door for him.

"I was in a meeting at the church," he explained, quickly going over to Roseanna and feeling her pulse. "What happened here?"

"Dori came by and when Roseanna saw her, she remembered everything. She became very distraught and picked up a poker and tried to hit Dori. She might have killed her if I hadn't got here in time."

168

"Oh, no," Jesse gasped. "I hate to think what this is going to do to her." He looked at Brad and asked, "How did she react to you?"

"She was hurt and angry. She screamed at me, then, grabbed her head and toppled backwards. I caught her, and laid her on the couch. Angelina wasn't home so I called you."

"I think maybe this is something I need to handle," Jesse remarked. "She can't have pain medicine, so there's not too much Angelina can do."

"What can I do to help?"

"Get me a cold wet cloth and then get out of here. It might upset her more if she sees you."

Brad bought the washcloth, then went into the bedroom, fell on his knees and prayed.

Jesse gently stroked Roseanna's face with the cloth. "Honey, this is Jesse. Can you hear me?"

Roseanna's eyes flitted wildly as she tried to focus on him. "Jesse?"

"Yes, sweetheart, I'm here."

"Where is she? I'm going to kill her."

Jesse put his hand over her mouth gently. "Relax, Roseanna, she's gone."

"But I want her dead, Jesse," Roseanna cut in. "I tried to kill her but Brad grabbed my arm. I-I guess he didn't want me to hurt his little-little..." She burst into tears. "She deserved to die so why did he stop me?"

"Honey, he did it to protect you," Jesse said compassionately. "He couldn't let you take a life. It would have destroyed you."

She grabbed her head again. "Jesse, my head," she cried, clutching his hand. "Can you give me something?"

"No, I can't do that," he told her. "Just lie real still and I'll try to make it stop hurting." He massaged her neck and shoulders. "You need to lie down on the bed. It will be much more comfortable." He helped her to her feet.

Brad got up off his knees when they walked into the room. "I'll leave you two alone," he mumbled, then, walked out of the room.

About a half an hour later Jesse walked into the den. "She's asleep now," he said. "Stay close by her in case she wakes up during the night."

"I will," Brad answered. "How is she? Did she talk about what happened?"

"Yeah, she talked about it," Jesse replied. "She in a state of depression and the coming days are very essential to her well-being. You've got to be very careful how you deal with her. She's fragile right now and one wrong word or move could send her over the edge."

"I'm staying right by her side and I will be very careful what I say or do. Is there anything specific I should do?"

"Just keep doing what you're doing," Jesse said. "I believe if anyone can bring her out of this, it's you."

"I will do whatever it takes to pull her through this depression and then I'll try my best to get her to trust me again."

"I'll pray that it happens, but I'm not sure she can ever trust you again. I'm having a problem believing your story that nothing happened between Dori and you."

"I guess I can't blame you for that," Brad said. "Oh, by the way, the meeting at church, is it something I should know about?"

Jesse fumbled around for words to say. He had wanted Deacon LaPree to talk to Brad when the decision was made, but he had to answer his question. "It was concerning Dori and you being at the cabin together and..."

"Are you firing me?"

"I don't know, Brad. I left before the meeting was over. But I voted before I left. I said I want to wait on any decision until we know the whole truth."

"Well, thanks for that, Jesse."

Jesse looked at him with a worried look. His whole future was on the line and he didn't seem upset. Maybe it hadn't sunk in yet. "Brad, are you all right? This must be a real shock. Maybe if you go to Deacon LaPree and tell him your side of the story…"

"No," Brad said. "I'm not leaving Roseanna for even one minute. Let the committee do what they feel is right."

"Is there anyway you can prove that you are telling the truth?"

Brad shook his head. "Dori and I are the only ones who know what went on between us, and nobody is taking our word for anything," he said. "These folks have known me for years. They either believe me, or they don't. Roseanna is my only concern right now. I really don't care what they decide to do."

Jesse put his arms around him and embraced him. "Hang in there, man," he said, then hurried to his car and drove away.

Brad dressed for bed and lie down beside Roseanna. His thoughts were troubled as his mind replayed the events of the last few days. How did things get so mixed up? Roseanna was hurting right now and she wanted him with her. But what about when her mind became clear and she had time to think about the cabin, and Dori and him. Could he convince her that nothing happened between the two of them? He had no proof to offer so would she take his word for it. "I don't think so," he mumbled aloud. But he couldn't think of his future right now. There were more important matters at hand. He had to be sure Roseanna got over this depression and out of the fog she was in. And he would make it happen no matter how things turned out for him. His love for her would see to that.

Chapter 17

Angelina sighed as she gazed at the calendar on the desk in her office. It was Friday. Andy had been gone a week and she had not heard a word from him. What did it mean? Had she driven him away forever with her accusations about Roseanna and him---or had she struck a chord in his heart that made him realize that he was still in love with Roseanna, and no longer wanted a life with her. "Oh, Andy," she whispered, as the phone rang, cutting into her thoughts. "Hello," she said, hoping to hear his voice on the other end. "Mama," she said, with a bit of disappointment in her voice when her mother answered.

"You sound a little down," Mama said.

"I'm sorry. I was hoping it was Andy on the phone."

"You haven't heard from him?"

"Not a word and I wonder if I'll ever hear from him again. Mama, I don't think he's coming back, not to me anyway."

"Angelina, he loves you very much and he will be back, so put those thoughts out of your mind," her mother said. "The reason I'm calling is to see if it is okay for the twins to go to New Orleans with your daddy and me for the night. Belle is giving a sleep over at her house for the boys at church so we're taking Will and Alex by there, and we've decided to go on to New Orleans, and we'd like for Drew and Abby to go with us."

"Are you sure you want to do this? Hadn't you rather go to New Orleans just the two of you and get some rest and relaxation?"

"You know how much your daddy and I enjoy being with our grandkids, so the answer is no, we wouldn't rather go alone---so how about it?"

Angelina thought a moment before answering. "They have missed their daddy, and the trip would be good for them, so it's okay with me. What time will you leave?"

"We'll pick them up at school and leave from there."

"Okay, I'll pack an overnight bag for them and have it with me here at the clinic. That way I can get a big hug and kiss from them before you take off."

After work that afternoon, Angelina pondered the wisdom of letting them go as she sat in the den facing a night alone in the big empty house. Thoughts of Andy raced through her mind. "Oh, Andy," she said aloud, "where are you and why don't you call?" She laid down on the couch and put a pillow under her head. She closed her eyes and sighed wearily, determined to put thoughts of him out of her mind. But before she had a chance to do that, the phone rang.

"Angelina," her mother said when she answered. "Can you come to New Orleans right away?"

"What's wrong, Mama? Has something happened to the kids?"

"Oh, no, the kids are fine," Mama assured her. "They are having a great time and we're planning a big day tomorrow and they want you to come and share in all the fun."

"I don't know," she said. "I've had a very tiring day. I'm not sure I want to drive all the way to New Orleans tonight."

"It would mean a lot to them; and honey, I believe it would do you good to get away. I think you need a day of fun with the kids."

"You're right about that. I do need to get out and have fun so I'll do it."

"That's great," Mama said with a sigh of relief. "We'll reserve a room in your name so all you'll have to do when you get here is pick up the key at the front desk. See you later."

"There has been a big mistake made here," Angelina exclaimed, hours later when the bellboy opened the door to the honeymoon suite and motioned her inside. "A regular room was reserved in my name."

"I don't know about that, ma-am," the young man said politely. "This is where they told me to bring you and your luggage." He sat the overnight bag down on the floor. "You'll have to call the front desk and talk to them about the mix-up." He turned to leave and she handed him a twenty-dollar bill. "Thank you, ma-am," he said walking out and shutting the door behind him.

"The honeymoon suite," she snorted in disgust. "This is supposed to make me feel better?"

"I sure hope so, cause if it doesn't I've gone to a lot of trouble for nothing."

"Andy!" She cried out with surprise and glee at the sound of his voice.

"I've missed you, sweetheart," he said, taking her in his arms and kissing her. "I'm sorry about everything and I hope I can make it up to you."

"I was worried sick," she said, stepping out of his arms. "Where have you been and why didn't you call me?"

"I've been traveling around to different places tending to company business for my father; and as to why I didn't call you I was afraid. I thought maybe you wanted out of the marriage and my leaving had given you the excuse you needed to do so."

"You should have called me, no matter what," she said. "The kids were asking all kinds of questions; questions that I couldn't answer."

"I know and I'm sorry," he said meekly. "But I wanted to meet with you somewhere special to try to explain things to you. So I called Mama and we planned this little rendezvous here in the honeymoon suite. I hope you will stay."

"I'll stay, but I do need answers," she said firmly. "I need to know how far things have gone between Roseanna and you, and, if you're still in love with her. And, Andy, don't lie to me."

"Sweetheart, I'd never lie to you," he told her. "I know that by not telling you what happened between Roseanna and me that Christmas night, years ago, it must seem like I lied to you, but I didn't mean it that way. I knew how much it would hurt you and I didn't know how you would react, especially since you were pregnant, so I kept quiet."

"Well, tell me now," she insisted. "I have a right to know."

"As God is my witness there's never been anything except those kisses between Roseanna and me, and nothing has happened since that night. I'm certainly not in love with her and haven't been since the time in Friends Harbor when I bumped into you. I fell in love with you that night and all feelings, except friendship for Roseanna, slipped from my mind forever. I do love her in a special way and probably always will, but there is not, and never again will be, anything romantic between us. I love you, Angelina; nothing is more important than my love for you. I'd rather die than to live on this earth without you."

"Oh Andy, I remember another time when you said practically those same words to me, and was ready to prove it," she cried, caressing his face. "Remember, it was the night I graduated from college and we were on our way to Nashville for Roseanna's concert and that car was chasing us. You speeded up trying to get away from them and couldn't make a curve and the car skidded off the road, stopping just short of plunging into a deep ravine. That other car turned around and was coming back. They were going to finish the job and push us into the ravine. You unfastened your seatbelt, but mine was stuck and we couldn't loosen it. I begged you to get out of the car and save yourself. But you wouldn't. You held me close, and said you'd rather die with me than to live on this earth without me." Tears were rolling down her face. "How could I have forgotten such an unselfish love like that? I know now that you love me and not my sister. Oh Andy, can you ever forgive me."

"There's nothing to forgive sweetheart," he said, pulling her close and kissing her. "Can you forgive me for betraying our love by kissing Roseanna that night, and for keeping it from you? I didn't tell you then because I knew it would hurt you, and, I was afraid you would leave me and I couldn't stand the thought of losing you. Then after time passed and Roseanna had moved to Nashville, there didn't seem to be a need to tell you, so I didn't. I didn't think you would ever find out, but secrets have a way of coming back to haunt us. I hope you will believe me, sweetheart, when I tell you that I'm through meddling into Roseanna and Brad's affairs. I've done a lot of soul searching this week and I've come to realize that I've been a butt-in-ski where Roseanna was concerned. I wouldn't blame Brad if he punched me in the nose, and honey, if you want to slug me; I've got that coming too."

She laughed and put her arms around him. "I don't think that will be necessary, and I'm not sure I could get used to a 'mind his own business' Andy Winslow, or, if I even want to. I knew you were obnoxious when I married you but I loved you anyway, and I still love you just the way you are."

"Come here, you," he said pulling her close and kissing her.

Chapter 18

A week had passed since Brad and Roseanna were at the ranch and Isabelle was no closer to forgiving her father than when they left. She didn't know about what was going on back home; Brad had made sure of that. He knew she would think she caused all the trouble Roseanna was having because of the fight they had, and she didn't need anything else on her, so he had told everyone not to tell her.

"I've got to get on with my life. I can't sit around and mope." She said the words to herself with determination. "Mama you made your choice and I've made mine. I'm never going to forgive daddy even if it means I'll never be a part of our family again." She picked Brady up from out of his crib and continued. "Sweetie, you and I are going to make it. I've got a good income and we have Mimi to take care of us. We don't need anyone else. There's no way I'm going to let you be influenced by my father who is nothing but a hypocrite."

She had to snap out of this mood she was in. She had a concert tomorrow night and she had to get ready for it. She nodded in approval as a plan formed in her head. "I don't have to live by Daddy's rules anymore and I'm not, starting right now," she said, determinedly. "Mimi," she called, "can you watch the baby for awhile? I've got some shopping to do."

The next night Isabelle pranced out on stage wearing an outfit that was little more than a black bathing suit with fringe from the waist down to her thighs, with glitter all over it that sparkled with every move of her body. Black decorative boots rounded out her attire. She started singing 'I'm Your Woman' with all the gusto inside her. Some men in the crowd stood up and whistled and yelled their approval. But most of the audience sat there in bewilderment; wondering what had gotten into Isabelle; why was she acting this way?

It was all Bo could do to stay seated. He wanted to march up on that stage and drag her off, out of sight of those men who were cheering her on. But knowing that the guards would stop him, he sat there, tears rolling down his face, and watched as she made a spectacle of herself. He breathed a sigh of relief when the concert ended and Isabelle took a final bow and ran off stage.

He didn't have a backstage pass so he waited at the exit he thought she would use when she left the auditorium. A few minutes later she walked through the door.

"Issy!" His voice was loud and sharp.

She whirled around. "What are you doing here?"

"I might ask you the same question," he stormed. "What in the world do you think you were doing up on that stage tonight---dressed like that."

"Bo Abbott, it's none of your business. I'll dress like I want to and I'll sing like I want to, so butt out of my life!"

"I'm concerned about you, Isabelle." His voice was gentle now. "Do you know what kind of men you will attract by acting the way you did tonight?"

"Are you jealous because those men were whistling at me?" She smirked. "Well I liked it and I'm going to keep on singing like I sung tonight. This is the new me and if you don't like it, then don't come to my concerts."

"You don't know what you're getting into," he said sadly. Then an idea popped into his head. He grabbed her, pulled her close and kissed her in a very offensive way.

She shoved him away from her and slapped him so hard that it sent him tottering backward. Then she burst into tears and ran away.

"That's the kind of treatment you can expect from men as long as you act like you did tonight." He flung the words after her as she disappeared into the auditorium. He stood there almost in shock. Why had kissed her like that?

What had possessed him? Was she right---did he do it because he was jealous? He had to apologize to her. He walked around the celerity parking area until he found her car, then, stood by it, waiting for her to come out again.

"Are you waiting for Isabelle?"

He turned to see a pretty young woman standing there. "Yes," he replied. "I'm Bo Abbott and I need to find her."

"I'm Lily," she said. "If you are a friend of hers you'd better go after her quick. He's going to hurt her."

"Who's going to hurt her?"

"Ray Butler. He's my ex-boyfriend and also the new drummer in the band," she explained. "He talked her into going to his apartment to look at a new song he's written; said it was just her style and would go to the top of the charts if she recorded it. But that's not true. He's getting her there so he can sleep with her."

"Isabelle would never do that," Bo said

"He'll get her so drunk 'til she won't realize what's going on."

"Isabelle doesn't drink."

"She won't know she's drinking," Lily said. "He'll fix her a soft drink and lace it with liquor and after a few drinks she won't know what hit her. I know. I've been there."

"Where does that scum live?"

"Follow me," she said and handed him a key. "This is the key to his apartment. I won't need it anymore." She jumped in her car and sped away. Bo followed. They twisted and turned through the streets of Nashville until she came to a stop before a red brick apartment complex. "He lives in 5 B," she called.

"Thanks," he yelled as she speeded away, then he ran around looking at each number. "This is it," he mumbled, putting the key in the lock and turning it. He stepped inside unnoticed.

"Get your hands off her," he yelled making a flying lunge at the man who was forcing Isabelle down on the bed. He knocked him across the room and landed on top of him in a heap on the floor.

The man shoved Bo off him and stood to his feet. "Who are you?" he demanded angrily. "You're trespassing and I'm going to call the police."

"Go right ahead," Bo said smugly. "Be sure and ask to speak to my dad; Chief Abbott. He loves Isabelle like a daughter and he'll be very interested in what you're trying to do here tonight."

"Chief Abbott; I've heard of him. He doesn't play around," the man uttered. "Okay, just go and I'll forget about the charges."

"I'm taking Isabelle with me," Bo said leaning down to pick her up.

"She stays," the man said firmly, looking Bo square in the eye. "She's eighteen and she came here of her own free will..."

Bo grabbed him by the collar. "She didn't get drunk of her own free will. Now step aside or I'll make that call to police headquarters myself."

Begrudgingly, the man stepped aside.

Isabelle opened her eyes just as Bo picked her up. Her eyes flitted wildly as she tried to get focused. "Bo? Whatcha doin' here?"

"I'm taking you home."

"I don't wanna go home. I wanna stay here with Ray. He's my friend. I like him." Her words were slurred and ran together.

"He's not your friend and we're getting out of here." He carried her out the door, keeping an eye on the man named Ray. He set her in the front seat of his car and belted her in. He ran around to the driver's side and sped away.

"You're mean, Bo. Why did you make me leave? It was a party. We were having fun."

"The only one that was going to have fun was that sleazebag," he told her gently. "I walked in just in the nick of time. He was fixing to rape you."

"I wouldn't have let him done that," she lisped.

"You're so drunk you wouldn't have known what was going on 'til it was too late."

"I don't drink," she said indignantly turning her back to him.

"You did tonight," he told her. "That creep put liquor in your soft drink so you wouldn't realize you were drinking until you were stoned out of your mind."

"He didn't. He's my friend," she pouted and sat with her arms crossed, glaring straight ahead.

They had gone several blocks before she spoke again. This time her voice was sweet as she looked over at Bo. "Do you like me Bo? I like you. I like you, a lot."

"I like you a lot, too," he replied.

She unfastened her seatbelt and crawled over close to him and put her arms around his neck. "I like you a whole lot, Bo, and I want to kiss you." She leaned over and kissed his face over and over. "Do you want to kiss me, Bo?"

He tried to push her away. "Isabelle, get back over there. You're going to make us have a wreck." But she held on to him even tighter. He pulled over to the curb and moved her back over to her side and fastened the seatbelt around her. "My apartment is just a couple of blocks from here. I'm taking you there."

"Bo, I'm gonna be sick," she yelled, a moment later.

"Hold on, we're pulling into my apartment," he said, looking at her anxiously. He parked the car, jumped out and ran over to her side, opened the door and lifted her out. "Hold on, just another---yuck."

She had thrown up just as he raised her up shoulder high so it was all over both of them. She groaned and laid her head on his shoulder, getting it on her face and in her hair. He hurried into the house and ran to the bathroom. He set her down on the commode, yanked off her boots, then holding on to her with one hand he reached in the bathtub and turned on the water and after adjusting it to the right temp, he put her in the bathtub. He stepped in behind her and turned on the shower.

She hit him with her fist. "You pervert, get out of this shower. I'm not that kind of girl."

He grabbed her arms and held them to her side. "Isabelle, we have our clothes on," he pointed out with a twinge of exasperation in his voice. He poured shampoo into his hand and rubbed it into her hair. He tilted her head backward and rinsed the shampoo out of her hair. He turned the showerhead on himself then on their clothes. As soon as all the mess was off, he stepped out of the tub and pulled the shower curtain closed. "Pull your clothes off and hand them to me."

There was no defiance from her, only a moment of silence. "Bo," she called. "I can't undo my blouse."

He had noticed that it fastened in the back. He pulled the curtain back and unfastened her blouse, then closed the curtain again. "Hand it to me." As he took it from her, he said. "Now pull off your jeans."

Another moment of silence followed. "Bo," she lisped almost sweetly.

"What now?"

"My jeans are stuck. I can't get them off."

"That's because they're wet," he told her. "Lie down, stick your legs over the side of the tub and I will pull them off." It took a couple of minutes but she finally managed to do what he said. He tugged with all his might. They didn't budge. He put one foot on the tub, braced the other one firmly on the floor and pulled with all his might.

"Bo, I've unfastened them now," she called, as the jeans came off and Bo went flying back against the bathroom door.

"If I get through this night still in one piece," he grumbled as he began to regret his decision to bring her here instead of taking her home to the ranch. "I've been trained to deal with drunks, but it was never anything like this," he groused, getting up off the floor. He picked up her clothes and walked out into the hall. He came back a few minutes later. "Here's a big towel and a bathrobe," he called, laying them on the floor of the bathroom. "Get dressed and I'll dry your hair."

He could hear her grumbling through the door. Finally she came out. "I'm not going to wear this bathrobe," she said. "It's big and bulky and I don't like it."

He grabbed her before she could get it off. "The bathrobe stays on," he ordered, pulling it snugly around her and tying the belt tightly.

"Bo, I'm not going to...." She passed out and fell into his arms.

"Thank You," he whispered, lifting his eyes upward. He carried her over and laid her down on the bed. He pulled the covers up over her. He felt sure she would sleep through the night so he relaxed a bit. He called his dad and made arrangements for him to get Isabelle's car home. Then he grabbed a pillow and a quilt and settled down on the couch for a good night's sleep.

He was awakened the next morning by moans coming from the bedroom.

"My head! I'm dying. Help me! Help me!"

He jumped up and ran to her side. "Isabelle..."

"Bo, what are you doing here?"

"I live here."

"What am I doing here?"

"I brought you here last night to sober you up."

She leaned up on one arm, then moaned, grabbed her head and laid back down. "Sober me up---I don't understand, Bo. I don't drink."

"You did last night," he said, then, told her the whole story of how Ray had put liquor in her soft drink.

"Oh, my head, Bo," she cried. "I can't stand the pain. Give me a pain pill."

"Issy, I'm sorry, but I can't do that," he said. "I'm not sure how pain pills and the booze will react in your system so..."

"I don't care about that; I've got to have something. My head is about to explode, so, please Bo, give me something," she pleaded.

"Sorry," he replied, shaking his head.

"You like to see me suffer, don't you?" Her voice was raised, angry. "This is your way to get back at me; well I'll get the pills myself." She jumped out of bed and stood to her feet only to totter and fall.

Bo caught her before she hit the floor. He picked her up and carried her over to the couch. He took her head in his lap and began to massage her temples. "Maybe this will help," he said gently. "Just close your eyes and lay perfectly still."

She lay there moaning and groaning while he gently massaged her head, neck and shoulders. After a good amount of time had passed, the pain in her head eased and she sat up. "Thank you, Bo; that helped a lot."

"Now let's get some coffee into you." He stood up and went into the kitchen. He came out a few minutes later carrying two mugs of black coffee. "Drink up," he said, handing one mug to her. He sat down beside her.

"Thank you, Bo, for taking care of me," she said, between sips of coffee.

"It was the least I could do after the way I'm been acting." He sat his cup down on the coffee table and turned to face her. "Issy, I'm sorry for the way I acted last night---

for kissing you the way I did. I'm ashamed of myself and I hope someday you can forgive me."

"I'm the one who should be ashamed for the way I acted, and I am," she said. "I never should have been out on that stage dressed like that; and the way I acted was beyond shameful; but I had lost faith in everything I held dear."

"I know it had to be something really bad to make you act that way and I know it all started with me. Want to talk about it?"

She nodded. "It did start when you tricked me into thinking we were married, then left me; but you are not entirely to blame; there have been other things since then. I fell in love with Brock and I trusted him with all my heart; then he left me too. Then on the day that was supposed to have been our wedding day, he called me..."

"He called you; why?"

"He wanted to see how I was doing but before the conversation ended he mentioned how happy he was and that Susan was pregnant. That was more than I could bear to hear and I hung up on him. Then not long after that you showed up at the door with the baby and he was wearing the shirt you had bought him. And you know what happened next."

"I'm sorry, Issy, I would not have been so pig-headed if I had known what day it was; no wonder you jumped all over me."

"After that fight with you I wanted to find out about a legal matter so I went to see Ross Turner. He was late so his secretary took me to his office and told me to wait there. She had brought Mama's file by mistake and when she left I scanned through it. I didn't mean to pry but I saw the word, 'divorce' so I checked it out. It said mama was suing daddy for divorce on the grounds of adultery. I couldn't believe it so I read further. It stated that daddy was having an affair with Dori, and that he was planning to marry her as soon as the divorce from mama was final. That was the final straw. I ran from the office and called Mama on her cell phone. Daddy answered and I screamed at him, calling him a hypocrite and telling him I hated him. He and Mama showed up a few hours later and we had one of the biggest fights ever. Mama defended him but I wouldn't listen to anything she had to say. I said I didn't have a daddy anymore and she told me if I didn't have a daddy then I didn't have a mama either, and she forbid me to call home again until I was ready to ask daddy to forgive me. Then she stormed out, taking him with her and I haven't heard from them since."

"Isabelle, I'm so sorry," he said, taking her in his arms. "I had no idea. No wonder you snapped. Can you forgive me for the shoddy way I've treated you?"

"Bo, after what you did last night, how could I not forgive you? I can't imagine what I would have done if you hadn't been there for me. But how did you know what was going on and where to find me?"

"That creep's ex-girlfriend told me, and she gave me the key to his apartment and showed me where it was."

"The Lord was watching over me even after all I had done."

"That's the way God is," Bo commented. "He loves us even though we're not always as good as we should be." He paused. "Isabelle, I'm sorry, too, for the grief I've put you through concerning Brady and I promise…"

"No, Bo," she said, interrupting him. "I'm the one who has been unreasonable about the baby. I promise I won't try to keep you from seeing him again. After all you are his father and he needs you in his life."

Bo could hardly believe his ears. "Thank you, Isabelle," he said gratefully. "And I want to help support him financially. I'll…"

"That's not necessary," she said, interrupting him again. "With my career going so well I make more money than Brady and I will ever need. So don't…"

This time he interrupted her. "But I want to help support my son, in fact, I insist on it. He's my responsibility too, so we'll draw up legal papers stating that I will pay whatever you feel is a fair amount each month."

"Well, I'll let you help but we don't need legal papers," she told him. "I know you will keep your word, so we'll work out something between the two of us."

He agreed and they talked on for awhile until she was totally sober, then he drove her home.

Chapter 19

"Mimi, I'm moving back home," Isabelle announced on Saturday morning.

Mimi stood there eyes wide with surprise, not able to speak for a moment. "You're moving home---but why?" she finally managed to mumble.

"I want Brady to grow up around his relatives."

"But why now? What caused this hasty decision to leave here?"

"I just realized it's time to go home," Isabelle answered. "I know I can't move back in with Mama and Daddy, but I can live with Aunt Belle and Uncle Jesse; they love me."

"When will you be leaving?"

"I'll pack today and we'll leave either this afternoon or early tomorrow morning."

"Will you fly home in the company jet?"

"No, I'm driving through in my car."

"Isabelle, I won't let you drive that long distance alone. I'm coming with you," Mimi said. "I can stay a couple of days, then, fly back to Nashville."

Isabelle threw her arms around her. "Thanks, Mimi; that takes a load off my mind. Now will you listen for Brady, I've got a lot of work to do."

Mimi nodded, then as soon as Isabelle left the room, she dialed Bo's cell phone. "Isabelle is packing to move back home," she said when he answered. "If you want to see her and the baby before they leave, you'd better get over here now."

"I'm on my way."

Meanwhile, Isabelle was busy packing. She fought back tears that tried to fill her eyes as she thought back to the real reason she was leaving; the reason why she couldn't stay in Nashville. Only a couple of days ago she was happier than she had been in almost a year. It was the day after Bo had rescued her from that awful man who had gotten her drunk and tried to rape her. She had come to realize that Bo was telling the truth about the night of their mock wedding. He was too drunk to know what he was doing. She now knew that was possible because she had done things she would never have done if she'd been sober. So that meant Bo had truly loved her and she had reason to hope that he still did. She had resolved to tell him that she understood and she still loved him. She'd wanted to tell him right away but she had invited Ellie and Rex to have dinner with her at their favorite restaurant on Friday night so she would have to wait to talk to him.

A tear rolled down her face as she thought back to last night. She'd been waiting on Ellie and Rex for about thirty minutes when her cell phone rang.

"Honey, we're in the worst traffic jam ever," Ellie explained. "We've been sitting practically in the same place for about thirty minutes and it looks like we're going to be stuck here for an hour or more. Rex is starving, so we're going to exit off the first chance we get and find a place to eat. I'm sorry."

"That's okay, Aunt Ellie. I understand," Isabelle said. "I'll talk to you later." She was just about to leave the restaurant when she spied Bo sitting at a nearby table with an attractive woman. "I didn't know Bo was dating anyone," she mumbled aloud, squinting to get a better look at the woman. As she was watching, he reached out and took hold of the woman's hands.

Isabelle couldn't hear what they were saying but she could see what they were doing, and even though she knew it was rude to stare, she couldn't take her eyes off them.

Bo looked into the woman's eyes and said something to her. She smiled and nodded her head happily. Whatever he said she agreed to it. Isabelle looked on in disbelief as he took a small box from his pocket, pulled out a ring, and placed it on her finger. Then he leaned over the table and kissed her. Isabelle gasped in horror. Bo had proposed and she had accepted. She jumped up and ran from the restaurant pausing only to tell the waiter to put what she owed on her bill. Tears stung her eyes and her heart pounded as she drove to the ranch. Bo was in love with someone else. He was going to marry her. She had lost him again and this time for good. Her thoughts were interrupted by a knock on the bedroom door.

Not waiting for Isabelle to invite him, Bo walked in and took her by the hand. "Come on, Issy, we're going for a ride," he stated flatly, pulling her into the den. "I've got something to tell you."

"Bo, I'm very busy," she protested, knowing what he wanted to tell her.

"You go ahead. I'll do your laundry and have everything ready for you to pack when you get back," Mimi said. She had overheard the conversation and was not going to let this chance for Bo to talk to Isabelle slip away.

They rode along in silence. Isabelle's heart was breaking as she sat so close to him, but yet was so far away from him. She knew she had no right to be angry with him for falling in love with someone else. She had told him over and over how much she hated him. She knew now that she had never stopped loving him and that the love she had felt for Brock was not the real thing. Now just when she realized she loved Bo, she had lost him forever.

"I don't understand, Issy," Bo said, breaking the silence. "Why are you leaving?"

"It's time for me to go home," she answered feebly.

"But the other day when we talked, you said you wanted me to be a part of Brady's life and promised that I could see him anytime I wanted to."

"That's still true," she said. "You can come see him anytime."

"That will be a little hard to do with you living hundreds of miles away."

"I'm sorry, Bo but this is the way it's got to be."

He didn't answer and they sat in an awkward silence until Bo drove up a mountain and parked on the top.

Isabelle stepped out of the car and looked around. "Why did you bring me here, Bo?" she demanded angrily. "How could you hurt me like this?"

"Issy, this is a special place to us and I wanted to be here with you when I tell you what…"

"I already know what you're going to tell me, and I can't believe you would bring me to this place to tell me something like that."

"You already know?"

"Yes, I know you're getting married."

"You do?"

"I was at the restaurant last night and I saw you propose to her."

"Oh, that," he said flippantly, then he leaned over and kissed her. He caught her hand just as she reached out to slap him. "Not this time, you don't," he said, kissing her again.

"Bo Abbott, you're the most detestable person I've ever met; kissing me when you're about to marry someone else."

"Let me explain, Issy," he said. "You didn't see what you thought you saw."

"I know a proposal when I see one," she huffed.

"Oh, I proposed to her alright," he admitted. "But I didn't propose for myself. You see, a friend of mine is in Iraq and the woman I was with last night is his girl. He's coming home in about a month for a thirty day leave. He wants to marry her the day he gets home, but he knows she wants a nice church wedding and that she would need time to get ready. He didn't want to propose over the phone so he sent me the words to say and ordered the ring online so I could pick it up. So you see she didn't agree to marry me; she agreed to marry him."

"You're not going to marry her?"

He looked at Isabelle as realization hit him. "That's what this is all about, isn't it? You're leaving because you thought I was marrying someone else." He picked her up, and swinging her around he yelled at the top of his voice. "Hey, world, she loves me! She really loves me!" But not being willing to rely wholly on the fact that she loved him, he sat her down on the magical bench, the one where the girl always said yes to her young man when he proposed to her. Kneeling down he took her hand and looked into her eyes. "Issy, I messed things up before, but I never stopped loving you. I never could; cause you're the only girl in the world for me. So, Isabelle, I'm going to ask you again, will you marry me?"

She started laughing. "Bo, this is so funny," she said between giggles. "I thought you were in love with someone else and you thought I was still in love with Brock. I thought you were bringing me here to tell me you were getting married, and you were really bringing me here to propose to me. How could we both be so wrong and so right at the same time? Isn't that funny Bo?"

"Yeah, I guess so; but will you marry me?"

"Of course, I will marry you," she said, still laughing.

Bo pulled her into his arms and her giddiness rubbed off on him, and even though he didn't really know why, he started laughing too.

A little squirrel on the ground holding an acorn between his front feet heard the commotion and scampered up a nearby tree. A group of birds sitting on a branch right above the bench, fluttered their wings and flew away; but Isabelle and Bo didn't notice. Their world was right again and laughter filled their hearts.

"I needed that," she gasped, finally regaining her composure. "I haven't had a good laugh in a long time.

The last time I laughed like that was on my eighteenth birthday."

"Our wedding day," Bo asked, a little put out that she would find something to laugh about on their special day. "I didn't feel like laughing that day."

"Well at first neither did I," she told him, sensing the hurt in his voice. "I came up here that morning and I sat on this bench and cried and cried. I tried to find the answer as to why you would betray me, and the only thing I could come up with was that the thousand dollars meant more to you than I did. I was heartbroken, Bo."

"But you had a good time later on?"

"Yeah, I met Brock that day," she explained. "He was at my birthday party and as his gift to me he invited me to have dinner with him that night. We ate at his house and afterward watched videos that were so funny I laughed 'til I cried. That night the healing process began inside me; that night I started getting over you and falling in love with him or so I thought."

"I spent that day thinking of you and our wedding. I cried as I thought of the love I had thrown away," he said. "Issy, I don't see how you could have forgotten our love so quickly."

"Bo, did you expect me just to sit home and wait for you to come back to me?"

"I guess that's what I hoped would happen," he answered truthfully. "How about changing the subject now? I can think of a lot of things I'd rather talk about than your love for Mr. Wonderful. You did just agree to marry me, didn't you?"

"I'm sorry," she said, "but I must talk about Brock just a little more. The other night I realized the love I felt for him, even though it was real and it was good, it wasn't the kind of love that I feel for you. Bo, I know now that I never stopped loving you and I never will, and I want to spend the rest of my life with you, so let's seal our engagement with a kiss."

"I don't know if I should chance it," he said teasingly. "The last few times I kissed you, I got my face slapped."

"Well, not this time," she whispered leaning over and kissing him. "I'm so happy, Bo."

"Me too," he said, then took her in his arms and kissed her over and over. "I'm not dreaming am I? If I am dreaming, don't wake me, for I'd rather spend the rest of my life in a dream world married to you, than to be awake without you."

"I could stay here in your arms all day, but we've got some plans to make," she reminded him. "We need to set a date."

"Let's get married right away," he said. "I don't want to chance losing you again."

"How about next Saturday," she suggested.

"A week from today?"

"You don't want to marry me that soon?"

"Of course I do, but can you be ready in a week?"

She laughed. "Bo, Mama has planned two weddings for me this year. She can do this one with her eyes closed. Let's call right now and tell her." She dialed the number.

"Hello."

"Daddy," Isabelle answered cautiously, not really knowing how things stood between them. She still believed he was guilty but she didn't hate him anymore. She wasn't sure how he felt about her.

"Isabelle, it's so good to hear your voice.

"It's good to hear your voice too, Daddy, and, I love you."

"I love you too, sweetheart."

"Daddy, I'm so happy," she said. "I'm getting married and..."

"No, Isabelle, it's too soon," he blurted out. "You haven't had time to heal since Brock walked out on you. Sweetheart, give yourself time to get over all the hurt you've been through this past year---date the man, if you must, but don't make any long term commitments until you're absolutely sure."

"But, Daddy, I am sure," she said. "I've never been happier in my life."

"Honey, it's just a rebound thing. Please don't do something you'll regret later. You just can't meet someone and fall in love with them."

"I thought you fell in love with Mama the first time you saw her."

"That's right, I did," he admitted, knowing that he couldn't put up a convincing argument against love at first sight.

"Relax, Daddy," she said. "I've known this man all of my life and he is the love of my life; in fact he always has been---it's Bo, Daddy, we're back together. We're getting married."

"Bo? But sweetheart, he hurt you so badly."

"We've gotten through all of that, Daddy. I know now that Bo has always loved me. I'll explain everything to you when I see you." She paused, then, when he didn't say anything, she continued. "Daddy, we're getting married at the church there next Saturday and..."

"A week from today," he gasped. There was shock and apprehension in his voice.

"Yes, and I need to talk to Mama so we can start working on the wedding plans."

"Sweetheart, your mama can't come to the phone right now," he said. "Tell me your plans and I'll make a list and give it to her."

"Basically, everything's the same as my first wedding plans," she explained. "We're getting married there. I want you to walk me down the aisle, but I also want you to marry us; is that possible?"

"Well, I suppose Andy could do the preliminaries, then, I can take over and do the main part of the ceremony."

"Daddy, could Uncle Jesse do it? He's my favorite uncle and I'd love it if he could be a part of my wedding."

"Well, he is a deacon, so I don't see a problem, but I'll check into it."

"Thanks, Daddy, and the only changes we really want in the plans for our first wedding is we don't want fancy catered food; we want a good old home cooking sit down kind of supper where everyone can relax and have a good time."

"I believe we can handle that with all the relatives we have here and of course the ladies at the church with want to pitch in too."

"Well, that's it, daddy. I'll see you one day next week."

"Okay sweetheart," he said, hanging up the phone and yelling for Roseanna.

"There's one more phone call I need to make," she told Bo as she dialed another number.

"Hello."

"Brock"

"Isabelle, is that you?"

"Yes, and I have wonderful news. I'm getting married next Saturday."

"No, Isabelle; it's too soon," he said worriedly. "You're about to make the biggest mistake of your life. Give yourself more time."

She laughed. "Relax, Brock, I've just been through all of that with Daddy, so I'll tell you right up front; I'm marrying Bo. I realized a couple of days ago that it was Bo that I really love; and it's always been him. I thought what you and I had was the real thing but I know now it wasn't.

You said you couldn't be completely happy until you knew I was happy too. Well, I'm happy now, so you can relax and enjoy all the happiness you deserve. Brock, I want you to know that I will always care about you and wish only the best for you and your family. I also want to invite the three of you to the wedding. I hope you can come. I'd like to meet your wife and daughter."

"I would like to be there to help you celebrate your special day, but we already have plans for next week-end. And, Isabelle, I will always care for you too."

"Who knows," she said, "maybe someday the four of us can be good friends."

"I'd like that," he said, then, they said their goodbyes and hung up.

She took Bo's hands in hers. "I hope you don't mind that I called Brock. Bo, he was good to me and I don't know that I could have survived if he had not come into my life. From the day I met him, he's been there for me. When I found out I was pregnant I thought my life was over but he stood by me, and I was able to get through that difficult time because of him. And the media had a hey-day when it was learned that I was pregnant. A reporter hired a woman to confront me in the grocery store. She pulled my coat open revealing the fact that I was pregnant, then she slapped me and was going to hit me again, but Brock stopped her. Of course they got it all on film. The next morning the story and pictures were splashed all over the front page of that newspaper. The article was very cruel." Tears filled her eyes as she remembered the humiliation she had felt. "It was a really bad time but Brock stood by me and I did weather the storm. Bo, I owed it to him to let him know that my life is back on track so he can get on with his life and be happy with his wife and daughter without any feelings of guilt over me."

Bo took her in his arms. "Honey, I'm glad Brock was there to pick up the pieces of your life when your world crumbled because of me. I realize the two of you will always have special feelings for each other and I'm okay with that. I am the most blessed man on earth, and the happiest one, because, come next Saturday the most wonderful and beautiful girl on earth will become my wife." He pulled her close and kissed her. "Now, let's go share our good news with the rest of the world."

Chapter 20

Roseanna stood in the den thinking about the wedding preparations. Had she done everything right? Would Isabelle be pleased? She knew she was not in the frame of mind to think straight. What if she had forgotten some important detail? Belle had helped plan everything, but still she had nagging doubts. She shook her head trying to clear the cobwebs from her mind. Would she ever be able to think clearly again or must she go through life with her mind muddled and confused? Her thoughts were interrupted when Brad walked in and put his arms around her.

"Sweetheart, don't worry, you've done a great job planning this wedding," he said, as if reading her mind. "Isabelle is going to be so pleased."

"Do you really think so," she said, snuggling close in his arms. "I want everything to be perfect for Isabelle, but I'm scared, Brad. What if she senses something is wrong with me. You know I can't think straight; what if I fall to pieces and spoil her wedding day. I'd never forgive myself."

"Roseanna, that's not going to happen," he assured her. "I'll be with you every moment and if you feel like you can't handle the situation, I'll know, and I will handle it for you. Please don't worry sweetheart. You're gonna do fine."

Roseanna didn't have time to ponder the situation further, for the cars carrying Isabelle, Bo and the others from Nashville pulled into the driveway. "Please stay close to me, Brad," she pleaded as they walked outside to welcome their guests.

"I'm here, baby," he whispered squeezing her hand.

Amid the happy hello's, hugs and kisses, and play time with her grandson, Roseanna was able to relax a little and things went off without a hitch. Before she had time to worry too much, a couple of days had passed and the wedding was almost ready to begin. A big test as to how well Roseanna could handle things on her own came when she was alone with Isabelle in the bride's room.

"You're the most beautiful bride ever," Roseanna remarked. "I love you so much and I'm so proud of my little girl."

"I love you too, Mama," Isabelle said. "You are the best mother in the world and I'll always remember the things you taught me. I only hope that Bo and I will always be as happy as you and daddy are."

Roseanna trembled as thoughts of Brad and Dori in the cabin flashed through her mind. She had to control her feelings for Isabelle's sake. "Honey, I feel certain that you and Bo will be as happy as we've been. You love and trust each other and that's the basis for a long and happy marriage."

"Amen to that," Brad said, stepping into the room. "Roseanna, I believe they're about ready to seat the mothers," he added, giving her a kiss. "And may I say there has never been a more beautiful mother of the bride."

"Thank you," she said, then after giving Isabelle another kiss she walked out.

"I guess this is it, sweetheart," Brad said. "This is the time I've been dreading since the day you were born; the day I would have to walk you up the aisle and give you to another man." Tears misted his eyes. "Are you sure you don't want to back out?"

"I'm sure, daddy," she said, laughing. "But you don't have to worry. Even though I marry Bo today; I'll always be your little girl. Nothing on earth can change that."

"Okay, let's go." He took her by the arm and headed over to the church.

Isabelle watched as her attendants marched up the aisle, one by one. Beth looking radiant in her gown of soft yellow silk went first. She was met by Mikey who had a big crush on her and was happy to get this opportunity to escort her to her place on the stage. Next, Cassie dressed in a matching gown of mint green looked lovely even though she could give birth to a little baby boy any day now. Duke beamed as he escorted her to her place. Brianna, dressed in a pink gown that matched the other two, was the last one to march up the aisle. Lee met her and took her to the place for the maid of honor.

As Isabelle watched Lee and Brianna, she thought of her earlier conversation with Lee. He had asked her to go with him to Roseanna's special place to talk about a decision he had to make.

He had gotten right to the subject. "Isabelle, I'm in love with Brianna and I want to ask her to marry me."

"I happen to know she's in love with you too, so what is the problem?"

"I haven't told anyone this but I've received the call into the ministry and I plan to pursue that calling in the near future. I know there won't be much money coming in, and I don't know if I have the right to ask Brianna to share that kind of life with me since she has always been rich."

"Brianna is a down to earth kind of girl and having money doesn't mean that much to her," Isabelle told him. "I'm sure I know what her answer will be, but even if I'm wrong, you've got to at least give her a chance to decide for herself. Don't wait, ask her right away. I'd like to know her answer before we leave on our honeymoon."

Now as she stood here, Isabelle wondered if he had asked her, and if she had accepted. She forced her thoughts back to the present as she watched the twins, Abby and Drew walk, side by side, up the aisle. Abby spread flower petals on the white runner and Drew carried the velvet pillow that held the rings. "They're so cute," she remarked and Brad nodded.

"Get ready," Brad said as the wedding march peeled forth. He brushed away tears that were misting his eyes, took her arm and stepped inside.

Isabelle saw the tears and squeezed his arm. "It's all right daddy," she whispered. "Remember, I'll always be your little girl."

They reached the front and Jesse read a scripture concerning marriage. Then he turned to Brad and asked; "Who gives this woman to be wed?"

"Her mother and I do," Brad replied, placing Isabelle's hand into Bo's hand.

Jesse stepped aside and Brad took his place as Roseanna and Kent sang "You Raise Me Up." Roseanna had panicked when Isabelle asked her to sing; and she asked Kent to help her. Now, her fears were quickly dismissed as the words rang throughout the sanctuary and tears filled the eyes of the wedding guests.

Brad turned to Bo. "I believe you have something to say to Isabelle."

Bo took hold of her hands. "Isabelle that song must have been written especially for you and me. I can stand on mountains and walk on water when you are by my side. I'm strong only when you are with me. I know I messed things up between us the first time, but I never stopped loving you, I never could. I promise you that I will cherish the love we share every day, for the rest of my life. I will never treat that love carelessly again. I not only make promises to you today but to our son as well." Mavis walked over and placed Brady in his arms. Bo looked down at his son. "Brady, I don't deserve you nor your mother, but I'm glad she gave me another chance to be a husband to her and a father to you, for I truly love you both with all my heart and my emotions. I promise to take care of the two of you, provide for you, and give you all the love and tender care that I have inside of me." He leaned down and kissed his son, then handed him to Mavis. He took Isabelle's hands again.

"You are the love of my life and when I think that in a few minutes the most beautiful and wonderful girl in the world will become my wife, I know that I am the most blessed man on earth."

Brad nodded to Isabelle and she began her vows to Bo. "Bo, I've always loved you even when I was too young to understand the meaning of love. When you left me and I thought that you didn't love me, my world crumbled and I made myself believe that I hated you, even to the point of convincing myself that I was in love with someone else. But it was always you Bo. I love you so much today and I will love you for all of my tomorrows. I'm so thankful that God in His wisdom knew that we could only be happy with each other and He brought us back together. We are both blessed."

They repeated the regular marriage vows and Brad pronounced that they were now husband and wife. Bo kissed his bride and their journey together began.

After pictures of the wedding party and relatives were taken, they were escorted to the head table and their meals were set down before them, then, the other guests lined up to go through the buffet. They were about half finished when Roseanna spied Dori in the serving line.

"What's she doing here?" she gasped and began to tremble.

Belle saw Dori, and worry lines formed on her face. She grabbed Roseanna's hand and turned to Mavis. "Let's go to the ladies room," she said, nodding in Dori's direction.

Mavis stood up and they walked on either side of Roseanna holding her hands. They looked to see if Isabelle had noticed, but she was busy talking to her guests and she didn't see them leave.

Belle leaned over and whispered in Jesse's ear as they walked by. "Dori is here. Meet us in the ladies room in a couple of minutes."

Jesse waited a few minutes, then, stood and walked out. He hurried to the ladies room. "Lock the door," he said. "I don't want anyone coming in and finding me here."

Roseanna was heaving for breath. Panic showed on her face. Jesse put his arms around her. "Take a deep breath and let it out slowly," he coaxed. "Now do it again."

Roseanna did as he said and after a few minutes her breathing was almost normal. "Jesse," she cried. "Why is that woman at my daughter's wedding? She knows she's not welcome. Is she here just to torment me?"

"I don't know why she showed up, but you can handle it," he answered, trying to calm her down. "Honey, you've got to be strong for Isabelle's sake." He wet a paper towel and put it on her brow. "I will go and tell her to leave so just stay calm for a little while longer."

Meanwhile Brad noticed Dori and anger rose up inside of him. "I'm going to tell her to leave," he said and stood up.

Jesse walked up just then. He put his hand on his arm. "No, let me do it," he said. "You don't need to be talking to her." He walked over to Dori and grabbed her by the arm. "Where do you get off coming to this wedding."

"Isabelle wanted me to help with the serving."

"You could have said no," he said bluntly.

"I tried," she told him. "But she wouldn't take no for an answer, and short of telling her the truth about what's going on, I couldn't give her a reason not to be here, and if I leave before my job is finished, she might ask questions."

"Well, see that you leave as soon as possible," he said. "Roseanna saw you and she is having a hard time coping."

"I know Roseanna has been hurt in all of this, and I'm very sorry; and don't worry I'll leave at the earliest possible moment. I don't exactly relish being treated like a tramp by all these good church people."

Jesse felt a twinge of guilt. He was a deacon and it was his job to treat others kindly, even under adverse circumstances. "I'm sorry I jumped on you like that. I should have been more compassionate."

She didn't answer but turned and walked away.

Meanwhile, Brad leaned over to Bo. "I need to talk to you. It's very important."

Bo whispered something to Isabelle, then, got up and followed Brad out of the room. "What's up?"

"I need you to get Isabelle out of here as soon as possible," he answered with a look of worry on his face. "I can't explain why right now, but I promise I'll tell you everything when you get back from your honeymoon."

"Sounds serious," Bo said.

"It is."

"I'll do it, but what do I tell my wife?"

"Tell her that the flight to the place where you're spending your honeymoon will take several hours and that you need to get to the airport as soon as possible."

"And, you're not going to tell me what our destination is?"

Brad shook his head. "We want it to be a surprise. But I can promise that it will be a nice surprise." Their honeymoon trip was a gift from Brad and Roseanna and all that they would tell them was that it was a wonderful place.

They walked back to the table and Bo leaned over to Isabelle. "Honey, we need to be leaving as soon as possible. Brad told me that the flight to our secret honeymoon place will take hours and the company jet is waiting at the airport."

"Did he tell you where we're going?"

"No, he just said it will be a nice surprise," he told her. "I need to make the announcement that we will be leaving soon."

"Okay, she said. "We need to cut the cake and throw the bouquet first."

Bo stood and got everyone's attention. "We'd like to thank all of you for coming to help us celebrate our special day. But my new father-in-law just informed me that we need to get to the airport right away as our flight will take several hours. Our destination is still a secret to Isabelle and me; but I have been assured that it will be worth waiting for. So without further ado, we will cut the cake and throw the bouquet." He took Isabelle's hand and they walked over to the wedding cake. They cut two small pieces and fed them to each other; then drank punch from two long-stemmed glasses.

"Now, young ladies, line up," Isabelle said, and turned her back to them. She had seen where Brianna was standing and she aimed the bouquet in her direction. It fell right in her hands.

"Now it's time for the young men to line up," Bo said, as he took the garter from off Isabelle's leg. He tossed it and Lee reached out and grabbed it.

"I couldn't let Brianna be the next young lady to be married without me being the next man, since she has already said yes to my proposal," he said, grinning big as cheers went up.

Roseanna watched as Dori walked out the back door.

Hugs and kisses were given all around; then Bo and Isabelle ran to the waiting limo amid rice and shouts of well wishes. They jumped inside and the limo raced away from the church and headed for the airport.

"I'm taking Roseanna home," Belle told Jesse as soon as the limo was out of sight. "She's had about all she can take for one day."

He nodded. "We'll stay here and help clean up. Call if you need me," he said, giving her a quick kiss.

A few moments later his cell phone rang.

"Jesse, hurry," Belle shouted hysterically, when he answered. "Roseanna has gone off the deep end. She's threatening to get Brad's gun and kill Dori."

"We're on our way," he said, grabbing Brad's hand. "We've got to get home quick." He touched Steve's hand to get his attention as they rushed out the door. "Tell Mama we've got to go and we'll call her later."

They rushed to the car and in record time were pulling into Brad's driveway. Jesse had explained the situation to Brad as they sped down the highway and he jumped from the car before it came to a complete stop and bolted across the lawn and into the house. Jesse followed close behind.

"Where is she?" Brad's voice was filled with fear.

"She's in your bedroom. I think she has the gun."

Brad started down the hallway, but Jesse stopped him. "Let me handle this," he said. "In her state of mind she might shoot you."

"Jesse," Belle called out fear ringing her voice.

"I'll be okay, sweetheart," he said, trying to put her mind at ease. "She won't hurt me." He walked to the bedroom as Brad and Belle joined hands and prayed.

"Roseanna, I'm here," he said, calmly, walking over to her.

"Don't try to stop me, Jesse," she said in a threatening tone. "She has to die; that's the only way she will ever leave my family alone."

"Sweetheart, let's talk about this," he said pleadingly, trying to find a way to get the gun away from her.

"No! I'm going to kill her," she screamed. "Now, get out of my way, Jesse!"

"No, I won't let you do this," he said, grabbing the gun and trying to wrench it from her grasp. A deafening explosion was heard as the gun went off in their hands.

"Jesse!" Belle screamed as she raced to the bedroom.

"Sweetheart," Brad gasped as he followed on her heels.

Roseanna lay limp in Jesse's arms as they rushed into the room.

"Oh no, sweetheart," Brad cried, running over to her. "Is she...?"

"No, she just fainted," Jesse said. "We're both okay but I'm afraid that your room didn't fair so well." He pointed to a big hole in the ceiling. He laid Roseanna down on the bed and took Belle in his arms. "It's over, honey."

"Jesse, I was so scared," she said, tears running down her face. "I couldn't bear the thought of either one of you being hurt or..." She laid her head on his shoulder and wept.

He held her close and turned to Brad. "Roseanna can't take anymore," he said. "I hate to think what tonight will do to her. She may try again to kill Dori."

Brad shook his head. "No, she won't," he said. "I'm getting her out of here first thing tomorrow. She won't ever have to see Dori again."

"Where are you going," Belle asked.

"I'm taking her to Nashville," he said. "She loves the ranch."

"Good," Jesse said. "She needs to get away from the pressures here."

"The company plane won't be back from Hawaii by then, will it?" Belle knew that's where Bo and Isabelle were going on their honeymoon. "You can use the Pecot Company plane. I'll have to check with Lance, but I'm sure it will be all right. I'll call him now." She made the call and it was all set for Brad and Roseanna to leave early Sunday morning.

"We'll spend the night and drive you to the airport," Jesse offered. "I would like to stay close by in case Roseanna needs me when she comes to." He thought it best to let her come around on her own; forcing her might make matters worse.

"Thanks, Jesse," Brad said. "Just pick any bedroom you want and make yourself at home. And, Belle, you know where Roseanna's things are so feel free to use anything you need. See you in the morning."

They had barely left the room when Roseanna came to. "Jesse," she screamed, with a look of horror in her eyes. "I killed Jesse."

Brad grabbed her and held her close. "No, you didn't sweetheart," he tried to assure her. "Jesse is okay."

"No, he's dead," she screamed. "I shot him."

Jesse and Belle heard the screams and rushed into the room. Jesse walked over to her. "Roseanna, I'm okay," he said, taking her hand. "The gun went off. You fainted, but no one was hurt."

"Belle, help me," she cried, looking over at her sister.

Brad stood up and let Belle sit down on the bed beside her. A tear ran down his face. Roseanna had not wanted comfort from him but from her sister.

"Belle, what's wrong with me?" she asked as Belle pulled her into her arms. "I wanted to kill Dori tonight; I still want to. Help me, sis, please help me."

"It's going to be all right, honey," Belle said. "We're all going to help you. Brad has come up with a plan that will make things a lot better."

"I don't want to hear anything that Brad has to say," she snapped. "He doesn't love me; he loves Dori. He asked her to the wedding so she could be near him."

Belle didn't know how to answer so she looked at Jesse for help. He came over and sat down beside Roseanna.

"Honey, just listen to what Brad has to say and then if you don't like the plan, we'll think of something else." He motioned for Brad.

Brad walked over but he didn't offer to take her hand. "Sweetheart, I'm taking you to Nashville; to the ranch. We're leaving in the morning and we'll stay there until you're better."

"Are you taking me away so I won't kill your precious Dori?"

"No, Roseanna, I don't care about her. I'm only thinking of you. I know how much you love the ranch and I believe it will be good for you to get away from here for awhile." There was a look of hurt in his eyes. "Please say you'll go."

"Do I have a choice," she asked sarcastically. "You make all the decisions now since, thanks to you, I'm in no shape to think for myself."

Her words cut deep. He couldn't stop the tears that misted his eyes. She had never actually blamed him before, not out loud anyway. It hurt to know she felt that way about him. "We'll go or we'll stay," he said. "The choice is yours."

"Jesse," she muttered looking at him for an answer.

Roseanna, Brad is thinking of you and what's best for you, and Belle and I agree with him. I think the ranch would be very good for you right now. I think you need to do what Brad suggests."

"Since I'm outnumbered I'll agree to go, but only if he will agree to bring me back if I want to come home."

"Of course, I will bring you home anytime you say," Brad assured her. "Now lie back and get some sleep. We're leaving early in the morning."

"What about my things? I'll need to take some things with me."

"I'll pack for you," Belle offered. "I know the things you will want to take so you rest now."

"I'm sorry she treated you that way," Jesse told Brad when they were out of earshot of Roseanna. "Maybe being at the ranch together will soften the hostility she has toward you."

"I hope so but I'm not going to hold my breath," he said. "She talked about me as if I wasn't even in the room. I think tonight set her back a long way and I don't know if I will be able to help her through it."

"I pray that you can, and if you need help just call and I can be there in a few hours," Jesse replied, then, he changed the subject. "Things went well at the wedding, don't you think?"

"Everyone treated me well, but I felt an undercurrent; no one there believes that I'm innocent and they were just being nice so Isabelle wouldn't get suspicious."

"Well, there's at least one person who believes in you---Andy."

"Andy thinks I'm telling the truth?"

"I know that it's hard to believe, but he actually went to bat for you with the committee."

"Will wonders never cease," Brad said shaking his head. "I'll have to remember to thank him." He looked over at Jesse. "What about you? Do you think I'm guilty?"

Jesse didn't answer right away. When he did his words were slow and guarded. "I love you like a brother. I couldn't love you more if you were my blood brother; but there's just too many unanswered questions; too many things that point to your guilt."

"Well, thanks for being honest," Brad said. "Someday I hope to prove to everyone that I am not a liar and a hypocrite. Now, if you will excuse me I'm going to my wife and see if I can undo some of the damage that tonight caused."

"Brad, I'm sorry and I pray that one day soon you will give us proof of your innocence. I'd like nothing better than to trust you again, but the evidence…"

Brad walked away without saying a word. He wanted to lash out but he needed to sleep on this before he said things that he might regret later. He hated this rift with

Jesse; and he hoped he could mend it before leaving tomorrow but however it turned out, Roseanna was his main concern, and, they would fly to Nashville in the morning whether or not things were right between Jesse and him. He hoped and prayed that tomorrow would be a new beginning for Roseanna; and, that in time she would learn to trust him again.

Chapter 21

Two weeks had passed since Brad and Roseanna came to Nashville. Isabelle and Bo had gotten home from their honeymoon late the night before and Brad had brought the baby home this morning. He came alone because he wanted to tell Isabelle the truth about the things she had read in Ross's notes concerning the divorce.

"I believe you, Daddy," she said, after Brad explained the things that had happened between Dori and him in South Africa. "I know now you could never knowingly break your marriage vows to Mama or your commitment to God. I'm sorry I said those horrible things to you. I should have trusted you."

He took her in his arms. "Thanks, sweetheart, for believing in me again, but there's more that I must tell you and I'm not sure how you will react to it."

"Is it something about Mama? Are you having problems again?"

He nodded. "It deals with Roseanna's reaction to you when you found out about the divorce."

"I don't understand."

"I saw the look of hopelessness on your face when your mother told you not to call home unless you were calling to apologize to me; practically disowning you 'til you did," he said, choosing his words as to not make her blame herself. "I was very upset with Roseanna and by the time we got home I could barely stand the sight of her, but I couldn't talk to her about it, so while she was asleep I took off to the cabin to sort things out."

"I guess Mama was upset that you went without her."

"That was the least of our problems," he said and told her what had happened with Dori, and how Roseanna found out; and had overdosed on pain pills and almost died; and how it had affected her mind.

"Oh, Daddy, is she okay now?"

"She's doing better, but if I had not brought her here to Nashville, I don't know what would have happened. She went off the deep end because Dori was at your wedding, and when she got home she got my gun and was going to kill Dori, but Jesse was able to get the gun away from her."

"It's my fault that Dori was there," Isabelle cried. "I insisted that she come and be one of the servers. "Daddy, I'm so sorry. I invited Dori to the wedding for the wrong reason. I wanted to see the two of you together so I could detect if anything was going on between you; and because of my suspicious mind, Mama got hurt. Is there anything I can do to make her better?"

"Just love her and be there for her," he said. "The pills should be out of her system soon and we'll know more if any permanent damage was done. If it does affect her permanently, I'll never forgive myself, for I am to blame for all of it."

"Don't say that, Daddy," she said. "Everyone knows that you wouldn't do anything to hurt Mama."

"Sweetheart, no one at home believes me and they hold me responsible for what happened to Roseanna. They think I'm lying about the whole thing and there is no way I can prove otherwise."

She ran over and put her arms around him. Daddy, I believe you. I know you're innocent."

He shook his head. "Even though I didn't sleep with Dori, I am guilty of bad judgment in letting her stay when she showed up at the cabin that night. I knew how it would look but I let it happen, and now only she and I know the truth, and no one is listening to us."

"God knows the truth, Daddy, and I believe that sooner or later everyone else will too."

"Thank you, sweetheart," he said, giving her a big hug. "It means the world to me that you believe in me. Now, I need to get going. I want to be there when Roseanna gets up. I don't like to leave her very long at a time." He started out the door, then, stopped. "Why don't Bo and you come over for supper tonight? It would be good for Roseanna, and we'd all like to hear about your trip to Hawaii."

"It was great, and thanks again for giving us such a wonderful wedding gift, and, we'll be happy to join you for supper tonight."

Roseanna awoke early one morning two weeks later and sat up in bed. Brad was sleeping peacefully. Not wanting to disturb him, she eased off the bed, dressed in jeans and shirt and pulled on a pair of boots. Then she slipped out the door and out to the barn. She saddled Midnight Thunder and rode out of the corral and down the path that led to the lake. It felt good being out by herself, without anyone watching over her. She took a deep breath and inhaled the fresh morning air. She was so much better today. Her mind was clear, not fuzzy. She knew that she was back to her old self, one hundred percent. "Thank you, God," she whispered as she rode up to the lake, dismounted, and looked out across the water.

The sun was coming up and spreading its rays over the lake, causing ripples of brightly colored hues, to dance across the water. She couldn't remember ever seeing anything more beautiful. It reminded her of the beautiful life she'd had with Brad. Her countenance changed as she thought of her marriage and how it had been affected by his affair with Dori. She put her arms around Midnight Thunder. "Boy, if only you could help me through this," she whispered in his ear. But she knew her only help would come from the Lord. "Lord, I'll need strength from You to be able to stand, and to do what I have to do," she prayed, then, mounting her horse she rode slowly toward the house.

"Rex, will you take care of Midnight Thunder for me," she asked getting off the horse. "I have something to take care of and it can't wait."

"Sure thing," Roseanna," he replied. "You went riding alone; does that mean you're feeling better."

"Yes, I feel much better," she answered, giving him one of her famous smiles.

"I'm glad," he said hugging her. "We were all concerned about you."

"I know, and it made me feel good to know so many people cared about me."

"Sweetheart, I've been looking everywhere for you," Brad said, walking up just then. "You didn't go riding alone, did you?"

"Yeah, I did, and it felt great," she assured him. "Brad, do you have a few minutes? I need to talk to you."

"I always have time for you, Roseanna." He sensed urgency in her voice that worried him. What was so important that she had to talk to him now; something that couldn't wait until they'd had breakfast.

"Let's go to the gazebo where we won't be disturbed." She took his hand and walked into the back yard. She sat down on the swing and motioned for him to join her.

"What's this all about, Roseanna?"

"I'm out of the fog" she said. "My mind is not cluttered anymore. I'm back to my old self."

He pulled her into his arms. "Oh, sweetheart," he cried, holding her close. Words could not express his joy so he just held her.

She looked at him through tear-dimmed eyes as she cupped his face in her hands. "Brad, you've been so good to me through all this; you've taken such good care of me; but now I…" She left the sentence unfinished.

Worry filled his heart again. "Roseanna, what are you trying to tell me?"

"Brad, I've sensed for a few days now, that I was getting well and it's a wonderful feeling; but when I look at you, I see you and Dori at the cabin together, and I feel myself being drawn back into that fog and it scares me. I don't ever want to go there again."

His muscles tensed as he began to realize what she was trying to tell him. "What's this all about?"

"This is the hardest thing I've ever had to do, Brad, but I can't afford to let the sight of you send me back into the place I was in. So I'm asking you to leave."

"You don't mean that, Roseanna..."

"Yes, I do mean it," she replied. "I'm sorry, Brad."

"You're sorry," he yelled jumping to his feet. "After all I've done for you these past weeks..."

"Don't you mean after all you've done *to* me," she yelled back. She jumped up and got in his face. "Whose fault was it that I was in that condition?"

"You're the one who swallowed those pills; and may I add there was no reason for you to do so, except for your insane jealously!"

"How dare you say that to me?" There was anger and hurt in her voice. "You took that woman to our cabin and you're trying to make me feel guilty!"

"I've told you the truth about that, but you don't believe me," he said in disgust. "By not believing me you are calling me a liar and a hypocrite. Someday when it's too late you will find out that I'm telling the truth, and when that day comes I want you to remember this moment."

"Brad, my mind is clear now; so don't try to con me into believing that nothing happened. Why else would you take her to the cabin?"

"Forget it," he said. "I'm through trying to convince you. I'm out of here."

"Are you going to Dori?"

"What if I said I was?"

"At least it would be better knowing you were with her, rather than wondering if the two of you were sneaking around behind my back, carrying on your little affair."

"That does it!" His eyes flashed with the fury he felt building up inside him. "Don't you worry, Roseanna, I'm leaving as soon as I can make the arrangements."

"As long as it happens today," she said, her eyes flashing fury right back at him. "I'm going to the office and I want you out of my house by the time I get home this evening."

"Your house! Your Company! Your money!" He was yelling again. "Well, keep it; I'm tired of being a 'kept' man living off your wealth. I'll call the kids when I get settled and they can come visit me anytime they want to; but Roseanna, don't come with them because I never want to see you again!" He shoved her aside and stalked off.

"Brad," she cried out as she lost her footing and fell, but he kept walking; he didn't even look back.

She got up and checked herself over and since she was not seriously hurt she went into the house and dressed quickly then left for the office, her heart beating between hurt and anger.

The house seemed large and empty that afternoon when she got home so she knew Brad was gone. Her world always seemed empty without him in it. "I don't care what he's done I can't live without him," she said aloud. "Mimi," she called.

Mimi came walking in from the kitchen. Her eyes were bloodshot from crying. "Did you have a good day?" Her words were stiff and formal.

"My day was fine," Roseanna answered, noting a hint of anger in Mimi's voice. "Is he gone?"

"Yes, he's gone."

"Did he tell you where he was going?"

"No, but I know where he is." Mimi was polite but distant.

Roseanna could detect hostility in her voice and she knew that Mimi thought she was being unfair to Brad and wouldn't offer information about him willingly, so she asked her outright. "Would you tell me where he is, please?"

Mimi didn't answer; she just stood there looking at Roseanna.

"Tell me." This time it was an order not a request.

"There's a cabin here on the ranch; he's staying there until he can figure out what to do, now that his life is turned upside down."

"You're blaming me, aren't you?" This time there was a twinge of anger in Roseanna's voice.

"Well, he wouldn't have left on his own."

"Tell me where the cabin is," Roseanna demanded, ignoring Mimi's cutting remark.

"It's hidden in a clump of trees about a quarter of a mile up that road." She pointed to the road that led to the north end of the ranch.

"Thanks, Mimi," Roseanna said, heading out the front door and walking to the stables. She put a saddle on Midnight Thunder and climbed up on him. "We're going to bring him back," she said as she patted the horse's neck and then headed out to the road leading north.

A few minutes later she stopped in front of the cabin. It was rustic, unpainted and very small. Roseanna flinched as she thought of Brad living in a place like this. She got down off the horse, hurried up to the cabin, and fearing that he wouldn't let her in if she knocked on the door, she opened it quietly and started to step inside, but then she stopped. Brad was on his knees praying.

The wheels in her brain started turning. "Whatever Brad says to the Lord will be the truth," she said under her breath. She felt sure the Lord had led her here so she could finally hear Brad admit his affair with Dori. She listened intently as he prayed.

"Father," he began, "I made a horrible mistake and I don't think I can ever make it right. Roseanna almost died because of it. Now, no one back home believes a word I say. I know I acted foolishly. I know what the Word says about shunning the very appearance of evil, yet I allowed Dori to stay at the cabin with me. I've told Roseanna and the others that nothing happened between us; but there's no way I can prove that I'm telling the truth. Lord, You know nothing went on between Dori and me; if only You could show them that I am telling the truth; they sure won't listen to me."

"Oh, no, what have I done," Roseanna gasped as she turned and ran to her horse, mounted him and raced for the ranch.

She stumbled through the door and fell into Mimi's arms. "Oh, Mimi, he was telling the truth all the time. Brad is innocent and I've ruined his life. I've taken away everything that was precious to him; his family, his ministry, his reputation." She burst into tears and told Mimi the whole story.

Mimi held her until the tears subsided. Then she looked her in the eye and said, "You get right back to that cabin and tell Brad that you know he is telling the truth, and beg his forgiveness..."

"No, I can't do that," Roseanna cried. "I've ruined his life enough already. By not believing in him I was calling him a liar and a hypocrite; and he could never forgive me for that. Anyway, he'll be better off without me around messing things up for him."

"Roseanna, Brad loves you and he can forgive you for anything. Go to him, child, and make things right before it's too late."

"It's already too late, Mimi," she said. She turned and walked to her bedroom and shut the door behind her.

The next morning Roseanna walked into the kitchen, her eyes bloodshot from crying all night.

Mimi took one look at her. "Did you sleep at all last night," she asked handing her a cup of coffee.

"No," she answered. "I don't know if I'll ever sleep again. I miss Brad so much and I'll never stop loving him. I'm going to the cabin and stay with him if that's what it takes. Now that I know he's telling the truth; maybe that will make a difference." She started out the door just as the phone rang.

"It's for you," Mimi called.

"Hello," Roseanna said, hoping she could cut the conversation short and get to the cabin; to Brad.

"Roseanna, this is Ross and I need to talk to you as soon as possible."

"Can it wait," she asked. "I'm on my way to see Brad and it's urgent."

"That's what this is about," he told her. "Brad has left town. He came by my office early this morning and signed divorce papers. He said you'd be in later to file for the divorce. What's going on between you two?"

"We're having serious problems, ones that can't be resolved."

"I'm sorry Roseanna, but are you sure divorce is the answer?"

"He signed the papers, isn't that proof enough?" She thought a moment then said, "I'll get back to you on this."

Mimi came in and put her arms around her. "Roseanna, what's wrong? You're as pale as a ghost."

"That was my lawyer on the phone. Brad wants a divorce. Mimi, I've lost him forever."

Mimi held her close trying to console her. "Maybe he'll change his mind and call you," she said, hoping that was the case.

Brad drove away from the lawyer's office with dark and ugly thoughts raging in his mind. "I don't need you, Roseanna. I don't need any of you," he scowled angrily. But he did need someone. Loneliness like he'd never felt flooded his very being, and for the first time in his life he felt utterly alone. He needed someone to lift him up, a friendly voice to comfort him. "I'll call Dori," he mumbled aloud. "At least she doesn't hate me." He dialed her cell phone.

"Hello Brad," she said, recognizing his number. "What's up?"

"I just wanted to call and check on you," he said. "Are things better between Mac and you?"

"No, and they never will be," she answered. "He's gone too far this time. He threw me out of the house and with the help of a lawyer got legal papers declaring me to be an unfit mother. Now I can't see my kids until after the divorce proceedings."

"He can't do that," Brad said angrily. "I'm coming home. I'm going to talk to him and I'll be there for you."

"I'm not there, Brad. I'm in Kansas at my parent's home," she told him. "And it won't do any good to talk to Mac. His mind is made up; as far as he's concerned I'm a tramp, and he wants nothing to do with me."

"I'm coming to Kansas then," he said. "Tell me how to get there." He wrote down the directions then turned the car around and headed in the direction of Kansas.

Hours later he knocked on Dori's front door. When she opened it, he pulled her into his arms and kissed her, over and over; kisses that spoke of more than friendship; much more.

She pushed him away gently. "Brad, it's not that I didn't enjoy those kisses, but I've got to know the reason behind them."

"Roseanna's mind is clear, the pills are out of her system with no harm done. She's herself again..."

"That's wonderful," Dori exclaimed, then with a puzzled look she said, "I don't understand; if Roseanna is well, why are you here with me? Why did you kiss me?"

Brad told her of the fight he'd had with Roseanna and about the divorce papers he had signed before leaving Nashville. "And since Roseanna thinks I'm a liar and a hypocrite, I feel certain she will file for divorce right away and in a couple of months I will be a free man."

"Is that what you really want, Brad?"

"Yes it is," he answered. "I thought about it on my way here and I'm tired of putting up with Roseanna's doubts about me. I'll be happy when she is no longer a part of my life."

"What about your ministry?"

He hung his head. "When I give up my life with Roseanna, I'll be giving up the ministry as well; for I'll no longer be worthy to preach the gospel."

"And you can live with that?"

"I can if I have you with me," he answered. "Dori, I'm asking you to marry me as soon as our divorces are final."

"A proposal of marriage...I'm speechless."

Maybe this will help you get your voice back," he said, taking her in his arms and kissing her again. "Well?"

"Yes, I will marry you," she said, kissing him. "And since you obviously don't have a place to live, you can move in here with me and we can start our life together now."

"Sounds good to me." He took her in his arms again and kissed her passionately; struggling to shake the feelings of guilt and condemnation that consumed him. Did she feel guilty too? We have the right to be happy, he reasoned. Roseanna doesn't love me and Mac doesn't love her so we've got to find our happiness with each other. He convinced himself that he was right and moved his stuff into her house. But their plans for a long happy future were cut short when the ringing of the phone woke them up in the middle of the night on Saturday.

She leaned over and answered it while Brad turned on the light. "Oh, no," she cried. "I'll be there as soon as possible."

"What's wrong?"

"There's been an accident and Mac's been hurt; they don't know if he's going to make it." She wept as he pulled her into his arms. "Oh, God, please help him; he can't die. I've got to go to him, Brad, he needs me; and the kids, what they must be going through; their daddy is hurt and their mother is gone. I'm sorry but I've got to leave now."

"I'm going with you."

"No, it wouldn't be good for us to show up together. You stay here and I'll be back as soon as I can, and we'll go ahead with the plans we made."

"Okay," he said. "I'll drive you to the airport."

Roseanna was beside herself. Days had passed and still no word from Brad. He wouldn't answer his phone when she called him. Anger set up in her heart as she remembered how she had forgiven him for the things that happened in Africa; now he wouldn't forgive her for simply not believing in him. By Friday her anger had grown to the point that she went to her lawyer's office and filed for divorce.

Saturday morning Roseanna awoke early. "I've made a decision," she told Mimi as she sat down to breakfast. "I'm going home. Brad is never coming back and I need the comfort of my family around me."

"Are you sure, honey?" There was sadness in Mimi's voice. "What if he does come back?"

"He won't," Roseanna replied. "He made it perfectly clear that he never wants to see me again, and, that he wants a divorce, so I filed for one yesterday."

"Oh, no, Roseanna, it's too soon. Give yourselves time to heal. Give your marriage another chance."

"No, Mimi, it's over this time and the sooner I get on with my life, the better; so I'm going home today."

"I'll miss you; we all will."

"I'll miss you too and I promise I'll come back real often, and who knows I may even move back here one day; but for now I've got to go home." She called Harriet and made arrangements to fly to Louisiana in the company jet. Then she called Jesse. She felt the need to talk to him. She confided in him about the trouble she and Brad were having and also about the divorce.

"I'll pick you up at the airport," he said. "We need to talk." He hung up the phone and went to his office and made a phone call. If he was right, there were plans to be made and they had to be made quickly, correctly, and secretly; there would be no room for error. By the time he went to the airport the plans were completed. Now all he needed to put them into action was Roseanna's cooperation, and that might not be easy.

"How are you, Roseanna?" he asked when he picked her up at the airport late that afternoon.

"I'm making it," she answered. "The pills are out of my system and mind is clear so I'm doing fine physically, but emotionally I'm a wreck."

"Tell me what happened with Brad," he said. "What led to the divorce?"

"I don't know what got into him," she answered. "I told him that I was well; but that each time I looked at him I thought about Dori and him at the cabin together, and I felt like I was being pulled back into that fog. Then I told him to leave. He became very angry and shoved me so hard that I fell to the ground. He didn't even look back. Why would he do that, Jesse?"

A worried look crossed Jesse's face as he mulled it over for a few minutes. "You told him to leave? Honey, that must have been hard on him," he answered. "Brad has been under a great deal of stress ever since this started. He blamed himself for you taking the pills; then no one believed him when he said nothing happened between Dori and him. We know now that he was telling the truth, and he was being falsely accused. I can see how that could make him very angry. And he did put his life on hold to stay with you every minute you were ill. The night of Isabelle's wedding I could tell he was at the breaking point. I was almost as worried about him as I was about you. He was about ready to explode then, and when you told him to leave that was the last straw and he reacted violently. I'm concerned about him, Roseanna. He's vulnerable right now and that leaves room for the devil to get a foothold in his life. I know---I've been there."

"I'm sorry if I added to all the stress in his life, but Jesse, I'm at my breaking point too. I don't know how much more I can take."

"I'm sure it's been hard on you," he said, whispering a prayer under his breath. "Honey, I think you need a change from all this turmoil in your life."

"Tell me, Jesse, how do I get that?"

"You need to go some place where you can be alone and relax."

"No matter where I go, people recognize me, and there's no way I can relax."

"There's nowhere at all?"

"Nowhere except Brad's cabin," she said, "and, I certainly can't go there."

"Why not? It sounds like the perfect place."

"You think I could go there after all that's happened?"

"You know, now, that nothing happened between Brad and Dori, so it shouldn't bother you, and honey trust me on this, I think it's just what you need."

"Jesse, you're about the smartest man I know and I do trust you," she said. "Even if it didn't work out I could always visit with Mom and Dad; and since the boys will be in camp for two more weeks it might be just what I need. I'll do it. I'll leave first thing in the morning."

"Roseanna, I think you should go to the cabin for a few days before you get in touch with any of the family. It will only worry them to see you like this."

"You're right again, Jesse. No one but you will know I'm here."

"Good," he said. "It might be hard for you to get to sleep your first night there so take this tomorrow night before you go to bed," he added, handing her a bottle with one sleeping pill in it. He pulled into her driveway and took her luggage from his car. He carried it into her house, then, he hugged her and smiled. The first part of the plan was in motion. He said goodbye and walked to his car. He dialed his phone. "She's coming tomorrow," he said. "Do you think you can put the wheels in motion there?"

"Yes, we'll get things ready here and we'll make sure he arrives at the right time," Brad's mother answered. "I believe our plan is foolproof and there's no way it can fail. They're as good as back together."

Chapter 22

Roseanna arrived at the Lefourche home late the next afternoon. There was a big meal waiting and visiting afterward. It was almost dark when she got ready to go to the cabin.

"I was thinking about that cell phone of yours," her father-in-law said. "You won't get much rest with folks calling you a lot. Why don't you leave it here?"

"But what if there's an emergency back home?"

"We'll answer your calls and we'll let you know if something important happens," he promised.

"Okay," she said, handing him the phone.

Janet Lefourche spoke up. "Honey, I hate to impose on you, but I have an early appointment tomorrow and my car is acting up. I planned on driving William's truck but something came up and he has to have it, so would it be possible for me to borrow your car?"

"Of course you can borrow it, but I'll either have to stay here tonight or you'll have to take me to the cabin."

"I'm redoing my bedrooms and both of the guest rooms are too messed up for anyone to stay in them, so I'll drive you there."

When they reached the cabin she helped Roseanna unpack the car then visited for awhile. "You're probably tired from your trip and here I am running my mouth. Why don't you get ready for bed and I'll be leaving soon."

"Jesse gave me this pill to help me sleep; and I really do need to sleep so I'll take it now." She went into the bathroom and returned a few moments later dressed for bed. She yawned. "I'm sorry. It's been a long day and I am suddenly very tired."

"Don't apologize, I understand," her mother-in-law said. "Go on to bed. You'll probably be asleep in a few minutes. I'll sit in there with you until you fall asleep, that is, if you don't mind; and I'll turn the lights out when I leave."

Roseanna walked over and hugged her. "I don't mind at all," she said. "You're like a mother to me and tonight I think I would like to be tucked into bed by my mother."

Janet sat beside her and held her hand until she fell asleep. Then she pulled her over to the far side of the bed and tiptoed out of the room. She walked over to the fuse box, unscrewed the fuses, took them out, and with a flashlight to guide the way, she put them in a drawer in the kitchen cabinets. She then walked to the door, opened it, and drove away.

About an hour later Brad showed up at his parent's home. He felt awkward not knowing how his mother would feel about him being here. His father had called around noon and asked him to come home.

"Brad, what are you doing here," his mother asked when she opened the door and saw him standing there.

"Dad called and said you weren't feeling well and that a visit from me would cheer you up."

"Well, he was right. I feel better already," she said, putting her arms around him and giving him a big kiss. She motioned him inside.

"Thanks Mom. I wasn't sure how you'd feel about me after what happened at the cabin."

"I was upset then," she answered. "Sit down and have a cup of coffee and a piece of apple pie. Your father will join you in a moment."

"You know I can't resist your apple pie; it's my favorite."

"Hello son," William Lefourche said, walking in and shaking his hand. "It sure is good to see you."

"You, too, Dad," Brad answered. "It's been much too long."

Janet poured coffee into two mugs. She dropped a sedative into one and placed them on the tray with the pie. She handed the coffee mug with the sedative to Brad and the other one to her husband. She set the pie down in front of them. She poured another cup of coffee and joined them.

They asked Brad lots of questions while they ate, like where he was going and what he was going to do with the rest of his life. He was able to hedge their questions. He certainly didn't want them to know his plans.

"I'm suddenly very sleepy," he said yawning big. "Can we continue this conversation tomorrow?"

"Of course son," his father said.

"Mom, am I sleeping in my old room?"

"Oh, Brad, I'm sorry," she said apologetically. "I'm in the middle of rearranging the guest rooms and they are both in a mess."

"I'll crash on the couch…"

"No, I've got a better idea," his father broke in. "Why don't you spend the night at the cabin?"

"Okay, I only hope I can stay awake long enough to get there."

"Nonsense, I'll drive you and then come and pick you up for breakfast."

They arrived at the cabin a few minutes later. Brad got his overnight bag from the back seat and got out of the car. "Goodnight Dad. See you in the morning."

"Goodnight," his father called and drove back down the road.

Brad opened the door of the cabin and stepped inside. He flipped the light switch, but nothing happened. He tried it again, but still no light. "I'll check that out tomorrow," he mumbled. "I'm going to bed now." He felt his way into the bedroom and fell down on the bed. He was asleep in less than five minutes.

Roseanna awoke the next morning and when she opened her eyes she saw the form of someone lying in bed beside her. Terror like she'd never known gripped her. Had a homeless tramp wandered in during the night to find a place to sleep; but why had he not noticed her? He was probably drunk and would not have turned on the light. Then another even more terrifying thought crossed her mind; what if he were a prison escapee trying to avoid getting caught. What ever the case, she would be in danger if he saw her. Her only chance was to get out of the cabin without waking him. She'd run into the woods and hide. "Oh, Lord, help me," she silently prayed as she eased out of bed and tiptoed quietly around the end of it.

Brad awoke and sensed that someone was in the room. "Most likely a thief, thinking no one is here," he mused to himself. "If he sees me he can't realize that I am awake, so I'll lie perfectly still and wait for a chance to jump him," he mused further. He opened his eyes just enough to see what was happening; then when the thief got within range he made a flying lunge and knocked him to the floor.

Roseanna screamed as the man knocked her to the floor and held her there. She was helpless to defend herself against this strong man. She screamed again as he forced her face upward.

"Roseanna!"

"Brad!" She was relieved, but very angry. "Not only did you scare me out of my wits, but I think you dislocated my shoulder as well," she fumed. "What are you doing here, anyway?"

"This *is* my cabin," Brad snapped standing up and helping her to her feet. "Now, tell me why you're here?"

She moved her shoulder around until she was sure it was still intact, then, she answered his question. "Jesse thought I needed to get away and rest and..."

"And he suggested you come here, right?"

"Yes, he did, he thought..."

"They did it to us again," Brad blurted out.

"I don't understand."

"Do you remember the last time you and I accidentally showed up here at the same time?"

"But that was no accident; Jesse and Mom planned it...You don't think..."

"Yes, I do think; in fact I'm sure of it," he answered and told her how he happened to arrive at the cabin late last night. "They plotted to get us together, here in our special place, in hopes that we will make up."

"Well, it looks like the first part of their plan worked; here we are," she said. "But as to the rest of it, they can't make us stay here against our will. We can leave anytime we want to."

"I'm not too sure of that," he told her. "I didn't see your car last night. Is it parked in the back?"

"No, Mom had an early appointment this morning and she needed to borrow it so she dropped me off, and she is coming to pick me up as soon as she is finished."

"Don't count on it."

"We can use your car..."

"No, we can't; they've got it too," he said and explained how his father drove him to the cabin last night.

"Well, in spite of all of that, their plan is not going to work," she declared. "We'll call a taxi." She started to reach for her phone. "We'll have to use your phone. I left mine with Dad."

"At his suggestion, I'll bet," Brad said, reaching for his phone. "They got mine too," he exclaimed, after searching his pockets and not finding it. "It looks like we're stuck here until they decide to come pick us up."

"They wouldn't leave us here very long would they? I only brought a small amount of food."

"Let's check something out," he said walking toward the kitchen. "Unless I miss my guess our cupboards will be well stocked." They opened up the cabinets and looked in the refrigerator and freezer and found them filled with their favorite foods.

"Brad, they're holding us hostage," she cried. "Just wait 'til I get my hands on Jesse Lawrence."

"Don't forget Mom and Dad," he reminded her. "Jesse could not have pulled it off without them."

"Well, they can make us stay here, but they can't make our decisions for us. We're still free to decide for ourselves."

"That's true, they can't bend our will to their way of thinking," he said. "Now since we know that we're not going anywhere, how about we fix breakfast? I'll get the coffee started."

He filled the coffee pot and plugged it in while Roseanna got out a pan and put the bacon on to fry.

"Brad, something is wrong," she said after a few minutes. "The bacon is not frying."

He felt the coffeepot. It was cold. "Come with me," he said, remembering that the lights were out last night. "I think I know what's going on." He checked the fuse box and all the fuses were gone. "This was part of the plot to keep me from seeing you when I went to bed. They thought of everything didn't they?" They searched for the fuses and finally found them in the cabinet drawers, screwed them into the fuse box, and finished cooking breakfast.

Midway through eating Roseanna gasped, "I only brought a couple of changes of clothes. What am I going to do if we're here for a week or two?"

"Well, stop whining," he said. "I only have my overnight bag and just one change of clothes."

"Maybe, one of us could walk to your parent's house," she suggested. "Ten miles is really not that far if…"

"By one of us I suppose you mean me," he groused. "But it wouldn't do any good to go. They have planned this thing down to the smallest detail; they would know that we might try that; so Mom and Dad won't be there, and they'll take the keys to the house and the cars with them."

"But what if there's emergency at home, Dad promised to let me know…"

"Oh, they won't go that far away," he assured her. "They've probably rented a room in town. That's another fifteen miles, and I'm sure not gonna walk that far."

"So I guess we need to figure out how to wash the clothes we do have."

"Any suggestions?"

"We could go swimming in the lake with our clothes on, or better still, get in the shower with them on."

"I guess that would work."

"Okay, now that the issue of our clothes is settled, how do we pass the time? There's nothing to do; no TV, no radio, no CD player; my guitar is at home, and I didn't bring any books or magazines, so what am I supposed to do for the next week or so?" Her voice was harsh, accusing.

"This is certainly not my fault," he said. "I'm not the one who blabbed to everyone about the divorce. That's why we're here, you know."

"I only told Jesse…"

"Well it appears that you didn't need to blab it to anyone else," he yelled.

"I should have known you would blame me," she yelled back. "Nothing is ever your fault, Mr. High and Mighty!"

He stood up, threw his napkin down on the table, and stormed out the door.

Roseanna's boiling point had reached its limit. She would show him; she searched until she found a piece of chalk, and then she went thorough the house drawing walkways. "We may have to stay here together but we sure don't have to associate with each other," she said aloud with a smirk on her face.

It was dusky dark when Brad got back to the cabin. He walked in and saw the chalk lines. "What's all this?" he quizzed.

"I've divided the cabin off into sections; one for me and one for you," she replied. "I will sleep in the bedroom and you will sleep on the couch. I've drawn a walkway through my bedroom so you can get to the bathroom without trespassing on my property."

"Hold on," he said. "Why am I sleeping on the couch?"

"Because you're a man and men always sleeps on the couch."

"Who gets the kitchen?"

"We share that," she said. "We'll take turns. I've already had my supper so you can use the kitchen when you get ready to eat."

"I'm not hungry," he snapped. "I'm going to bed, so if you will kindly remove yourself from my premises."

Roseanna walked into the bedroom and having nothing else to do, she dressed for bed, laid down, and turned off the light.

Three days of trying to stay out of each others way proved to be more than Brad could bear. On the third night he had been in bed for about three hours when he was ready for a truce. "Roseanna," he called out. "I'm going to die of boredom if I have to lie here one more minute. Can we talk?" He got up off the couch and walked into the bedroom before she could say no. He lay down on the bed. "This will be like old times, the two of us lying in bed talking."

"Say what you want to say and make it snappy."

"Roseanna, I haven't been able to tell you why I went to the cabin alone. May I tell you now?"

"If you wish," she said as if she didn't care one way or the other.

"It started when Isabelle found out about our divorce," he began. "You remember how upset she was and how she hated me and called me a hypocrite."

"I knew that hurt you, but it doesn't explain why you went to the cabin without me."

"I saw the look on Isabelle's face when you shut her out of our family unless she apologized to me. It was more than I could bear to see the look of hopelessness and hurt in her eyes. I thought you were unfair to her and I was upset with you for treating her that way. By the time we reached home I was so angry that I couldn't stand the sight of you, and I was on the verge of hating you. That's the reason I had to get out of there and also the reason I couldn't take you with me."

"Why didn't you tell me this? We could have worked it out."

"Roseanna, I couldn't tell you how I felt, especially since you were defending me to our daughter. So I went to the cabin to try to sort out my feelings."

"That doesn't explain how Dori ended up with your cell phone and why she was at the cabin with you."

"I couldn't tell you about that before; it would have only made things worse."

"Tell me now." Even though she knew he was innocent, she still wanted to know how it happened.

"When I got to New Orleans I was sleepy. I stopped for coffee at the hotel we stay in when we're there. I heard someone speak to me. I looked up and saw Dori standing there. She was attending a seminar on Agriculture and was staying at the hotel. I was upset for I wanted to be alone; but you know Dori; she sat down, poured herself a cup of coffee and insisted on knowing why I was there so early. I tried to get rid of her but she wouldn't budge. I finally told her what was bothering me and that I was on my way to the cabin to sort things out. She advised me to go back home and talk things out with you, but when I said I couldn't, she suggested that I go up to her room and sleep 'til she got out of her meeting; then we would talk. She handed me the key to her room and left. I decided to take her up on her offer and went to her room. I laid down on the bed and tried to go to sleep, but I couldn't, so after about thirty minutes I got up, wrote her a note and left. I knew what folks would think if they knew that I was in her hotel room so I kept quiet about it."

"How did she get your phone?" Roseanna's voice was impatient.

"I didn't realize it but I left my phone in her room, and when she came back from her meeting she found it. She knew that Mom and Dad were gone on vacation, and in case of an emergency I could not be reached, so she decided to bring the phone to me. That's why she answered when you called," he explained. "I know it was dumb for her to come to the cabin, and it was just as dumb of me to let her stay. The other stuff I told you is true; she slept in the bed and I slept on the couch. The next morning we talked about my problem and she was getting ready to leave when Mom showed up with the news that you had overdosed on pain pills and they didn't know if you would make it."

"Brad, I remember that I didn't take those pills intentionally. My head was hurting so badly that I took a couple, and I carried the bottle of pills and some water and set them on the coffee table in case I needed more. I remember waking up several times and taking more pills because my head was still hurting; then I don't remember anything else until I woke up in our bed on Thursday morning," she explained. "And, I know now that you were telling the truth; I know nothing happened between Dori and you here in the cabin." She waited for him to say something but when he didn't, she leaned up on her elbow and looked over at him. He was sound asleep. "Well, this is just great," she grumbled, grabbed her pillow, yanked the cover off of him, walked into the living room, fell down on the couch, and pulled the covers over her head.

Brad awoke the next morning and realized he was on the bed instead of the sofa. Would Roseanna be upset? She was already up so he would soon find out. He walked into the living room and saw her sleeping on the couch. "Oh, no, I'm going to get it for sure," he mumbled. She looked beautiful lying there asleep. He wanted to go over, take her in his arms and kiss her; but he couldn't. Their life together was over; soon they would be divorced and he would begin his life with Dori. He had to stay focused on reality. He walked to the kitchen and started breakfast.

A few minutes later Roseanna woke up to the aroma of coffee perking, and the sound of bacon sizzling in the pan.

Brad walked in. "You're awake," he said. "I'm sorry about last night. I didn't mean to go to sleep and I sure didn't mean for you to sleep on the couch."

"But you did go to sleep and I did sleep on the couch."

"I feel doubly bad since I'm the one who wanted to talk."

"You made it fine as long as you were doing the talking; it was when I started talking that you fell asleep."

"I heard the part about the pills, and it wasn't that I didn't want to hear the rest of it," he assured her. "I was just so relaxed that I fell off to sleep without realizing it. But I'd love to hear it now."

"Forget it, it's not important," she snapped and headed for the bathroom.

When they sat down to breakfast, Brad looked over at her. "Roseanna, we can't go on like this," he said. "We've got to stop treating each other like the enemy. We need each other. Can't we try to get along, at least, while we're here?"

"That would make things a lot easier," she said. And as angry as they were at each other they became comrades to fight against a mutual foe: boredom.

After a couple of days of forcing themselves to be friendly, Roseanna and Brad realized it wasn't working. They were like strangers, polite, but not really connecting.

Roseanna woke early on the third day of their truce. She looked at Brad lying on the couch asleep. Love for him swelled in her heart. "Oh, Brad, what are we doing to each other," she muttered and hurried over to the couch. She knelt down and put her arms around him. "I love you, Brad," she whispered leaning over and kissing him.

He opened his eyes. Wildness and rage showed in them. "Stop that!" he yelled, shoving her away from him. "Don't ever touch me again!"

Roseanna looked at him with bewilderment on her face. "I don't understand, Brad," she cried. "I love you."

"Well, I don't love you and I want you to stay away from me." He jumped up and raced out the door, cursing under his breath.

Roseanna sat there stunned. She had never heard him use foul language before. Had these past few weeks been too much for him? Had he broken under the load? She fell to her knees and cried out to the Lord. "Oh, God, that wasn't Brad just now. He would never speak your Name like that. It's like an evil force is controlling him." She remembered Jesse's concern that Brad might be vulnerable to the devil. "Is that it, Lord, is he bound by Satan---if so, he needs to be set free; but what can I do?"

Scriptures flashed through her mind. 'God is love. God so loved...' "That's it," she said. "If love can't set him free, then nothing can."

She stood and walked outside to look for him. He was standing down by the lake. His back was to her so she crept up behind him and clasped her arms around him.

Startled, he tried to get free of her grasp, but he couldn't pry her arms loose. "Roseanna, let me go," he screamed. "You bitch, I told you to let go of me!"

Roseanna felt strength surge through her. It was as if God had his strong arms clasped over hers and formed a force that Brad couldn't break through. "I love you, Brad," she whispered in his ear. "I love you, no matter what, and I always will."

"You make me sick," he said with disgust. "I can't stand the sight of you."

"I love you sweetheart," she said ignoring his harsh words. "I love you."

The demon inside him trembled at the mention of love. He used Brad's voice to speak words he felt sure would stop her. "You're a fool, Roseanna to think I could still love you. I'm with Dori now; she's my kind of woman. I'm living in her house and sharing her bed."

"Even if that's true, I still love you," she said, determined to keep focused on the goal. She leaned around and kissed him on the face. "Honey, feel my love going through you. Let it set you free. You always said that love is stronger than hate, and that good will overcome evil. My love for you is strong and it's good, and it will last through out eternity. Sweetheart, take my love; let it break this hold that Satan has over you." She laid her face against his as tears ran down her cheeks. "I love you, Brad. I love you so much," she whispered again.

A tear rolled down his face as the devil took his flight. "Roseanna, help me. Please help me," he pleaded.

"Of course, I'll help you, sweetheart, but most of your help must come from the Lord."

"I'm not worthy to ask for His help or to even utter His name," he said, hanging his head. "I've sinned against the Lord and against you, Roseanna. I can't believe I let the devil defeat me like that."

"Brad, the devil may have won a battle against you but he certainly has not won the war and he never will. We're going to pray until you are back on track with God; until you feel peace in your heart again."

"No, God doesn't love me anymore. He couldn't, not after what I've done."

"Brad, you know better than that," she said. "God's love for us was so great that it sent Jesus to the cross; so do you think He's going to stop loving you just because you failed Him? Whose arms do you think was holding you just now? It certainly wasn't mine alone for I'm not strong enough to even hold you, much less the evil spirit that had you bound. Brad, it was God's arms that held you. He loves you and wants you to come back to Him."

Brad burst into tears and knelt there in the sand. Roseanna knelt beside him and put her arms around him. He cried out to God, repenting of the sins he had committed over the past few days, and prayed for forgiveness from the depths of his soul. With tears streaming down his face, he pulled Roseanna close. "Oh sweetheart, I feel clean inside again and God's sweet anointing is flowing through me once more. I know now that I am worthy to preach His holy word again, and it's all because of you Roseanna, and the love you have for me. Thank God you cared enough about me to help me find my way back to the Lord."

"I'll always love you Brad and I'm thankful that you have made peace with the Lord, but we need to talk about us. The things you said about Dori and you, are they true or was that just the devil speaking, trying to upset me?"

He hung his head. "I need to tell you about that."

"Then it is true. I really don't want to hear it."

"You must sweetheart," he said. "Until you know the truth you can't make a decision about our future." He took her hand. "That morning when you told me to leave, something snapped inside me and I went berserk. I knew you fell when I shoved you, but I had so much anger and hatred in my heart against you that I didn't care if you were hurt. I guess that's when Satan got control of me."

"But, Brad, I heard you praying later. I went to the cabin to get you to come back to me, but when I got there you were praying and I listened cause I knew whatever you said to the Lord would be the truth, and I fully expected to hear you admit your guilt but instead I found out that you were telling the truth all along."

"Why didn't you stay and talk to me?"

"I realized that I had ruined your life and I couldn't face you."

"I'm thankful that you learned the truth through my prayer; but I haven't prayed since then. I thought that prayer would never be answered and it just seemed useless to pray since my heart was far from God." He paused. "Now, let's get back to what I need to tell you."

"I'm listening."

"I let my anger for you fester in my heart until by the next morning I was so angry that I convinced myself I didn't want a life with you; and I wanted to make sure you knew it, so that's why I signed divorce papers. After leaving Ross's office I had nowhere to go so I started driving. That's when the devil started putting ideas in my head. He planted the seed in my mind that I needed to hear a friendly voice and that Dori was the only person who still felt friendly toward me, so I called her. I told myself I was calling to see how she and Mac were doing, but that wasn't the truth. I was lonely and I wanted to see her. When she answered I found out that Mac had thrown her out of the house, and had papers from a judge declaring her to be an unfit mother, and she was not allowed to see the kids. That made me angry and I decided to go to her. She was living in her parent's home in Kansas, so I went there." He was quiet for a moment trying to choose the right words to say to make this easier on Roseanna but there was no easy way to say it. He knew it would hurt her, but he had to tell her all of it. "I know now that I was being controlled by the devil but I didn't realize it then. I kept right on telling myself that I was only going to her so I could help her with the ordeal she was going through, but when I got there..."

"What happened?" Roseanna already knew but she wanted to hear it from him.

"Oh Baby, please forgive me." His words were filled with shame and remorse. "When she opened the door I pulled her into my arms and kissed her. After several kisses she pushed me away and asked me where this was leading. I told her about our divorce and that I wanted a life with her; and if she wanted that too, we would be married as soon as we were both free. She said that she also wanted a life with me, and we made plans for our future. She suggested that I move in with her so we could start our lives together that day and not have to wait until the divorces were final. So I moved my stuff into her house and—and we lived together until Saturday night when she received the call that Mac had been seriously hurt in an accident and she left to go to him. I was going to stay at her house until she got back but Dad called the next morning and asked me to come home for a few days and you know the rest."

Roseanna was in tears. "You've been living together and..."

He pulled her into his arms. "Oh, sweetheart, I'm so sorry about that," he said, holding her close. "If I could go back and change one thing in my life, I would change what happened between Dori and me. I would even choose to be stranded for months on that island rather than betray you. But I have betrayed you and I won't blame you if you never forgive me."

"Brad, I'd give everything I own to be able to forgive you as completely as God has forgiven you, but I just can't, not yet."

"So that means the divorce will go though?"

"No, I don't want a divorce," she said. "I love you and I want our marriage to be good like it was before, but it's going to take a while for me to get over this and you may not want to wait until..."

"Sweetheart, I'll wait forever," he blurted out. "Knowing that you love me and want our marriage to work is more than I could ever hope for. I love you so much, Roseanna." He took her in his arms and held her and they sat there in the sand content to be together again.

"You can sleep in here with me," Roseanna said that night as they got ready for bed. "There's no longer any reason for you to sleep on that lumpy couch."

"My back is forever grateful to you," he said lying down beside her. "Thank you sweetheart for rescuing me from the clutches of Satan," he added kissing her tenderly.

"Brad, we've been here almost a week so why did the devil wait until today to raise his ugly head?"

"He wasn't worried as long as we were at odds with each other but when you said you loved me he had to try to stop you, for he can't survive where love abounds." He took her in his arms and kissed her again. "Goodnight Roseanna, I love you."

"I love you too." She lay awake staring into the darkness. "Please help me, God," she prayed silently. "I need to forgive him completely. I know he was under the control of Satan when he slept with Dori, but until I can get the picture of them out of my mind, I can never truly forgive him." She finally fell asleep only to wake hours later with feelings of joy bubbling up inside her. "Brad, wake up," she said nudging him. "A miracle has happened."

He sat up in bed. "What?" he asked, opening his eyes and looking around.

"Brad, God performed a miracle in my heart while I was asleep," she said happily. "I can now forgive you for being with Dori. I can forgive you for everything."

Sweetheart, that's wonderful," he cried and held her as tears ran down their faces. Then a serious look crossed his face. "Roseanna we came much too close to destroying our marriage this time. When we allowed anger and hatred to consume us, we stopped caring about each other; and the love we felt was covered over by the hatred we nurtured in our hearts against one another."

"Brad, let's make a promise right now that no matter how hurtful the problem is, we will talk it out and not give up until things are good between us."

"I do so solemnly promise," he said. "But we've got to do more than that. The devil has been trying to destroy our marriage for years. He knows the folks in our congregation, especially the young couples, look to us for guidance for their own marriages; and not only them, but our marriage is also an icon for your fans. If the devil could cause our marriage to end in divorce, he could destroy a lot of other families who look on us as their example of a perfect marriage. So, we've got to put a stop to him right now."

"How do we do that?"

"First we talk," he said. "Even though you have forgiven me there will still be problems in our marriage until you can get over the feelings you have against Dori."

Tears misted her eyes. "How do I get rid of them?"

"Before we do anything I've got a confession to make. I've been jealous of Andy all these years," he admitted. "After all you did fall in love with the guy and almost married him; and there have been times when I've doubted your love for me and wondered if you regretted your decision not to marry him."

"Brad, you don't have to be jealous of Andy," she said. "I made the decision between the two of you years ago, and I haven't changed my mind, and I never will. Remember I only fell in love with him when I thought you were dead. The minute you walked into that hospital room, alive and well, the choice was already made; my heart had made it the day I fell in love with you."

"Oh, sweetheart, please forgive me for ever doubting your love for me."

"No, I'm the one who should be apologizing," she said. "I caused all this mess because I couldn't trust you. Even though there was no proof that you were telling the truth, I should have trusted you anyway."

"I can't blame you for not believing me," he said. "But we must never let doubt slip into our marriage again."

"How do we do that, Brad?"

"We pray and ask God to help us; for only He can truly give us that inner healing that will get rid of all the bad feelings we have inside."

They knelt beside the bed and prayed that all the jealously that was rooted deep in their hearts against Dori and Andy would be gone. The sun was coming up the next morning when they finally got the assurance their prayers had been answered. They knew they had won the battle against the devil's attempt to destroy their marriage. "Thank you, God," they whispered standing to their feet.

"Brad, God truly performed an inner healing in me," Roseanna said. "The feelings of jealously are gone and I'm going to make sure they never return."

"I feel the same way about Andy, and even when he butts into our business again, as I'm sure he will; I'm not going to let it bother me." He took her in his arms. "I'm so happy things worked out for us. The only regret I have is losing the church. I'm sure they have fired me by now."

"Maybe not," she told him. "I told Jesse that nothing happened between Dori and you at the cabin, and I feel sure he has told the others by now."

"So you think there's a chance that they will keep me on as pastor?"

"I think there's a good chance."

He smiled, obviously delighted and relieved. "I want that, but I'll only go back on one condition."

"Brad, if they decide to keep you on, I'm not sure you should put a condition on going back."

"Well I won't go back any other way."

"Brad, if you really want this…"

"Sweetheart, I'll only go back if you go with me, 'cause I'll never go anywhere on this earth again without you by my side. So do we go back or not?"

"We go back," she said leaning over and kissing him.

"What happens when they find out about what just happened between Dori and me?"

"They don't find out," she said. "You have asked for and received forgiveness from both God and me; and it will never be mentioned again. Agreed?"

"Agreed."

Days passed but things were different now. Love had returned to Brad and Roseanna's hearts, and life was beautiful again. All too soon the end of two weeks was approaching.

Feeling certain they would be going home in the next day or two, Brad and Roseanna got up early on Friday in order to see the sunrise over the lake one last time.

"It's so beautiful here," she sighed snuggling in his arms.

He nodded and pulled her close. "The beauty here is great, but it pales in comparison to the beauty of our love," he said. "No artist, past, present, or future, could ever capture on canvas the splendor of the love I feel for you."

"You're right Brad, and I wish we could pass that splendor down to future generations; what a heritage that would be." She thought a moment. "That's what I'm going to do," she exclaimed. "I'm going to write a book about our family!"

He grinned. "It certainly should be a best seller."

"It won't be that kind of book," she said. "I'm not going to market it. It will just be passed down through our family from generation to generation. Brad, I want our descendents to know us; not only as names on a family tree, but as real people just like them. I don't want to just pass our money down to them; I want to pass the wisdom we have acquired through everyday experiences. I want them to know the importance of love by learning about the love we've shared through the years; and I want them to embrace the spiritual inheritance that is handed down through your faithfulness." She stopped to get her breath, then, added. "I'll write about the whole family, including your parents; and I'll start with Grandma."

"What an awesome idea; what an amazing legacy to leave behind for our descendants," he said. "But don't fail to write of your contributions; for your singing has added a lot to the spiritual inheritance we'll leave behind."

"I'll write about everything," she said. "I'm so excited I can hardly wait to get started." She took his hand. "Let's hurry back to the cabin."

"Yeah, today just might be the day we get to go home."

"Brad," she yelled excitedly when they approached the cabin. "My car is here."

They ran to the car, opened the doors and looked inside. The keys were in the ignition, their cell phones were on the dash and a note was lying on the seat. Roseanna picked it up and read it.

"Brad," she exclaimed. "Mom wrote that Jesse called and the church is expecting their 'pastor' to be there for the Sunday morning service; and he also said that Mac is doing fine and he and Dori are back together and doing good; thank God for that." She read further. "Honey, Dori was at church last Sunday...I didn't think she'd ever go back to church after they treated her like a tramp."

"Thank God she did," he said. "But sweetheart can you deal with her living next door after what happened between us? I don't want to put more pressure on you. We'll move back to Nashville before I'll let that happen."

"I'll be fine," Roseanna said. "When God does something He does it right. I'm not the least bit jealous of her now. I hope we can work things out between us and be friends again."

At eleven o'clock on Sunday morning Brad and Roseanna walked hand in hand into the church back home amid cheers and a lot of hugs and kisses.

Brad walked to the pulpit amid more cheers.

"Glad to have you back, pastor," Earl yelled out.

"Glad to be back, Earl," Brad said, smiling at him. "It's so good to see all of you, and, under such happy circumstances; Roseanna has regained her health and I'm back in this pulpit again. God has blessed us abundantly. Roseanna is going to sing now before I preach."

"I wrote this song this past week after realizing just how weak I am on my own. As you know I've made some huge mistakes these past weeks; mistakes that caused all of us a lot of pain and heartache. God showed me through the words of this song that if I had been closer to the cross I would not have been so easily caught up in the trap that Satan had set for Brad and me." She paused and picked up her guitar and started strumming. The song is entitled, "Just Beneath The Cross" and I hope it blesses you as much as it has blessed me."

"Day after day I know that I'm guilty of from time to time,
Not keeping you on my mind;
I know I may often do, things unpleasing Lord to you,
I confess, Lord, this flesh I wear it is no good.

Keep me on my knees, and my eyes on Calvary,
Not one minute without a vision of those nail prints in my mind;
Though this fleshly vessel falls, I know you paid it all,
Keep me on my knees, just beneath the cross.

When I think what love you showed as you stumbled 'neath the load,
While scoffers mocked you just beneath the cross;
The crown of thorns that cut your head, that streamed of crimson red,
Were mercy drops that fell beneath the cross.

Keep me on my knees and my eyes on Calvary,
Not one minute without a vision of those nail prints in my mind;
Though this fleshly vessels falls, I know you paid it all,
Keep me on my knees, just beneath the cross.

Just beneath the cross, just beneath the cross,
May I ever stay, Lord, just beneath the cross;
For it's there I know I'll find, the strength to stand through time,
Keep me on my knees just beneath the cross.
For it's there I know I'll find, strength to stand through time,
Keep me on my knees just beneath the cross."

Shouts of praise rang through the sanctuary as people raised their voices in worship to the One who gave Himself on the cross for them. When the praise died down, Brad took his place behind the pulpit. "My sermon today deals with how to thwart Satan's plans for your life. Since Roseanna and I have just fought a battle with him, and spoiled the plans he had to ruin our lives, I want to share with you the steps to overcoming him. Let us pray."

Roseanna walked over to Dori when the service was over. "I need to talk to you," she said, taking her aside. "Dori, I want to apologize to you…"

"No, I'm the one who should be apologizing," she said. "I'm sorry about everything and I'm thankful that Brad and you have worked things out."

"I know what happened between Brad and you. He told me everything."

"I'm surprised you don't hate me," she said. "Mac sure will if he ever finds out…"

"He won't hear it from me," Roseanna promised. "I'm so happy things have worked out for Mac and you. And I hope the two of us can be friends again."

"I'd like that," she said, hugging Roseanna.

"There's somewhere we need to go before we go home," Brad told Roseanna after everyone left, taking her hand and walking the short distance to her special place.

She smiled. "It's been so long since I've been here; I'd almost forgotten how special it is to me."

"To us, sweetheart," Brad said. "We came here on the two most important days of our lives; the day we met, which was also the day we fell in love, and again on our wedding day. I wanted to come here today to tell you that as much as I loved you back then, I love you even more today. We have weathered many storms in our marriage and they have made us stronger, and we have truly become one because of them. I love you, Roseanna."

"I love you too, Brad, now and forever."

"Though out all eternity," he whispered and kissed her; and as she stood there in his arms, Roseanna silently thanked God for weaving the threads of their lives into a tapestry that brought them back to each other; threads of love that bound them together so strong that nothing or nobody would ever separate them again; and into a pattern which brought them home to stay.

Home. How good that sounded.

Roseanna Series Books

Roseanna
Belle's Restless Heart
Beyond The Tempest
Rainbow's End
Girl On The Run
Two Roads
A Summer's Dream
Betrayal

For more information or to order books call toll free:
 Viti Tackett   1-877-518-9575

To purchase books online
Email vititackett6@yahoo.com